# Listening to your
# inner sleuth . . .

D1714415

"For a mild-mannered PR woman you seem to have been involved with more than your share of murders."

"That's not *my* fault," I sputtered. "You sound as if I go out looking for violence. It's just an unfortunate coincidence—a tragic coincidence—that deaths happened to have occurred when I was around."

Nick raised one eyebrow. "That's probably true about Caroline Marshall's death and then those murders at the center. But you did choose to play amateur detective." He grabbed a hold of the hand I'd just pulled away. "What I'm saying, Liz, is be careful. You're not directly involved in this one—unless you choose to be."

His blue eyes peered intently into mine. "Please steer clear of Kate. There's something about her that doesn't seem right to me. I might be wrong, and I know I didn't think so at first, but the more I learn about Kate Quinlan the more I think she might be a very dangerous woman."

Was she? A dangerous woman or the victim of some malicious killer? "I have absolutely no intention of getting involved in any dangerous situations," I said.

For some reason Nick did not look relieved. "You didn't the other times either."

**Liz James puts a new spin on sleuthing
in the previous mysteries by
Karen Hanson Stuyck . . .**

# Cry for Help
# Held Accountable

## MORE MYSTERIES FROM THE
## BERKLEY PUBLISHING GROUP...

**THE HERON CARVIC MISS SEETON MYSTERIES:** Retired art teacher Miss Seeton steps in where Scotland Yard stumbles. "A most beguiling protagonist!" —*New York Times*

*by Heron Carvic*
MISS SEETON SINGS
MISS SEETON DRAWS THE LINE
WITCH MISS SEETON
PICTURE MISS SEETON
ODDS ON MISS SEETON

*by Hampton Charles*
ADVANTAGE MISS SEETON
MISS SEETON AT THE HELM
MISS SEETON, BY APPOINTMENT

*by Hamilton Crane*
HANDS UP, MISS SEETON
MISS SEETON CRACKS THE CASE
MISS SEETON PAINTS THE TOWN
MISS SEETON BY MOONLIGHT
MISS SEETON ROCKS THE CRADLE
MISS SEETON GOES TO BAT
MISS SEETON PLANTS SUSPICION
STARRING MISS SEETON
MISS SEETON UNDERCOVER
MISS SEETON RULES
SOLD TO MISS SEETON
SWEET MISS SEETON

**KATE SHUGAK MYSTERIES:** A former D.A. solves crimes in the far Alaska north ...

*by Dana Stabenow*
A COLD DAY FOR MURDER
DEAD IN THE WATER
A FATAL THAW

A COLD-BLOODED BUSINESS
PLAY WITH FIRE

**INSPECTOR BANKS MYSTERIES:** Award-winning British detective fiction at its finest ... "Robinson's novels are habit-forming!"
—*West Coast Review of Books*

*by Peter Robinson*
THE HANGING VALLEY
WEDNESDAY'S CHILD
INNOCENT GRAVES

PAST REASON HATED
FINAL ACCOUNT
GALLOWS VIEW

**CASS JAMESON MYSTERIES:** Lawyer Cass Jameson seeks justice in the criminal courts of New York City in this highly acclaimed series ... "A witty, gritty heroine." —*New York Post*

*by Carolyn Wheat*
FRESH KILLS
MEAN STREAK

DEAD MAN'S THOUGHTS

**LIZ JAMES MYSTERIES:** Featuring Liz James, public relations officer for the Houston Mental Health Center. Now she has her work cut out for her as someone targets clinic employees for murder ...

*by Karen Hanson Stuyck*
CRY FOR HELP
LETHAL LESSONS

HELD ACCOUNTABLE

# LETHAL LESSONS

## Karen Hanson Stuyck

BERKLEY PRIME CRIME, NEW YORK

If you purchased this book without a cover, you should be aware that this book is stolen property. It was reported as "unsold and destroyed" to the publisher, and neither the author nor the publisher has received any payment for this "stripped book."

LETHAL LESSONS

A Berkley Prime Crime Book / published by arrangement with the author

PRINTING HISTORY
Berkley Prime Crime edition / April 1997

All rights reserved.
Copyright © 1997 by Karen Hanson Stuyck.
This book may not be reproduced in whole or in part,
by mimeograph or any other means, without permission.
For information address: The Berkley Publishing Group,
200 Madison Avenue, New York, NY 10016.

The Putnam Berkley World Wide Web site address is
http://www.berkley.com/berkley

ISBN: 0-425-15723-7

Berkley Prime Crime Books are published
by The Berkley Publishing Group,
200 Madison Avenue, New York, NY 10016.
The name BERKLEY PRIME CRIME and the BERKLEY PRIME CRIME
design are trademarks belonging to Berkley Publishing Corporation.

PRINTED IN THE UNITED STATES OF AMERICA

10 9 8 7 6 5 4 3 2 1

# LETHAL LESSONS

# Chapter One

KATE QUINLAN HAD ALREADY LAUNCHED INTO HER spiel by the time I arrived at the Powerful Woman workshop. She was standing behind a podium at the front of the high-school conference room, a thin, earnest woman with a halo of curly blonde hair. When she chuckled, her alto voice sounded husky. "Of course, that was *before* I became a Powerful Woman."

Apparently it was the punch line to a good story. The group laughed appreciatively. A few of the sixty or so women in the audience clapped.

I moved to the back row of folding metal chairs—as far away from Kate as I could get.

Unfortunately, eagle-eye Kate had spotted me. "Oh, there's somebody who just walked in I want you all to meet. Liz, will you please stand up so everyone can see you?"

Reluctantly, I stood.

"Liz James is my colleague at the Houston Mental Health Center," Kate continued, unfazed by the venomous look I was sending her way. "She's a genius writer, and she's going to help me write a book about what I have learned so far in my life. You want to say anything, Liz?''

I shook my head, my smile feeling like a death grimace.

"I'm thinking of calling my book *You Deserve Better*. You like that title?''

Amid what sounded like a murmur of assent, I sat down. We genius writers don't like calling attention to ourselves. Particularly when we are not at all sure that we will be in any way connected with the aforementioned sorry excuse for a book.

Why had I allowed Kate to push me into coming here on a Saturday afternoon? I had about two dozen more important things I needed to be doing. Planning my wedding, for instance. Granted it was very, very hard to say ''no'' to Kate, who reminded me of a pit bull in the tenacity department. Still I could have kicked myself for not trying harder.

But I was there, ruining my day off, so I decided I might as well sit back and listen. Maybe I could pick up a few helpful tips for telling Kate she deserved a better ghostwriter than me.

At the moment, she was informing the group about how she used to be—her pre–Powerful Woman days. Kate reached somewhere behind the podium and emerged with a poster-sized photo of herself. She held it high, moving closer to the front row so we all could see it.

A substantial number of the audience gasped. The young woman in the photo was an obese, depressed-looking college student wearing blue jeans and a shapeless denim work shirt. Only the frizzy blonde hair and rather prominent nose connected the Kate of today to this woman who virtually oozed misery.

The new and improved Kate looked at her own photo

and shook her head. "Didn't look much like a Powerful Woman, did I?

"Let me tell you about myself then," she continued. Her voice was softer now, wheedling, sucking us into her story. Confession time.

"I'd just finished graduate school when this picture was taken. Just arrived at my first job: a psychiatric social worker at a big, metropolitan hospital." She glanced at her old self and smile ruefully. "Don't I really *look* as if I'd be able to help people? Is that a face to inspire confidence in the hurting and needy?"

Kate moved closer to us, in front of the podium. "Yes, I was miserable. Yes, I was depressed. I was in a job where my boss treated me like his errand girl and otherwise pretended that I didn't exist. I was living with a man who refused to get a job, expected me to support him and then come home to cook his dinner and take all the verbal abuse he could dish out. In between my fulfilling work and home life, I scurried over to my alcoholic mother's house to take care of her too."

Kate's voice grew even quieter in the now silent room. "I hated my life. I hated the way I looked. I hated the way I felt, dragging myself through every day. I hated the contemptuous way every major person in my life treated me. But I never objected, never stood up for myself, never screamed: 'Hey, cut that out!' I was the classic people-pleaser, a good girl who suffered silently and never, ever offended anyone. And I was killing myself. Destroying myself as surely as if I were slashing at my wrists with a razor blade. Except my way—the smiley, silent, nice-girl routine—prolonged the agony."

Kate shrugged and favored us all with a knowing look. "Now, my therapist colleagues might say I was suffering from a dependent personality disorder. Or you might say I was just unassertive or even masochistic. I don't think the diagnosis is important. What *is* important is how I changed.''

Leaning forward, earnest now. ''Because, you see, right now I'm not at all like that poor young woman in the picture. I look different, sure, but that was just a reflection of how I felt about myself. The change *inside* came first. Once I decided I didn't deserve to be treated that way, that in fact, I would no longer tolerate being treated that way, everything changed. Everything! I stopped being everyone's doormat. I stopped being sweet. I left my boyfriend a note saying I'd moved out and he was now responsible for paying the rent. I gave my boss two weeks' notice and found another position where my skills were valued. I told my mother I wouldn't be coming around for awhile. And after I did all that, I suddenly stopped eating everything in sight. Within six months I'd lost sixty pounds without even going on a diet.''

Okay, I guess I was interested now. Kate, as I could personally confirm, was now anything but a doormat. Still, I wasn't sure the story was sufficiently gripping for me to willingly give up a precious Saturday to hear it.

Kate's large, hazel eyes scanned the room. She grinned at us. ''So you're saying, 'Yeah, that's nice, but what does this have to do with me?' You're probably not seventy pounds overweight or financially supporting an abusive slug or sitting there smiling at the Boss From Hell. In fact, right this minute you're probably telling youself that what I've been saying has nothing at all to do with you, with the way you're conducting your life. Right?'' She looked around the room, smiling encouragement like a kindergarten teacher trying to coax her shy little ones to participate in show-and-tell.

I saw a few women in the front rows nod their agreement.

Kate's smile faded, but her voice, when she finally spoke, was still quiet. "Well, you're wrong."

I could feel something change in the room. Perhaps a rapid decrease in the audience's comfort level. There seemed to be a lot of people fidgeting, especially when Kate moved closer, close enough to peer directly into evasive eyes.

"In some ways it's a lot harder to confront what's wrong when your life isn't terrible," she said. "My life was so utterly miserable that I couldn't use the excuses I hear every day: 'Oh, well, my life is as good as most people's. Nobody gets exactly what she wants. After all, everybody has to make *some* compromises.' "

Okay, now I was interested. Let's stop talking about boring old you and start talking about how this affects *me*.

"Now it is possible, I guess," Kate continued, "that your life really is just exactly the way you want it. And if it is, I'm truly happy for you. But most people have some areas in their life they'd like to change. Some of those areas are obvious to them, like the twenty pounds they want to lose before their high school reunion. And some areas are not-so-obvious: maybe a dream they had when they were younger, but then abandoned when they grew up and became realistic."

Kate nodded to the only other woman I recognized, Lorna Bell, a young social worker who worked in the mental health center's adult clinic with Kate. While Lorna passed out pencils and small pads of paper, Kate explained that she wanted us all to try a little written exercise. But first she wanted us all to take a couple of deep breaths together.

Along with everyone else I slowly sucked in air, and then slowly exhaled it.

"Okay, you have ten minutes to list everything in your life that you'd like to change," Kate said. "Write down any thought that comes to mind. No one except you is going to read your list."

Yeah, wonderful. Surely no one in the room was unsophisticated enough to find any revelations in this simpleminded workshop, I thought as I started jotting down things I'd like to change: Lose ten pounds before my wedding. Get a new car, one that requires virtually no maintenance. Get more sleep—I seemed to be exhausted all the time lately.

I stopped. Right offhand those were the only things I could think of. I noticed that several of the women in the rows ahead of me had stopped writing too.

"For those of you who are stuck, close your eyes, take a couple more deep breaths," Kate advised. "You don't have to be sure this is something you really want. Just try to fill the page with anything you can think of."

This was a mind-set I could identify with, the if-you-don't-get-off-your-ass-you're-going-to-miss-the-deadline mentality. This was my work M.O., the way I'd managed to produce dozens of brochures, hundreds of newsletters, and thousands of news releases despite a deplorable tendency toward procrastination. Under pressure, I produced.

I filled that page. What I wanted to change: Buy new furniture for my apartment. Live in Europe for a year. Take up weight lifting. Run a marathon. Quit the job I've had for the last eleven years and find a new, exciting one at twice the pay. Learn to play the harpsichord. Learn to paint with oils. Learn to make pottery. Write a novel. Get a bread-baking machine and have homemade bread for breakfast every day. Scratch the wedding. Divorce my sister Margaret.

"Okay, everybody stop," Kate's alto voice broke into my concentration.

I looked down at what I'd written. I wanted to divorce my sister? Forget my wedding? What was going on here? These were *not* things that I wanted—were they?

"Maybe some of the things you wrote surprised you," Kate was saying. "But before you dismiss them out of hand, I want you to seriously consider: Could this be something that would make your life better? Now I am *not* saying that if your wish list included murdering your impossible teenage daughter that you go out and buy a handgun." Kate grinned as participants chuckled. "But it could mean that you and your daughter need to establish some new guidelines, or go into therapy, or go off for a weekend together—at the very least stop ignoring the problem."

Our next assignment was to decide which changes on our list would most improve our life, and to jot down a few ideas on how we could start making those changes.

I spent the time staring at my paper. I didn't see how I could remove Margaret from my life; I wasn't sure I even wanted to. We'd just had a fight the night before, one of about ten million in our years as sisters. As usual, Margaret was too pushy, wanting, in this particular case, to take over my wedding, have the reception at her house and generally orchestrate the whole thing. I had walked out in a huff, furious that she was pushing me around. Still, if history continued to repeat itself, I'd eventually break down and give in to Margaret's demands. As usual.

I sighed. Moved on. The wedding. Surely I'd meant I didn't want a big, elaborate wedding. I'd already done the white-gown thing, and a simple, private trip to a justice of the peace was much more to my taste. That's what I meant by "Scratch the wedding." I didn't mean that I didn't want to marry Nick.

"Okay, now let's break up into small groups," Kate instructed us.

I found myself in a group consisting of a sharp-featured young woman with short, bleach-blonde hair; a squat, gray-haired woman in a beige pantsuit; a freckled redhead who seemed to ooze perkiness; and an earnest-looking young woman with long, center-parted brown hair who had to be a college student.

The blonde woman started our discussion. "You know, I guess I never realized how furious I am with my boss. I mean, I know he pisses me off with all his little sex jokes and the way he pats my shoulder when he talks to me. But I always told myself that he doesn't mean anything. He's not coming on to me; he's just an old guy who doesn't know any better. But today I realized I'm tired of taking his shit. I know *he's* the one who's kept me from being promoted. I can't prove it, but I know."

"So what are you going to do about it?" the long-haired young woman asked. I'd bet she was planning to enter one of the helping professions.

The blonde, whose stick-on name badge read ANNETTE, sighed. "I don't know. I suppose I could file a sexual harassment suit."

"That takes forever," Beige Pantsuit said morosely. She, like me, did not wear a name tag. "My sister-in-law did that. It took three years to come to trial, and then she didn't win. I told her, 'Mary Lou, why didn't you just find a new job?' All she got from the experience was an ulcer."

"I guess I could look for a new job," Annette said, not sounding very enthusiastic at the prospect.

"I think that's a great idea, Annette," said the freckled

redhead—LINDSY, her name badge announced in big, capital letters. "Now, what I want to change is getting my family to help out more with the housework. I've got four kids, two dogs and two cats and a husband who doesn't do squat once he walks in the door at night. I'm tired of feeling as if I'm the family servant."

"Good luck," Beige Pantsuit said.

"Have you ever told your family how you feel?" I was surprised to discover the voice offering this inspired advice was my own. "Maybe you could make a chore chart and list the jobs each person is responsible for."

"You know, that's a great idea." Lindsy beamed at me. "Maybe I could give the kids stars and some kind of reward for completing their jobs."

I grinned back at her, pleased at how easy it was to solve other people's problems.

We went around the group like that. Beige Pantsuit wanted to find an interesting job after spending the last thirty years as a full-time homemaker and mother. The earnest, long-haired woman—who was actually a kindergarten teacher—wanted to start her own business, preferably one having nothing to do with small children. And I? When everyone looked expectantly at me, I muttered something about my sister taking over my wedding plans.

"So tell her to butt out," Beige Pantsuit said. "It's your wedding."

"It's not as simple as that," I said, feeling like a wimp.

"Maybe you need to tell her how you feel," Lindsy volunteered. "You know, the way you told me to do with my family."

She did not look like she was being sarcastic, but it was hard to tell with those wide-eyed, wholesome types.

Fortunately, Kate chose that moment to take center stage again. She wanted to share with us a story she'd heard in another group. "Robin here"—Kate patted the shoulder of a pixieish brunette with a lovely, porcelain complexion—"has a husband who spends every free minute with his classic cars."

"And not only does he ignore me," Robin said in a surprisingly loud voice for such a small woman, "he won't ever let me near his precious cars unless he's driving and I'm in the passenger seat. John even has a special lock for the garage that he has the only key to."

"Get rid of him," Beige Pantsuit called.

I was tempted to advise her to rule out arbitration or customer-service positions in her career search.

"I don't want to get rid of him," Robin replied. "I just want him to pay attention to me, to act as if I still matter to him."

"Have you told him this?" Kate asked.

Robin nodded, her lips trembling. "He said I was being unreasonable. That he owns a very demanding business and needs a hobby to unwind, to help him cope with the stress, and I should stop bitching and moaning. According to John, I'm lucky he doesn't beat me or go out with other women. Apparently I'm supposed to be grateful that he's home at night instead of out drinking or gambling away our money." Suddenly Robin started to cry.

Kate patted her shoulder, but let her cry. Finally, when Robin was down to a few sniffles, Kate said quietly, "The first step is to believe that you do deserve better. Do you believe that, Robin?"

"Well, yeah." Robin studied her shoes. "I guess I do. It's just that John *is* very tired. I do need to see his side of it too. He's not really a bad guy."

Kate's face, so sympathetic a moment earlier, looked stern. "No! This is what women do all the time: make excuses. Make excuses for their husbands: 'Oh, he feels so ashamed after he hits me.' Make excuses for why they themselves can't change: 'I'll do it later when my kids are grown.'

"No more excuses, Robin. If you want to live with it—if you decide you don't want to change—fine. Then stop whining. Make the best of it. If you want to change your life, no one but you can do it. And you *can* do it, Robin. I know you can."

Kate looked around the group. "What do we want to tell Robin? You," she prompted, waving her hands for us to join in, "Deserve . . ."

"Better!" the group shouted.

Yeah, right, I thought, feeling sorry for Robin, who was smiling sheepishly. At least I hadn't had to pay for this workshop.

Kate gave Robin a big hug and whispered something into her ear. Robin nodded. "I *do* deserve better," she announced, as if she'd just made a momentous discovery.

The workshop participants clapped enthusiastically. "Give him hell, honey," Beige Pantsuit shouted.

I glanced at my watch: 3:15. Almost time to go.

After that, more participants stood up to share their stories. A woman whose teenaged son was skipping school and staying out all night announced she was going to tell the kid he could move out if he wasn't home by eleven every night. "I'm not taking this crap from him anymore." (Wild applause.) A woman whose mother phoned six times a day to criticize her daughter's every move said she was getting an unlisted phone number on Monday. "I'm telling her that from now on when I want to talk to her, I'll phone her." (More applause.) Another woman was going to ask for a promotion. A timid-looking white-haired woman was going to tell her husband she wanted more sex. ("Right on!" Beige Pantsuit screamed amidst the cheers.) Everyone, it seemed, was filled with hope, enthusiasm, ebullience.

I felt like I should be wearing a sign that read: BAH! HUMBUG!

Kate finally ended the discussion. "I'm so proud of all of you," she said, beaming at us like a proud parent. "And I hope you're all proud of yourselves too. A lot of you have already taken the first step today: convincing yourself that you deserve better."

I tuned out, glancing at my watch: 3:59. Time to go. Kate was saying something about many participants liking to return for a second or third seminar for followup and support; the additional workshops were half-price.

The minute she finished talking, I leaped up and headed for the door. I'd tell Kate on Monday that I had too many other commitments to write her book. But right now all I wanted to do was go home.

A tall, scowling bald man stopped me in the parking lot. "Excuse me, miss, do you know if that women's workshop is over yet?"

"It's just finished. Everybody should be out in a few minutes."

"Damned waste of time and money," he said, gesturing with his car keys.

I'd been thinking the same thing myself a few minutes ago, but I wasn't up to a discussion about the merits of the workshop. Plus there was something about the man that gave me the creeps. I grunted and hurried toward my car.

Because I'd arrived late, my Toyota was parked at the furthest end of the school parking lot. By the time I reached it, the parking lot was filled with departing workshop participants.

I saw what happened next only because I dropped my car keys. As I stooped to pick them up, I saw Robin—the tiny brunette who'd shared her marital problems with the group—start to run. And the scowling, bald man I'd talked to was walking rapidly after her. "Hey, what the hell do you think you're doing?" he yelled at her.

As I, and about a dozen other participants, stared in fascination, Robin raced to an older model Thunderbird convertible, its top down. She jumped inside and turned on the ignition.

The bald man was running now. "Don't you *dare*!" he bellowed.

Robin put the car in reverse and backed up.

Women scurried for cover. The bald man was almost to the car now, his face red, his fists balled up.

Robin backed into him.

Somebody screamed. A woman.

Robin's husband was sprawled on the ground. "Bitch!" he was yelling, pulling himself up.

Robin stopped and shifted gears again. "I'm not going to take this anymore!" she screamed as she plowed into him a second time.

# Chapter Two

NICK WHISTLED AS WE PULLED IN FRONT OF THE QUIN-
lans' River Oaks home.

"Other people's misery must be a lucrative business."

"Not *that* lucrative," I said, taking in the elegant two-
story white colonial. River Oaks was probably the most
expensive subdivision in Houston, a close-to-town, older
neighborhood filled with large, graceful old homes next to
humongous new ones that often resembled insurance com-
panies complete with tennis courts and guest houses. My
godson, Jonathan, had once taken a bus tour of Houston
for a school field trip and said the bus had stopped at a
home in River Oaks where a pony grazed in the front yard.
Even the more modest homes now cost over a million dollars. Which meant the neighborhood tended to be filled with
CEOs, long-time partners in Houston's most expensive law
firms, hotshot physicians, and elderly oil men who somehow managed to stay afloat when the oil market (and much
of Houston's oil-based economy) went bust in the mid-
eighties.

"Kate and Roger didn't buy that house on their salaries from the mental health center," I said.

Nick parked his black Maxima across the street from the Quinlan home, and we walked up the tree-shaded path to the front door. "Tell me again why we're going to this thing," Nick said before pushing the doorbell.

"Roger Quinlan is head of the symposium committee that I served on." The two-day center-sponsored symposium on Violence, Aggression and Psychiatry had just concluded, and Roger apparently wanted to reward everyone who'd worked for months to pull it off.

A sullen-looking, overweight teenager in a shapeless navy dress opened the door. "The party's in there," she muttered, pointing to the back of the house.

"Thanks." I smiled at her. She did not smile back. "I bet you're Dr. Quinlan's daughter. I'm Liz James." I held out my hand.

"Mel Quinlan," she said, barely touching my hand.

Nick nodded at the room she'd pointed out. "Is that where I get a drink?"

"They've set up a bar in the sunroom." Mel indicated a smaller room next to the other. "You're going to need a lot to drink to put up with this crowd."

Nick grinned down at her. "I was thinking the same thing myself."

We walked past an antique-filled living room to the sunroom. I waved at some friends while Nick headed for the bar set up amidst the plants and white wicker furniture.

"Liz!" I heard the familiar husky voice behind me. I took a swig of the red wine Nick had just brought me before turning around to face our hostess.

I told Kate how lovely her house was and introduced her to Nick. I wished I could figure out how to work into the conversation that I didn't want to write her book: Oh, Kate, your rose garden is exquisite—and did I mention that I don't intend to write a single word about your simplistic workshop?

Kate smiled and shook Nick's hand. She was wearing a short, scoop-necked black dress, backless high-heeled pumps, and dangly silver earrings. Her makeup was subtle and effective and her blonde hair had somehow lost its kinkiness and now curled softly around her face. It was very clear from the expression on Nick's face that he at least found Kate Quinlan highly attractive.

"I always read your stories in the *Chronicle*," Kate was telling him. "I loved that last one you did about the guy who was selling those bogus franchises. You really skewered him."

"Thanks." Nick's white teeth glinted in his sharply planed—and, to my eyes, at least, very handsome—face. "From what I've been hearing about you, you're pretty good at puncturing inflated egos yourself."

Kate smiled back. The two of them looked as if they were starting some mutual admiration society: only muckrakers, fighters and abrasive malcontents need apply. I— the meek, quiet one—felt left out.

Kate turned to me. "Did you see Robin on the TV news last Saturday?" When I shook my head, she added, "Some policeman was arresting her in the high school parking lot, leading her to the squad car, and this Channel 13 reporter stuck a microphone in her face and asked her why she had run over her husband. Robin looked right into the camera and said, 'I just decided I wasn't going to take his abuse anymore. I deserve better than that. I've never felt so empowered. Taking Kate Quinlan's workshop changed my life.' "

I groaned. "Her husband is going to live, isn't he?"

Kate nodded serenely. "Oh, yeah. I called the hospital.

He's got some cracked ribs and a broken leg, but that's about it. When Robin got out of jail, she called to tell me she'd moved into her own apartment.''

Roger Quinlan had sidled up during the description of the man's injuries. "We should have had Kate speak at the Violence and Aggression conference, don't you think, Liz?" He bared sharp, piranha-like teeth. "She seems to have a unique talent for turning passive women into homicidal maniacs.''

"At least," Kate replied cooly, "*I* have a talent for something, Roger." She nodded at Nick and me, then walked away, without giving her husband a second glance.

Roger smiled stiffly, pretending to be unfazed by her parting shot. He was a slight, nervous man, with elegant hands that looked as if they regularly received the attention of a manicurist. He was losing his hair. A psychiatrist in the adult clinic and the clinic head, he was rumored to be very bright but frequently caustic with coworkers. He and Kate had both started working at the center about a year ago, so the symposium committee had been my first prolonged contact with Roger. As committee chair, his attention to detail and his perfectionism had contributed greatly to the symposium's success—the same traits that antagonized almost every one of the committee members.

"Did Kate tell you that she talked with a reporter yesterday?" Roger asked me. When I shook my head, he said, "The woman interviewed Kate about her Powerful Woman workshops." Roger rolled his eyes. "And from what I gather, she also interviewed some of the women who attended Kate's banal little lecture.''

"But why?" I asked. Every day in Houston hundreds of workshops of one sort or another took place. Very seldom did they generate news coverage.

Roger shrugged. "My point exactly, particularly when

you consider how little media coverage we received for our symposium. Apparently the Houston media aren't interested in cutting-edge psychiatric research. You have to have one of the participants run her husband over with his car to catch the attention of our stellar local journalists.'' His thin lips curled into a sneer. ''Too bad we didn't have a knife fight during our closing panel. Think of all the news coverage that would have generated.''

The member of the stellar local media standing next to me looked as if he was about to dump his Scotch onto Roger's shiny scalp. ''Another possibility you might consider is that your research was less cutting edge than you think. Medical reporters often complain that physicians' inflated egos make them overestimate the newsworthiness of their topics.''

''Actually,'' I interjected, trying too late to calm the suddenly choppy waters, ''the *Chronicle* medical reporter told me she's going to do a long story about the symposium. It's supposed to run next Sunday.''

Neither man looked remotely interested in this information.

''Who the hell are you?'' Roger demanded of Nick. ''And what right do you have to come into *my* house and insult me?''

At the sound of Roger's raised voice Kate rejoined our group. She looked unperturbed but curious and rather amused—not at all my reaction to the scene. If there had been a large rock nearby, I would have happily crawled under it.

''This is Nick Finley, Roger, Liz's fiancé. He's that wonderful investigative reporter for the *Chronicle*. Presumably he's here as Liz's date—not to uncover any of your professional malfeasance, though that, too, is a possibility.''

Roger looked as if he couldn't decide which one of them

he most wanted to slug. "Go to hell!" he snarled, presumably at his wife, then stalked away.

"Roger tends to overreact," Kate said mildly. "By the way, did you hear about my interview yesterday?"

I stared at her. Was she really so unfazed by Roger's antics—or so used to them—that she could just shrug off the whole incident and move on to Topic B? Or was she just so self-involved that she was indifferent to any subject that didn't hinge directly on her?

Still, I was relieved to change the subject. I'd been afraid that at any minute Nick or Roger was going to throw the first punch. "Roger said a reporter interviewed you and some women who attended the workshop Saturday," I said. "Who was the reporter?"

"Sheila somebody-or-other—Lemont? A nice kid in her mid-twenties."

Nick nodded. "Sheila Lemur. A new lifestyle writer."

I'd never worked with Sheila. "What kind of story is she planning to do?"

"She said she wanted to do a feature on how my workshop empowered women," Kate said. "Sheila saw Robin interviewed on TV when the police were taking her to jail, and Sheila phoned her. Then another woman from the workshop called to tell me what had happened to her. Apparently she'd been having trouble with a sexually harrassing boss. When he walked into the office Monday morning she pinched his butt. He objected and she said, 'What's wrong, honey? Is it *that* time of the month?' Loud enough for everyone within half a mile to hear."

Nick laughed. I smiled, remembering the sharp-featured blonde from the workshop. Apparently Annette had found a way to vent her anger.

"So, the next morning, the boss fired her," Kate said.

"He told her that her work was shoddy, and he didn't like her attitude."

I groaned. "Poor Annette. Do you know what she's going to do now?"

Kate grinned. "She filed charges with the Equal Employment Opportunity Commission, and said she feels great—empowered. And she attributes it all to my workshop. Sheila interviewed her too."

I envisioned the headline on Sheila's story: WORKSHOP'S MESSAGE TO WOMEN—READY! AIM! ATTACK!

Nick raised his eyebrows at me. "Is there something I should be preparing myself for? Some imminent surge of aggression about to be directed at me?"

I ignored him. "Surely you're going to cancel next Saturday's workshop. If you want to be taken seriously, you don't need to be known as the workshop leader who incites women to violence."

Kate sent me a you-must-be-joking look. "But I didn't incite anyone to violence. You were there. Did you hear me say anything about revenge or attacks or violence?"

I shook my head. "No, you just told them they didn't have to put up with all the crap in their life. On their own, they carried your argument to the next step."

Kate nodded. "Exactly. So you can be there next Saturday?"

I swallowed, wishing I'd had this conversation with her earlier. I also felt vaguely disappointed that somehow I'd missed out on all this floating personal empowerment from Kate's workshop. "No, I can't. I've been meaning to tell you this earlier, Kate, but I just don't have the time to work on your book. I have too many other commitments right now."

Kate looked unperturbed by my bailing out. "Okay."

She smiled at both of us. "Nice meeting you, Nick," she said before moving on to another group.

We left the party a few minutes later. As we walked by I noticed our host in what looked like a library talking to a pretty, auburn-haired psychiatry resident I'd met once. I think her name was Brenda. Whatever Roger was talking about seemed to require his standing very close to Brenda and touching her arm a lot. I decided not to tell him goodbye.

"I liked Kate," Nick said as we got into his car. "Can't imagine why she stays married to an officious asshole like Roger."

"You think she deserves better?" I asked, chuckling.

He sent me a blank look. "Obviously."

"You'll get it when you read Sheila's article."

"I can't wait," Nick said.

The article ran Friday morning. It was a nice-size feature with lots of quotes from Kate explaining the goals of her workshop, a few paragraphs about Robin's car assault: "It was a real life-changing experience for me." And Annette's pinch: "Walking out of the workshop, I felt all this pent-up rage come spilling out of me." There was also a big photo of Robin's husband standing on crutches in front of his dented 1957 Thunderbird convertible.

I just wished the story hadn't mentioned Kate was a therapist at the Houston Mental Health Center. That also seemed to be the main sentiment of my center colleagues who'd read the story and popped into my office to share their views. "Giving real therapy a bad name" and "Duping naive people with this instant-transformation crap" seemed to be the common comments from the psychotherapists. The only administrator who talked to me warned that if any reporter phoned, I should make clear that the mental health center was in no way connected to Kate's workshop.

My friend Amanda O'Neil, a child psychologist, was one of the few center employees amused by the article. "I must say I almost envy you being able to work on Kate's book," she told me over lunch. "It sounds a lot more exciting than working on the stuffy old journal article I'm trying to finish."

"I am not," I said firmly, "working on Kate's book. I don't have the time or the inclination."

"Oh, well," Amanda said. "Then I guess I'll just have to wait until Kate writes her own book to get the lowdown on how to transform myself."

"Don't hold your breath," I said. "I can't imagine any reputable publisher buying Kate's autobiographical self-help book."

That evening Nick and I went out to dinner with some friends of his from the newspaper; then we decided, on the spur of the moment, to take in a late movie. By the time I got home and into bed it was close to 2 A.M.

I was not pleased when the phone woke me out of a deep sleep. "Liz, you sound like you're asleep," a familiar voice said accusingly.

"I am." I pried one eye open to see what time it was. "Hey, it's only 8:10."

"Well, get up!" Kate Quinlan ordered. "You need to get down here right away. All these women who read the newspaper article just showed up for my workshop. Hundreds of angry women. It's Thelma-and-Louise land down here."

She hung up before I could remind her I was no longer involved with her workshop.

# Chapter Three

IT WAS A ZOO. WHEN I ARRIVED HALF AN HOUR LATER about two hundred impatient women were standing in line in the high-school hall. "They're trying to move the workshop to a larger room," a young woman in jeans, sandals and a baggy T-shirt told me, "but there's a chance some of us will still be turned away."

"She'll probably give another workshop in a week or two," I said, intending to be reassuring. "If this one is closed, I'm sure you can get into that one."

The woman's narrow face suddenly radiated hostility. "I don't want to be in another workshop. I want to be in *this* one."

Right. Let's hear it for delayed gratification. I walked to the front of the line, looking for Kate and explaining to anyone who complained that I was "workshop staff." I didn't find Kate, but I did locate Lorna Bell, the young social worker who'd helped out at the last workshop. She looked uncharacteristically frazzled. "Liz, thank God you're here. None of these women are registered for the workshop. They all just showed up, expecting to get in. But we don't have enough room for everybody, and nobody wants to go home.''

I glanced behind me, seeing what she meant. Nobody, unfortunately, had that look of pleasant, smiling accommodation I associated with women of my mother's generation. Instead the women in this line—of varying ages, sizes and ethnic groups—all looked as if they were ready to rip off Lorna's head if she tried to send them away. And *my* head. I caught some of the women at the front of the line glaring at me too.

Suddenly I spotted Kate coming down the hallway. Moving rapidly, smiling, stopping at the end of the line to answer questions

She stopped in the middle of the line. ''Okay, ladies.'' (Ladies?) ''We've got everything worked out,'' she announced in a loud, take-charge voice. ''We're moving the workshop from the conference room to the auditorium, and there should be room for everyone.''

A couple of women near the back applauded.

Kate pointed a long, manicured finger at Lorna and me. ''Since most of you haven't pre-registered for the workshop, you can give your check or cash to me or my assistants, Lorna and Liz, as you go into the auditorium. I'm hoping to get everything rolling in ten minutes.''

I was now Kate's assistant? As I sat next to Lorna, taking checks and dollar bills, handing out change from Lorna's metal cash box, I wondered what I needed to do to convince Kate that I was *not* part of the Powerful Woman workshop family.

When at last we'd accepted money from every woman in sight, I stood up to leave. ''See you Monday,'' I told Lorna.

''You're not leaving, are you?'' She turned limpid, deer-caught-in-the-headlights eyes on me.

"Well, yes, actually I planned to." As succinctly as possible, I explained that, contrary to what Kate seemed to think, I wasn't really a member of the workshop staff. I'd only come this morning to help Kate deal with the unexpected glut of participants. "Everyone is registered now, so I'm leaving."

Lorna clutched my arm. "Please, Liz, stay for just one more workshop. There are so many women, and I really need your help to get them into groups and pass out the paper and pencils and everything . . ."

Her voice trailed off, but her fingers still bit into my arm. I jerked my arm away, feeling annoyed. "Look, Lorna, I have other plans. I'm supposed to go look for wedding dresses and check out caterers with my sister today."

The image of Margaret's small, petulant face floated through my mind. Ooh, would she be pissed if I canceled our outing! I tilted my head to one side, considering. "Okay," I told Lorna, "but this is absolutely the last time I set foot in a Powerful Woman workshop. After this Kate is going to have to find another assistant. I'll be in the auditorium in a few minutes after I make a phone call."

The phone call ended up taking more than a few minutes. I hung up after Margaret snarled that she didn't care that I was her only sister. She was never, ever going to forgive me for this.

By the time I got to the auditorium Kate had already finished her introductory explanations and was answering questions from the audience. I sat down next to Lorna in the back row. "Kate didn't do this in the last workshop, did she?" I whispered.

Lorna shook her head. "This is a different group from last time. A lot more aggressive. And some of the women from last time"—she pointed to a group of women in the front row—"came back to tell what happened to them."

Now that they were pointed out to me, I recognized Robin, the classic-car wife, and Annette, the woman from my group who'd been fired after pinching her boss' fanny.

"Unfortunately," Kate was saying, "there have been certain misconceptions about Powerful Woman in the media recently. No matter what you may have heard or read, I am not advocating violence against men in these workshops."

The two hard-faced young women sitting on the other side of Lorna looked disappointed. In the front row, Robin raised her hand.

Kate nodded at her. "Yes, Robin?"

Robin jumped up, reminding me of an aging, but still-perky, cheerleader on speed. "I just want to say that while I realize you never advocated violence in the last workshop, that nevertheless your workshop changed my life. I feel so *empowered*." Robin gazed adoringly at Kate, who, I thought, looked a tad embarrassed.

Robin turned around, facing the audience. "But you know what?" she said in a conspiratorial, just-between-us-gals voice. "Running over my husband was the best thing I ever did in my life. I mean, I guess I'm glad the bastard didn't die, but I'll always treasure the memory of the expression on John's face when I ground those gears into reverse and started after him in his precious car with me in the driver's seat."

Women burst into wild applause around me. Women who looked as if they'd like to run down their husband or their boss or their mother-in-law with a classic car—hell, with any car at all. Robin beamed at her fans. I was afraid that at any minute she was going to take a bow.

I rolled my eyes at Lorna. She shook her head. "Jesus, save us," she whispered.

Kate finally managed to calm down the crowd. "Some

other women who attended last week's workshop have also asked to speak," she said. "Since we've been discussing making changes in our own lives, I thought it might be interesting to see the kinds of changes other participants have made."

I braced myself. A gray-haired woman in a stylish red suit stood up. She looked vaguely familiar, but only when she started to speak in a familiar deep, gravelly voice did I recognize her as Beige Pantsuit, the acerbic, negative woman from my group. "After years of telling myself that I have to do something to get out of the house, I have gone back to college," she announced. "I'm going to get my degree in accounting and become a CPA." She sat down.

Lorna and I applauded wildly.

"That's wonderful," Kate said. "And now Annette, where are you?"

The sharp-featured blonde, also from my small group at the first workshop, stood up. She did not look empowered. Petulant was more the word I'd use to describe Annette's expression.

"I left your workshop last week thinking I didn't deserve to be treated like some blonde bimbo by my disgusting pig of a boss. So I decided to show him what it felt like to be treated with contempt. On Monday morning, when he made one of his little remarks about what a wild weekend he bet I had had, I turned around and pinched his butt." Annette ignored the smattering of audience applause. "And do you know what that dickhead did? He fired me!"

"So what's happened since then?" Kate asked.

"Nothing. I filed charges with the EEOC, but that will take forever to come to trial. And in the meantime no one will hire me because they think I'm a troublemaker." Annette glared at Kate—a you-got-me-into-this-now-you-get-me-out look. Apparently the futile job search had shattered Annette's previous euphoria.

Kate looked around the room. "Anybody have any suggestions for Annette?"

"Sue the bastard!" somebody who apparently hadn't been listening too intently called out. "He didn't have any right to fire you for doing the same thing he'd been doing to you."

"Apply for jobs with women bosses," a heavy woman in a denim jumper and black T-shirt called in a high-pitched voice.

A green-haired teenager with an earring in her nose yelled, "Slash the bastard's tires and phone him in the middle of the night."

A few women laughed. Several applauded.

Lorna and I looked at each other. "I think this might be my last Powerful Woman workshop too," she said.

Kate still looked calm. Unflappable. "Do you want to continue working as a secretary?" she asked Annette.

Annette shrugged. "Not really. But I need the money."

"So if you could be anything you wanted to be, what kind of work would you do?"

I waited for Annette to say, "I'd be either a brain surgeon or a ballerina."

Instead she volunteered, "I guess I'd have my own business. I like to design clothes. I sew all my own things, and sometimes I make outfits for my friends too."

I wondered if the multicolored silk jacket and flowing pants she was wearing were her designs. If so, Annette might well have a future as a designer.

Kate looked as if she was having the same reaction. "That's a terrific idea! So what's stopping you from doing it?"

"Money. I don't have enough to start a business and no

bank is going to give me a loan. Especially now.'' Annette was looking depressed again.

"How about making some clothes and trying to sell them at other dress shops for now? You don't have to start out with your own shop at first. And while you're doing that maybe you can research the steps in opening your own business.''

I thought it was a great idea, but Annette still had a yes-but expression on her face. "And while you're doing all that—designing your clothes, finding dress stores to sell them—you're probably going to have to have another job to support yourself. But maybe you can find work in a clothes store that will teach you about retailing and about what kind of clothes customers are buying. The important thing is that you've identified a goal you are willing to work for. Now all you have to do is figure out the steps you have to take to get there.''

Annette was nodding and smiling, like now she got it. I glanced around the room. Some of the participants seemed interested, but a significant minority looked restless and bored. The girl with the green hair looked as if she was asleep.

I turned when the auditorium door opened and a man in a blue messenger-service uniform peered into the room. Lorna got up to go talk to him.

"There's a big package for Kate,'' Lorna whispered when she returned to her seat. "I told the guy to leave it outside, but he insisted he had instructions that Kate needed it this morning for the workshop. So I told him to bring it in.''

Lorna looked worried. "I hope that wasn't a mistake. Kate didn't tell me she was expecting a package.''

"Don't worry about it,'' I advised. "If Kate wasn't expecting it, she won't open it.''

Kate was talking about creating the kind of life you want when the man returned pushing a dolly holding a large packing box, the size I associated with major household appliances. What could it be? I watched Kate's face to see if she was having any kind of reaction to the delivery, but her expression didn't change as the man unloaded the box at the foot of the stage.

Suddenly Kate grinned. "Now I realize all this talk of taking responsibility and meeting your goals sounds kind of grim and joyless. But it doesn't have to be. Part of taking responsibility for yourself is being kind to yourself, nurturing yourself, giving yourself gifts." She looked at the package. "Which it looks as if someone has done for me. Should we open it?"

So Kate had planned it after all! She recruited some women from the front row to help her open the box. Did anyone have a scissors or utility knife to cut it open? A tanned, hard-bodied woman in blue jeans and a denim work shirt produced an Army knife from her fanny pack.

As Kate and the two volunteers worked on the box, I glanced at my watch, wondering how long it would be before our lunch break. I'd rushed out without breakfast this morning and my stomach was signaling its irritation at my oversight. I was harboring uncharitable thoughts about showbizzy stunts—Was a clown going to jump out with party favors for everyone?—while the trio up front took forever to open the damn box.

But finally they'd slit it down the middle and pried it open. I saw Kate's face turn ashen as she saw what was inside. One of her helpers screamed.

It took me a moment to figure out what was going on. The people ahead of me were standing up and someone else was screaming to call the police. But finally I, too, saw what was causing the commotion. Sprawled on the floor in front of the box was the very dead body of Roger Quinlan.

# Chapter Four

KATE QUINLAN CRIED A LOT AT ROGER'S FUNERAL. FOR some reason that surprised me. Probably because I'd always considered Kate a stiff-upper-lip type and also because frankly I'd never thought she was all that fond of Roger.

But sob she did, sitting in the first row of the River Oaks Methodist Church next to Mel. The teenager, dry-eyed, stared straight ahead, looking as if she wished she were somewhere else. A tiny blonde woman in a navy suit sat on the opposite side of the girl.

"That's Roger's first wife," Lorna Bell whispered to me, nodding at the woman in the navy suit. "She's Melanie's mother."

Mel's mother, I noticed, looked as composed as her daughter. Not too many ex-wives got choked up at their former husbands' funerals. She leaned over and whispered something to Mel, who turned to her with a smile.

We were sitting with a group of mental health center employees, people who'd worked with either Roger or Kate. I glanced around the large, white-paneled church flanked by lovely stained glass windows, recognizing several doctors from the medical center.

Lorna leaned toward me again. "She has a drinking problem," she whispered in an ominous voice.

"Who?" Mel? The first wife? Kate?

"Sissy, the ex-wife." Lorna's round, earnest face sent me a You're-not-paying-attention look. "That's why Melanie started living with Roger and Kate this year." Lorna lifted her skimpy eyebrows in a telling And-is-there-a-story-there expression.

How did she know all this stuff? I was about to inquire about further details when Tricia Whitmore turned around in the pew ahead of us to glare at us.

When Tricia returned to her original position, Lorna sent me another meaningful eyebrow raise. This time I knew what she was getting at. According to center gossip, Tricia had been having an affair with Roger. It seemed strange that Tricia, a new (and self-important) Ph.D. who almost always dressed conservatively, had chosen a short, shocking-pink knit dress for her beloved's funeral. And when she'd turned around to shush us her pale, rather horselike face appeared more angry than sad.

Still, who can tell about grief? I focused on the elderly minister's sermon long enough to hear about what a tragedy Roger's murder was, and what a loss his death was to his profession. I heard in detail about Roger's contributions to the church in making counseling available to residents of the church's shelter for the homeless and his research into anxiety and violence and aggression. No mention was made of less pleasant topics: the fatal gunshot wound to Roger's head, the fact that the funeral had been postponed until the medical examiner completed an autopsy.

I tuned out the reverend. I surreptitiously inspected the people sitting around me, noticing a lot of solemn faces and a few obviously bored ones. But no one looked very sad. Roger, one of my fellow symposium committee members had once remarked, had long ago decided that it was better to be feared than to be loved. I wondered suddenly if that was the decision that had gotten him killed.

Finally, after a soprano sang "Amazing Grace" and the minister gave a few closing remarks, the service was over. I stood up with relief.

As we filed out of the church I noticed Tricia's stony face, a sharp contrast to her bright pink dress. A clinical psychologist in the same adult clinic as Roger, Tricia had only been at the center about eight months. When I interviewed her for our employee newsletter I'd thought her a bright, serious, young woman, pleasant but reserved. The only personal information Tricia had been willing to divulge was about her athletic hobbies. She'd been into mountain climbing and skiing during grad school in Colorado, she said, but figured that in flat, snowless Houston she'd have to make do with marathon running and working out at the gym.

Now, as Tricia filed out ahead of me, I could see the muscles in her well-toned arms and the hard lines of her butt in the tight knit dress. It was hard for me to imagine what this twenty-eight-year-old fitness fanatic would see in balding, waspish Roger. Middle-aged, married Roger.

In the church anteroom I spotted Kate and walked over to offer my condolences.

"Oh, Liz." She grasped my upper arm as if for support. "You are coming back to the house, aren't you?" Her eyes, I saw, were red-rimmed and swollen, her face pale.

It was the first time I'd seen her look even mildly vulnerable. Without the customary fierce glint in her eyes and her aura of barely-contained energy, she seemed like another person, an older, depressed version of herself.

I hesitated. I hadn't been planning to go, but Kate seemed so needy, desperate even, that I figured it wouldn't hurt me to stop in for half an hour. Nick and I were going to lunch and then out shopping that afternoon. "Sure," I said, "but I'm only going to be able to stay for a little while."

"Thanks, Liz." Kate squeezed my arm. "I really appreciate it."

The Quinlan house was only a short drive from the church. By the time I got to the house, cars were already parked halfway down the block. Apparently Kate had reached out to a large number of her acquaintances for comfort.

I parked and walked to the house, trying to analyze the effect Kate had on me. Why did I, who didn't particularly even like the woman, end up doing whatever it was she wanted me to do? No, I'd told her, I'm sorry, I don't want to write your book or help out with your workshop, and then I'd come immediately when she'd summoned me out of bed last Saturday morning. And now today, another treasured Saturday. I had intended to leave immediately after the funeral and run a few errands before Nick arrived. Instead, I ended up at Kate's house. Keeping her company along with fifty or sixty other intimate friends.

So why *did* I do it? Yes, Kate was highly assertive in her requests, but I regularly said no to dozens of other pushy people. Granted, Kate had a certain charisma. And yes, I suppose it was flattering that she always seemed to need me so desperately—only *I* could write her book or help out with her workshop. But none of these felt like sufficient explanations for why I now stood at Kate's front door, feeling put upon and annoyed with myself, but nevertheless ready to do the right thing.

Roger's daughter, Mel, opened the door again. She was

wearing a navy linen dress that looked a size too small, black flats, and lots of heavy eye makeup that gave her pale face a racoonish look. She regarded me impassively. "They're in the back."

"I'm very sorry about your father," I said as I stepped inside. "I'm Liz James," I added, in case she'd forgotten our previous introduction. "I was on a committee with your dad at the mental health center."

Mel studied me for a moment, her face devoid of expression. "I remember you from Roger's party. The one where he and Kate got into their big screaming match."

I nodded, not sure what to say. I wondered if it was significant that Mel called her father by his first name, not Dad or Pop or, in that fine Texas tradition, Daddy. Wondered too when the "big screaming match" had taken place.

"Where's your boyfriend?" Mel asked. "That tall guy who pissed off Roger."

She didn't miss much; I'd have to give her that. "He didn't come to the funeral."

"Lucky him," Mel said, then turned to greet the next arriving guests.

I wandered to the back of the house, to the same room where Roger's symposium party had been held. I had a sudden vivid image of Roger on that night. Brilliant, caustic, perfectionist Roger in his expensive tweed sports jacket and silk shirt, looking like a small volcano about to erupt onto Nick and Kate.

Without him the room seemed subdued, the hum of conversations lower and more sedate. Even Kate, standing in a corner, sipping a drink and talking to a white-haired couple, appeared somehow muted. It was as if all the tears she'd shed at the funeral had drained her of her usual frenetic energy, leaving only this pallid shell of her former self.

When the couple moved away I walked over to Kate. I would pay my condolences and leave.

"Liz, thank you so much for coming." Kate's deep-set hazel eyes, gazing into mine, were still a bit swollen, but she looked more in control now, less likely to burst into tears.

She glanced around the room with a rather bewildered expression, as if she were trying to figure out where she was. "You know, all of this—Roger's dying, someone sending me the body—didn't really sink in until this morning at the funeral. Before that it all seemed so unreal."

Yes, I said, I could imagine it would take time to get over the shock. The stunt-like quality of Roger's murder had made his death seem unreal to me too.

Kate lowered her voice so much that I had to lean forward to hear her. "Do you remember Robin Carter from my workshop, the woman who ran over her husband?"

Surprised, I nodded. Who could forget Robin?

"Her husband phoned me last Friday at work. He said it was my fault that Robin had turned on him, and that he was going to make me pay for what I did to him. That I was going to suffer the same way he did."

I stared at her. "He called you on Friday, and on Saturday morning someone sent you Roger's body? Have you told this to the police?"

She nodded, looking suddenly exhausted. "I told them. A homicide detective said he'd check it out."

From the corner of my eye I saw some other guests approaching. Kate apparently saw them too because she reached over and grabbed my wrist, keeping me from moving away. "Please, Liz, I really need your help."

Before I could inquire what kind of help, the guests,

another older couple, were by her side. Kate squeezed my wrist. "Thanks again, Liz," she said in her polite-company voice before turning her attention to the new arrivals.

I smiled weakly and started working my way out of the room, nodding at the few people I knew. What did Kate want me to do? I couldn't imagine what kind of help I could provide that someone else, someone closer to her, couldn't. And had Robin's husband actually killed Roger in retaliation for Kate inciting Robin's violence? In some sick way it seemed a fitting vengeance: You take my wife from me, and now I'm taking your husband. The only minor problems in the logic: Robin's husband was not dead, and Robin hadn't needed very much inciting—her latent violent streak was very close to the surface.

"Oh, Liz." Tricia Whitmore motioned for me to join her and a tall, raw-boned man with sandy hair who was dressed in a well-tailored pin-striped suit. "This is Kate's neighbor, Bobby Smythe. Bobby, this is Liz James, the PR officer at the mental health center."

Introductions over, hands shaken, Tricia got down to the important stuff. "I didn't realize that you and Kate were so close," she said in her bland, let's-discuss-this psychologist voice.

Not as close as you and Roger, I wanted to say, but didn't. "Not really. I just helped her out a bit with her workshop."

"That must have been fascinating." Tricia smiled maliciously, apparently having given up on bland.

I shrugged. "I need to get going. Nice to meet you, Mr. Smythe."

He smiled. "I wonder if you'd just satisfy my curiosity about one thing before you go, Ms. James. Were you by any chance at the workshop where Roger's body was delivered?"

I nodded, sensing that my chances of making a fast exit were rapidly dwindling.

I heard Tricia gasp, saw her eyes widen in surprise. Bobby Smythe, on the other hand, merely looked intensely interested. "Tell us what happened," he said. "Please," he added, like a little boy recalling his manners—or a high-priced executive suddenly remembering that those outside of his office were not required to unquestioningly follow his every order.

I did, briefly: the who, what, when, where I'd learned in journalism school, stripped of my opinions or emotions. Also minus the fifth "w" all journalism students were taught to cram into their stories: why. Why had someone sent Roger's body to the Powerful Woman workshop? Perhaps the threat from Robin's husband provided one answer to that question, but I was still far from convinced that it was the right one.

Smythe's hard eyes glinted as he absorbed the info and asked more questions. "Who had delivered the box? Was I certain the man was wearing the uniform of a bona fide delivery service? How had Kate reacted when she'd opened the box?"

His curiosity struck me as more than slightly ghoulish. "Uh, are you by any chance a reporter?" I finally asked.

He grinned, displaying large white teeth. "No, an attorney. I guess both professions tend to ask too many questions. An occupational hazard. Sorry. I guess I just got carried away."

"Well, I now know a lot more than I ever wanted to know about the subject," Tricia said, sending him an accusatory stare.

So why didn't she move on? As an unabashed question-asker myself, I refused to view curiosity as a major character flaw. "Were you a friend of Roger's?" I asked Bobby.

He nodded. "We golfed together. My wife is a psychiatrist too. Occasionally the four of us went out to dinner together, though sometimes"—he grinned again—"the shrink talk got kind of oppressive."

After almost eleven years of working at the mental health center, I could relate to that. Tricia, I could see, didn't. "Where does your wife work?" she asked Bobby.

Bobby nodded toward a tall, gaunt woman whose dark hair was scraped tightly into a bun. She was talking to Kate, nodding sympathetically. "Allison is in private practice. She's a child psychiatrist."

I surreptitiously glanced at my watch. It was almost 12:15, and I was meeting Nick at my apartment at 12:45. "I've really got to get going now. It was nice meeting you," I told Bobby Smythe. "See you Monday, Tricia."

"I need to leave too," Tricia announced. She nodded at Bobby, then followed me out the door. "God, I can't believe I came to this," she said, looking suddenly tearful.

Awkwardly, I patted her arm. "Funerals are difficult," I said. A truly inane remark if I'd ever heard one.

Tricia didn't seem to think so, probably because she wasn't paying much attention anyway. As quickly as it had come, her tearful phase seemed to have metamorphosed into anger. Her blue eyes blazed in her pale, horsey face. "I guess I just came to make sure the bastard is dead," she said, then turned on her pale pink pumps and stalked to the street.

# Chapter Five

KATE QUINLAN MARCHED INTO MY OFFICE MONDAY morning carrying a small cardboard box. "This is my book," she announced, handing me the package. "I'd like you to read it."

I studied her face for signs of the grief I'd seen only two days ago. I didn't detect any. Kate today looked as energetic and driven as she had before Roger died. Either she'd had a very short mourning period or she did a remarkably good job of hiding her pain.

"I'll read it," I said, "but as I mentioned before, I don't really have time now to do much work on it." Ghostwrite it, I meant.

"Oh, I understand," she said smoothly. "At this point I'm mainly interested in your reaction to what I've written so far." She nodded toward the box. "I know I need to add more chapters. This is just the bare bones, my first draft."

Mentally I groaned. Bare bones–first draft manuscripts did not bode well for scintillating reading. And I had a sinking suspicion that Kate, no matter what she said, wanted more from me than a simple reaction to her manuscript. Particularly if it was as bad as I expected it to be.

Kate, to my surprise, sat down on the plastic chair next to my desk. She fixed her intense eyes on my face. "You see, now that Roger is dead, it's very important that I get moving on my book."

Actually, I didn't see. Did she mean that with her husband dead she needed the extra income? Or perhaps she needed the distraction of hard work to help her through her grief. "I'll read it and get back to you by the end of the week," I said, hoping that I'd be surprised by the merits of her manuscript. It was possible, of course. Kate was an articulate and sometimes witty speaker. If she focused on stories about real women who'd overcome their problems the book might even be quite moving.

"I'd appreciate that," Kate said. "And I want you to be brutally honest, Liz. If you think it sucks, tell me. I can take it."

I assured her that I'd give her my honest opinion. I hesitated, then asked, "How are you doing—aside from the book, I mean."

Kate sighed. "Last night I called the homicide detective I'd talked to before. I just wanted to see what was going on, if they'd made any progress in finding out who killed Roger." She frowned. "He wasn't exactly forthcoming with information. About the only thing he would tell me about John Carter, Robin's husband, was that he was out of town at some conference that weekend; he didn't get back to Houston until Sunday night. Apparently Carter admits to calling and threatening me on Friday, but he said what he meant was that he was planning to attack me in the media. He'd been phoning different reporters, trying to get them to do critical pieces about me and the workshops."

I remembered the brief TV interview I'd seen of Robin's husband right after he'd gotten out of the hospital. Balancing on crutches, his right leg in a cast, the man had emanated fury. His deep voice cracked with passion as he'd blasted the seminar that "set my wife against me." John Carter had not looked like a man who would take an attack on himself lightly. Would his sense of vengeance have been satisfied by some nasty newspaper articles about Kate's seminars? From what I'd seen of him, John looked more like an eye-for-an-eye kind of guy.

"Didn't the police consider the possibility that Carter hired someone to kill Roger?" I asked. Surely the plaster-encased man I'd seen on TV was not physically capable right now of hoisting Roger's body into a box. But, as the owner of a large car dealership, he was certainly financially capable of hiring someone else to do the job for him. A pro who could handle all the messy details while John high-tailed it out of town for the weekend.

Kate nodded vigorously. "That's exactly what I said. He didn't need to be anywhere near Houston if he hired a hit man. But you know what this detective said to that?"

I shook my head.

"He said, 'By the way, where were *you* on Friday afternoon and evening?' He also wanted to know why I hadn't mentioned that Roger did not come home on Friday night."

These were not, I thought, unreasonable questions. Apparently my face registered my opinion because Kate added, a bit resentfully, "I was seeing patients all afternoon. After work I went out for a few drinks with Lorna and Lisa Grayson, our new social work intern. When I got home, around 8:30, no one else was home."

She raised her eyebrows at me. "Which isn't at all unusual. Roger and I lead very separate lives. I don't expect to see him on the weekends. If he hadn't shown up by Monday morning, then I would have thought something unusual had happened.''

She said it so matter-of-factly, as if most wives often didn't lay eyes on their husbands for an entire weekend. So where did Roger spend his weekends? I wondered, but couldn't get up my nerve to ask. Instead, I asked a more innocuous question. ''What about Mel? Where was she?''

''Mel spends the weekends with her mother.''

So did that mean that during the week, when Mel was living with them, that Roger and Kate inhabited the same house? I suddenly remembered the way Roger and Kate sniped at each other during the symposium party, the venomous looks they shot at each other. If these two people had so despised being around each other, why hadn't they just gotten a divorce? Roger had already left one failed marriage behind him, and Kate seemed like the kind of feisty, independent woman who would have walked out on him without a second thought. So why had they stayed together? For Mel's sake? For financial reasons? Because they were both too busy to file the papers?

Kate stood up. ''I appreciate you taking the time to read my manuscript, Liz.'' She started toward the door, then turned back with a wry smile. ''And not that it's any of your business, but Roger usually spent the weekend with his girlfriend—whoever she might be at the moment.'' Kate lifted her hand in a little wave, then turned and walked into the hall.

I spent the rest of the morning writing a brochure for mental health center volunteers, answering phone calls and attending a more-than-usually tedious planning meeting for an upcoming psychology conference. By noon I was ready for a break.

Amanda and I usually had lunch together on Mondays,

but she was out of town this week at a child psychology conference and I'd brought a sack lunch and a paperback copy of *The Red Scream*. Pushing my office door closed, I kicked off my low-heeled black pumps and arranged my lunch on my desk: gazpacho in a thermos, crackers and slices of Swiss cheese, a Diet Coke and an apple.

I munched on cheese and crackers, sipped my soup and read about poem-writing Texas murderers for a satisfying fifteen minutes before recalling the mystery in my own office. What kind of book had Kate Quinlan written?

I tossed the remains of my lunch into the wastebasket, wiped off my sticky fingers with a paper napkin, and started skimming Kate's manuscript.

It started out predictably, the written version of Kate's introduction to the Powerful Woman workshop. She was a better speaker than writer.

I finished my apple while skimming the next chapter. It was more autobiographical than the first, Kate's account of her unhappy adolescence and college years when as a depressed, obese young woman she'd tried desperately to make everyone like her, to fulfill everyone's needs but her own. Kate-the-writer captured very well her younger mindset, the mixture of accommodation and self-contempt. Her I-can't-take-this-anymore scene was masterful, showing the once-cowering woman confronting her tyrannical boss then stalking out of his office to start building her new life. When Kate wrote about herself, rather than listing psychological maxims, she was a powerful writer.

I turned the next page, wondering how Kate would handle the rest of her life: her Powerful Woman years. My life has changed, everything is wonderful, blah-blah-blah. I skimmed a few pages about Kate's satisfying career, her dramatic weight loss, her total recovery from the depression that had haunted her throughout her late teens and early twenties. Then I hit a subject that Kate hadn't talked about before: her marriage to Roger.

I kept reading and felt my mouth drop open. No wonder Kate had said that now that Roger was dead she wanted to get moving on her book. She hadn't been talking about transcending her grief. She was just being realistic about libel laws. Now that Roger wasn't around, he couldn't sue her.

I read in unabashed fascination about Kate's affair with the man she later married—a brilliant, witty, newly divorced psychiatrist. Kate described the passionate afternoons they spent in bed together, the heady evenings in which they argued over dinner and a bottle of wine about the relative merits of the views of Jung and Maslow and Skinner. They'd gotten married after knowing each other only two months, and within a year the marriage was visibly fraying. "After the sexual newness wore off, it was painfully clear that we'd been too distracted by lust to notice we were two basically incompatible personalities," Kate had written.

That wasn't the libelous part. Probably thousands of other people could have said the exact thing about their marriage. But then Kate launched into a description of Roger's response to the realization that things were not all rosy on the marriage front. She wrote that suddenly he had started coming home late, flirting outrageously with every woman in sight. Soon it had become obvious that Roger was having an affair—many affairs, in fact. "My aging psychiatrist husband—The Stud, I started to call him—apparently could not get enough female admiration, although, God knows, he was trying," Kate had written.

I glanced guiltily at my watch. I wanted very much to read on, but I didn't have the time. My lunch hour had ended a good fifteen minutes ago. Reluctantly, I put the manuscript in my desk drawer, wondering where Kate would go next with her narrative. Wouldn't a Powerful Woman (which Kate had spent pages claiming to be) bail out of such a marriage? And how had she expected Roger—not a man given to self-criticism—to react to her description of him?

I was about to open my office door when someone knocked on it. A rapid, urgent series of knocks.

I opened the door and found Lorna Bell staring, red-faced, at me. She looked as if she'd been crying.

"Lorna, what's wrong?" I drew her inside, closing the door after me.

"It's Kate!" She started to cry again.

"What about Kate? What happened?"

I waited for what seemed an eternity for Lorna to stop crying long enough to answer. But finally, sniffling, she did. "She's—-she's been arrested. The police just came to get her."

"But why?" Certainly the police couldn't think that Kate would have killed her husband and then had the body delivered to herself?

Lorna sucked air, trying to stop crying. "They said that the box with Roger's body was sent from Kate and Roger's house." She gasped before dissolving once again into tears.

# Chapter Six

"WHAT IS THAT WOMAN'S PROBLEM?" MY SISTER, Margaret, inquired loudly. "First she encourages the women in her workshop to run over their husbands with their cars and to assault their bosses. Then she goes and shoots her own husband."

Raoul, my handsome, dark-haired brother-in-law, glanced up from his veal. "At least she practices what she preaches."

I set down my fork, which was holding a mouthful of rather uninspired eggplant parmigiana. "Kate *didn't* kill her husband. Only an idiot would shoot him, then send herself the body."

Margaret finished chewing her salad, daintily blotted her mouth with her napkin, then came out swinging. Verbally, of course. Arguing had been Margaret's favorite form of fighting ever since a neighbor erroneously told her at the age of eight that she, Margaret, was a prodigy. "Actually sending the body could be a very clever way of diverting attention from herself. Because most people would assume just what you did—that no murderer would send herself a body. They'd think that if a bright woman like Kate killed her husband she'd do exactly the opposite: hide the body or dump it somewhere as far away from herself as possible. Or else she'd make the death look like an accident or some random crime, like walking in on a burglary and getting shot.''

Margaret took a sip of wine, holding up one finger in case anyone at the table was planning to usurp the spotlight. ''So can't you see how brilliant it was for Kate to send herself the body at her own seminar? Dozens of people are there to watch her open the box and witness how totally shocked she was when she encountered her husband's corpse.''

''Except,'' Nick pointed out, ''the police obviously think the same thing you do. So it wasn't that brilliant a scheme after all. Or''—he munched on a breadstick, his head tilted to the side—''maybe the police just always figure the husband or wife is the most likely suspect and they ignored the body-in-the-box aspect from the start.''

''I heard they arrested her because they found out the box was sent from Kate and Roger's house,'' I said.

''That does sound incriminating,'' my brother-in-law remarked.

''To put it mildly,'' Margaret added.

''But that's all the more reason why it doesn't make sense,'' I argued. ''Kate is not stupid. She'd realize that the police would investigate where the package came from. Would she send it from her own home? If she'd planned this convoluted scenario to make it look as if someone else was taking this grotesque vengeance on her, wouldn't she have sent the package from a place that couldn't be traced back to her? She could have hired someone to drop off the package at one of those mailing places, have the guy pay cash and give a fake return address. Only an imbecile would have the package picked up at her own house.''

Nick nodded. ''You're right. This obviously wasn't some impulsive crime of passion. Whoever did it spent a lot of effort in orchestrating the whole thing: getting the body in the right size box, having it picked up and delivered at a precise time.''

He turned to me. ''Didn't you say that the box was delivered just at the moment that Kate started lecturing to the group about give yourself a gift?''

Raoul chuckled. ''You're kidding.''

Nick grinned. ''No indeedy. It was a shame that the reporter didn't get that. Can you imagine the headlines?''

I cut him off before he had a chance to reel off some possibilities. ''But that's all the more proof Kate didn't do it,'' I argued above the general snickering. ''She'd never make fun of herself like that. She's very serious about her workshop.''

Margaret shook her head, making her blonde curls bounce. ''I doubt that Kate intended for the package to arrive precisely during the give-yourself-a-gift speech— which is a truly stupid idea, by the way. People are already too self-indulgent. Somebody needs to tell them to stop thinking of themselves for thirty seconds and buy someone else a gift.''

I glared at her. Margaret, though, was oblivious to my— or anyone else's—reaction to her and her know-it-all ways. Not for the first time, I wondered how I could share a gene pool with this woman whose prissy, octogenarian schoolmarm sensibility just happened to be located in a voluptuous thirty-year-old's body.

Margaret turned to me, her pretty, Kewpie-doll face set in the condescending look that always made me want to smack her. ''You're giving Kate too much credit, Lizzy. She probably figured that the police wouldn't be able to trace the package back to her or that the delivery service wouldn't keep the records. Lots of very smart people are also very arrogant. They think everyone else is too dumb to catch on to what they're doing.''

"Considering that you've never met the woman, you certainly seem to be an expert on the way she thinks," I said coldly.

"It's easier to see a situation more clearly when you're not emotionally involved in it," Margaret countered.

"Of course some people just always consider themselves the resident expert on every subject under the sun," I observed.

Margaret smiled. "Yes, some people are just blessed, aren't they?"

Despite myself I laughed. She was incorrigible. Always had been. Always would be.

My sister waited until my mouth was filled with eggplant before she launched her next volley. "We need to get our heads together on planning this wedding," she said, looking at Nick. "Since Liz seems to be so busy with this Powerful Woman seminar, maybe you should be the one who comes with me to the caterers next week."

Nick opened his mouth to reply, took one look at my face, and closed his mouth. He was by no means loath to offer his opinions, but only a fool steps willingly into the line of crossfire. And Nick was a very bright guy.

I set down the wineglass I'd been holding and met my sister's eyes. I was surprised at how calm I felt. "I've been meaning to clear up a few points with you," I said quietly. "This is Nick's and my wedding—not yours. It was generous of you to offer to plan the whole thing, but I think we'd rather do it ourselves. *Without* your help."

Margaret started to answer, but I cut her off. "The way I see it, Margaret, you have two choices right now: One.

Accept the fact that I'm not going to let you push me around anymore or Two. Stop seeing me.''

I watched two red blotches creep across my sister's pale complexion. Her eyes narrowed into furious slits as she leaped to her feet. "Come on, Raoul. I certainly don't want to stay where I'm not wanted. Someone might misinterpret my sisterly concern as pushiness.''

My brother-in-law hesitated, looking embarrassed and uncertain about what he needed to do next.

Margaret seemed oblivious of his reaction. She was focused on me now, leaning down so her face was inches from mine. "I can see what a great effect that workshop woman has had on you, Liz. How many lives does that homicidal bitch have to ruin before you wise up about her?''

She stalked out of the restaurant before I could think of any snappy reply. Raoul shrugged, sent us a raised palms, what-can-I-do look and followed her out.

I DIDN'T have time to get back to Kate's manuscript until my lunch hour on Wednesday. I pushed my office door closed, pulled the paper sack with my ham and cheese sandwich and carrot sticks from my desk drawer, and continued reading about how Kate had managed to live with a philandering jerk without thinking of herself as a victim.

Was she rationalizing her bad marriage? I wondered. Yes, Kate did seem to have forged an independent life for herself, apparently not overly concerned about Roger's affairs or their mutual dislike. But many people, including me, would not have called the latter years of their marriage a marriage at all. The Quinlans were more like two ex-spouses who happened to live under the same roof.

Still Kate was not writing a marriage manual. She was writing about taking responsibility for your life and choosing your own course. Viewing yourself, in the words of that hokey old poem, as the captain of your own fate. And that Kate had done.

The Roger of her manuscript might be a philanderer, a posturing snob and a small-minded tyrant, but she had never allowed him to make her unhappy. At least not in the written version of her life. Remembering her sniping at Roger at their symposium party, I wasn't so sure if her real life was as free of conflict as she claimed in her autobiography. But with Roger no longer around to refute Kate's assertions, who could say for sure that she was lying?

A sharp knock on my closed door interrupted my reading. Reluctantly I walked to the door, hoping I could convince whoever it was to come back in half an hour.

I pulled open the door. "Kate!"

She was standing in the hallway, smiling at me, dressed in jeans and a red plaid cotton shirt. She did not look like someone who had recently been in jail, even briefly.

"I'm out on bail," she explained as she marched past me into my office. She peered at the pages on my desk before plopping down into my guest chair. "Oh, good," she said, "that's just what I wanted to talk to you about." She flashed a broad grin at me. "So tell me. What do you think of my book?"

# Chapter Seven

KATE OPENED HER FRONT DOOR IN ANSWER TO MY knock. "Come on in. Consuela's making *huevos rancheros*, and everything is almost ready."

She was wearing tight blue jeans and a lavender T-shirt, her face free of any discernible makeup and her hair still damp from the shower. She grinned at me. "I'm really pleased you could make it, Liz."

Either she was enormously relieved to be out of jail or she was a morning person (I'm not)—or maybe both. In any case, she did not seem much like a grieving widow, I thought as we walked into her dark hardwood hallway with its long crimson and black oriental rug. Then I mentally kicked myself for my lack of generosity. There were dozens of ways to grieve. Just because Kate and Roger did not get along very well didn't mean she was glad he was dead. I glanced down at the manuscript in my hand. On the other hand, Kate's book certainly seemed to suggest that she wouldn't be all that devastated by Roger's demise.

I followed Kate into a sunny dining room with ivy-patterned wallpaper on the wall and a gleaming mahogany table that held place settings for two. "It's a little on the formal side," Kate said with a shrug. "But I figured we'd have room to spread out here. And who knows when I'll eat here again."

I sent her a questioning look.

"Oh, I can't afford to keep this house. It's ridiculously expensive. We only moved here because Roger was such a snob. He loved to let people know that he lived in River Oaks, even if it was the cheapest part."

Which wasn't, by any stretch of the imagination, cheap. "So you're selling the house?" I gratefully accepted a cup of coffee which Kate poured for me from a thermal carafe.

"Yeah, eventually. There's some legal things that need to be squared up first." Kate waved her hand dismissively, as if such legal details were too boring to contemplate. "I'll probably just move into an apartment or maybe a town house somewhere near work. I'm tired of wandering around this huge place anyway. It seems obscene for a couple of people to take up so much space, don't you think?"

A plump, gray-haired woman appeared at that moment, carrying two plates with a delicious-smelling egg concoction wrapped in tortillas. Consuela, I presumed. Her arrival saved me from answering Kate's question: Sure, it was obscene. So why hadn't Kate stayed true to her noble principles and moved out? Particularly since she didn't seem all that fond of her fellow occupants.

Kate introduced me to the housekeeper, Consuela Rodriguez. The woman nodded to me, but her wrinkled face remained expressionless. I had the distinct impression, as Consuela hurried out of the room, that Kate was not one of her favorite people. Or maybe she was just upset that she'd undoubtedly be losing her job when Kate sold the house.

In any case, the *huevos rancheros* were as delicious as

Kate had promised. If the rest of her cooking was as good as this, Consuela should have no problem at all finding another job.

"Do you want to give me the bad news now or wait until we're through eating?" Kate asked.

Actually, I would have preferred to tell her in my office in a succinct five-minute conversation, but Kate had insisted that no, we needed to discuss my recommendations. And she'd been meaning to invite me over to thank me for all my help. . . . So here I was once again doing Kate's bidding, this time over Saturday breakfast.

"It's not bad news," I said. "A lot of the book is very good. The autobiographical stuff in particular is very vivid."

"But . . ." Kate prodded. "Spit it out, Liz. I can take it."

Okay. "But the how-to part is kind of boring without any case histories to illustrate your points. The psychological research you cite is good; it gives your conclusions academic credibility, but you need to give examples too."

"Fine." Kate was making notes on a yellow legal pad. "What else?"

"Well, of course, the book needs to be much longer if you want a commercial publisher to take it. And"—I hesitated, not sure how far I should go.

"What?" Kate glanced up from her notes, looking impatient.

"You might want to tone down some of the parts about Roger."

"Why would I want to do that?" Kate asked.

"Because," an unfamiliar male voice answered, "you may well go to trial for murdering him."

I turned around to see the big, sandy-haired man I'd met here after Roger's funeral, Bobby Smythe, Kate's neighbor.

"Consuela, let me in the back door," he explained genially, in case either of us was about to accuse him of breaking and entering. He studied me for a moment before grinning in recognition. "We met after the funeral, didn't we? You work with Kate at the mental health center. Liz, isn't it?"

"That's right, Liz James." I smiled at him, noticing out of the corner of my eye that Kate did not look pleased to see him.

He leaned forward to offer me a huge hand to shake. He glanced in Kate's direction. "I'm representing Kate in her, uh, criminal proceedings."

"If it comes to that," Kate said tartly.

Bobby sighed. It will, his look said.

Kate explained that I was there to discuss her book. "So if you like, I'll call you when we're through," she added pointedly.

Bobby said that would be fine. They needed to discuss her defense. Today. He turned to me, looking very unlawyerly in his jeans, denim shirt, and cowboy boots. My image of a criminal attorney was someone considerably more aggressive than this genial man, though perhaps once he walked into a courtroom Bobby morphed into a barracuda.

"Nice to see you again, Liz," he said. "Will you try to convince my client here to start taking these charges seriously?" He didn't wait for an answer. "Because I wouldn't want her ending up in the penitentiary due to a sloppy defense."

"The case against her is that strong?" I blurted out. The image of Kate in prison shocked me. I'd just assumed that the only evidence the police had was the record of the box having been sent from this house. And—unless Kate herself had greeted the delivery man and instructed him to handle the box carefully, since there was a dead body inside—that certainly didn't seem like enough evidence to convict her, or, for that matter, to even go to trial.

Bobby clasped his big hand on my shoulder. "Within the next few weeks the grand jury will decide whether there's sufficient evidence to warrant a trial. But the police wouldn't have arrested Kate if they didn't think they had a case. It's circumstantial evidence, of course, but still it looks bad."

"Since I *didn't* kill Roger, I doubt that they can convict me," Kate said, looking amazingly bored by the subject. "They will never find my fingerprints on any gun. Or, for that matter, my signature on the receipt for that box that was supposed to have been picked up at my house."

"Who did sign it?" I asked.

"No one," Bobby said. "The package was left on the back porch with the necessary cash. Whoever phoned the delivery service—the voice was muffled; the clerk couldn't tell if it was a man or a woman—said that no one would be home and to pick up the package on the back porch."

"What name did the person give on the phone?" I asked.

"Roger Quinlan, Dr. Roger Quinlan," Bobby said.

Kate snorted. "You know, I wouldn't put it past Roger to have arranged the whole thing."

I stared at her, shocked.

Bobby looked interested. "You mean arrange for someone to mail you the body and then kill himself?"

"Sure. Think about it. You know how depressed Roger has been for the last six months or so. I always thought that car accident of his last summer could have been a botched suicide attempt."

"But then who sent you his body?" I asked.

Kate shrugged. "Somebody he hired. Maybe a hit man who he paid to shoot him, pack up the body and send me the package."

"But why bother with sending it to you?" I asked. "If he wanted you to discover his body, he could have killed himself here. It would have been a lot simpler, and he wouldn't have needed an accomplice."

"True," Kate agreed. "And I suppose I still might have been accused of murdering him if he shot himself, say, in the living room or, better yet, in my bedroom. But this way is so much more devious. So passive-aggressive. So very Roger. Now no one will think that he killed himself, and Roger hated for anyone to consider him weak or depressed or fallible. He was always very concerned about his image."

Kate stared out the dining room window. I followed her gaze, wondering if she was seeing the azalea bushes. "Even if Roger hadn't intended to set me up as his murderer," she said, "he certainly did want to humiliate me in public. You know how much he hated my workshops. Here was his chance to embarrass me and, he hoped, ruin my business at the same time. With one shot he could end all of his problems and cause a whole lot of problems for me."

It was an interesting theory. I thought back to the symposium party and Roger's diatribe about Kate's workshop. How unacademic the Powerful Woman workshop was, how crass and simpleminded. There was only one problem. "But the thing that seemed to irritate Roger the most about your workshops was all the publicity you were getting," I said. "Certainly sending you his body was a guarantee that you'd get even more media attention."

Kate shook her head. "But think of the kind of publicity it would be, the message that would be sent about Powerful Woman: What this crackpot means when she tells women to take responsibility for their lives is to get rid of any man who's standing in her way. Roger would be delighted if everyone in the country saw me as some kind of crazed, anti-male terrorist.''

"You are so full of shit!'' Mel stood in the door from the kitchen, her eyes blazing. "My father is murdered and all you think about is yourself. As usual. Everything that happens in the world has to be about you.''

"Well, she is possibly facing a trial,'' Bobby began in a calm, talking-sense-to-the-emotionally-overwrought voice. "She'd be a fool not to think of herself.''

"Particularly since she's probably the one who shot him!'' The look Mel hurled at her stepmother was as venomous as her words.

"Mel, no! I'd never—'' Kate stood up, looking genuinely upset.

Mel's round face wrinkled into a grimace, her shoulders heaving as she began to sob.

Kate started toward her, her arms open to embrace the girl. But before she could get to Mel, Consuela appeared from the kitchen. The housekeeper's face softened as she hurried over to the girl.

Mel fell gratefully into the housekeeper's plump arms, letting the older woman hug her close and croon low, singsong words into her ear.

I watched Kate watch them, her face pale. Standing no more than three feet from her stepdaughter, she looked alone and hurt and not at all powerful.

# Chapter Eight

TRICIA WHITMORE WAS THE KIND OF INTERVIEW SUB-
ject who set my teeth on edge. Sitting with ramrod-straight
posture, hands in her lap, smiling primly, Tricia seemed
incapable of uttering a sentence devoid of multisyllabic
gobbledygook. So far I'd sat in her office for twenty long
minutes, mentally translating simple thoughts couched in
complex language.

"I have high expectations that the results of our study
will allow us to interface more effectively with other agen-
cies and prioritize our needs in a mutually beneficial manner," she said.

Yeah, right. I wanted to tell her about my own private
I.Q. test for center M.D.s and Ph.D.s: The smart ones explained their ideas in simple English, while the dolts were
so unsure of themselves and their ideas that they had to use
big words. But if I told Tricia that, she would no doubt do
another of my favorite psychotherapist tricks: nothing. No
response, stony stare. Or maybe she'd smile tightly and say,
"Now *that* sounds hostile."

It was hard to believe that this uptight professional in

her navy blazer, khaki skirt and white blouse was the same person who, a few weeks earlier, had told me that she'd come to Roger Quinlan's funeral in her shocking pink dress just to "make sure the bastard is dead."

Apparently she'd grown tired of interfacing with Roger. I closed my steno notebook. "That's all I need, thanks." Tricia was going to be very surprised when she saw her pedantic insights on her study of interagency communication patterns reduced to three or four pithy paragraphs.

I stood up.

Tricia picked up a tabloid-sized newspaper from her desk. "Have you seen the story about Kate Quinlan?"

I shook my head. I also had never seen this newspaper, the *Houston Spectator*. It seemed as if everywhere I went there were stacks of some new special-interest local newspaper. Newspapers that usually didn't survive long enough to celebrate their one-year anniversary.

Tricia opened the newspaper to the story. "I thought you might like to read it," she said with a decidedly malicious smile. "Particularly since it mentions the mental health center."

I read the headline. Hell! The story was an interview with John Carter, Robin's car-obsessed husband. "INJURED HUSBAND CONTENDS ANTI-MALE SEMINAR BREEDS VIOLENCE" proclaimed the headline. A photo of John, bandaged and balancing on crutches, accompanied the article.

I skimmed the story. It recounted Robin's attack on John, which he seemed to blame entirely on Kate and the Powerful Woman seminar. Before she attended the workshop, John said, his wife had been "whiny" but certainly not violent. The seminar, he said, convinced Robin to act on her anger, to stop talking and start attacking. "That so-called workshop turned a passive, unhappy woman into a homicidal criminal," John said. "And she isn't even sorry about what she did to me. That Quinlan woman turned my wife into a monster.''

John went on to say that from what he'd observed, ''Violence against males is a direct outcome of that course. Even the leader's own husband turned up dead at one meeting. Kate Quinlan stooped so low that she had to use her husband's corpse for a show-and-tell exhibit.''

I wondered briefly if Kate could sue the *Spectator* for libel, then decided it wouldn't be worth the effort. By the time the case came to trial the tabloid would be long gone. ''Where did you get this?'' I asked Tricia.

''There's a pile of them in the clinic waiting room.'' Then she added, ''I don't think this kind of story reflects well on the center. It sounds as if our therapists are condoning, or even encouraging, violence against men.''

I glanced back at the article. Yes, it did identify Kate as being a therapist at the Houston Mental Health Center as well as the developer of the Powerful Woman seminar. Great.

But at least I could make sure that a minimum of people at the center read this trash. ''Did you see these newspapers anywhere besides the adult clinic's waiting room?''

Tricia shook her head. ''But they could be in every waiting room in the place, for all I know.'' She did not look displeased at the prospect.

I moved toward the door. ''Do you mind if I keep this?'' I held up the newspaper.

''Fine. I've already read it.'' Tricia paused. ''I wonder if the center can afford to get this kind of negative publicity right now. Especially when we're trying to get more state funding.''

I didn't answer her. I just wondered why she hated Kate so much.

A small stack of *Houston Spectator*s was still on a table

in the adult clinic's waiting room. I grabbed them, noticing that a haggard-looking woman in one of the chairs was reading a copy. I wanted to snatch it from her hands but refrained from acting on the impulse.

I hurried to the other waiting rooms throughout the center. There were none in the marriage and family clinic, none in the children's clinic. I was starting to feel less anxious— maybe only a handful of people had picked up the tabloid—as I headed down the front hallway of the center. Then I spotted the newspapers. On a table right next to the front door was a large stack of *Spectator*s. I snatched them.

"Hey, Liz, what you going to do with all those papers?" Tom Clark, a genial, freckle-faced social work student asked as he strolled by.

Bury them in the first Dumpster I see. "Oh, it's against the center's rules to distribute unauthorized publications in the building," I lied. "I can't imagine why anyone would want to read this one anyway."

Fortunately Tom seemed to buy my explanation. Indeed the *Houston Spectator*, with its too-dark photos, amateurish layout, and silly stories did not look like a newspaper that many people would be eager to read. I wondered suddenly why Tricia had bothered to pick one up.

I found no more papers in the geriatric clinic or in the cafeteria. I was returning to my office with my stack of confiscated papers when I ran into Kate in the hall. I could see her stiffen as she spotted what I was carrying.

"So you saw it too," she said, holding up her own copy of the tabloid.

She followed me into my office. "Did you read the story?" she asked as I pushed the door shut.

"Yeah. The only positive thing I can say is that this paper is not exactly a credible source of information. I've never heard of it before. Probably no one reads it."

"Enough people have. Including my new boss, Dr. Nelson. He phoned this morning to say he'd like to discuss it with me. We have an appointment tomorrow afternoon."

I wondered if he was going to be as censorious of the story as Tricia was. I hadn't yet met Dr. Nelson. He'd arrived earlier this week, a youngish psychiatrist who was going to head the marriage and family clinic. Nelson was supposed to be a specialist in both family therapy and short-term therapy techniques. I was scheduled to interview him for the newsletter tomorrow morning.

"I wonder how he even saw the story," I said.

"How did you get it?"

"Tricia Whitmore showed it to me when I interviewed her."

Kate's hazel eyes flashed, her thin lips pressed into a grim line. "That's who I suspect gave the paper to Dr. Nelson too. Lorna told me that Tricia was the one who showed her the story. A real busy little bee, our Tricia. I wouldn't be surprised if she was the one who dropped off the papers in the adult clinic's waiting room."

But why? I doubted that most women liked the wife of the man they were having an affair with, but Tricia's actions seemed excessively vengeful. Did she blame Kate for Roger breaking up with her? Or was her reaction strictly to Kate's workshops? Of course, to be fair, there was also the possibility that Tricia had done nothing other than show a few people the newspaper she'd innocently picked up in the waiting room. Maybe Dr. Nelson had done the same thing.

"Why would Tricia do that to you?" I asked. "I thought the two of you barely knew each other."

"I laughed at her," Kate said grimly. "About a month and a half ago she showed up in my office, introduced herself, and explained to me that I needed to 'let Roger go' because he loved her and wanted to be with her. And I laughed and told her she was a fool to believe Roger wanted any kind of permanent relationship with her. I said Roger was incapable of any long-term commitment to one woman, that all he seemed to be able to manage was a series of short-term affairs. And pretty soon he'd be trading her in for a new girlfriend.''

Kate suddenly smiled ruefully. ''I wish someone had told *me* that before I married him, though I probably would have refused to believe it the same way Tricia did.''

''And then Roger did dump her,'' I mused.

Kate nodded. ''A few weeks later. You didn't need a crystal ball to predict that. The question was only when. But Tricia was really pissed at Roger. I understand that she created quite a scene in his office. Screaming and throwing things. I heard—not from Roger, of course—that he was trying to get her fired. But he died first.''

I raised an eyebrow.

''Yeah,'' Kate said. ''I thought about that too. His death was very convenient for Tricia.''

The phone on my desk rang. I picked it up. ''It's for you.'' I handed the receiver to Kate.

''Yes?'' Kate said. Then, ''Mel? Is that you? What's wrong?''

I glanced over and saw all the color drain from her face.

''Oh, God,'' Kate said. ''Oh, God. I'll be right there, Mel. Call 911.''

Kate was halfway to the door before she remembered me.

''Kate, what happened?''

''It's our housekeeper,'' Kate said. ''Mel just came home from school and found Consuela's body.''

# Chapter Nine

I ENDED UP DRIVING KATE HOME IN MY CAR. AFTER running out of my office, she'd returned seconds later. "I forgot. I don't have a car today; mine is in the shop. Can you drive me home?"

The police cars were already there by the time we pulled into Kate's driveway. I wondered if folks who didn't live in posh River Oaks received such prompt service.

The minute I stopped the car Kate bolted for the front door. I hesitated for a moment, then, overcome by curiosity, decided to follow her. If anyone asked what I was doing, I'd say I'd come in to see if Kate needed anything.

Fortunately for me, the front door was left ajar. Kate must not have bothered to close it all the way when she ran inside. I walked into her house without knocking, feeling like an intruder.

I heard voices in the back of the house. The kitchen area, it sounded like. Is that where Mel had found Consuela's body? I heard a deep male voice and then Kate's voice, sounding shrill, demanding.

"Can I help you?" The unexpected noise at my shoulder

made me jump. I turned to face a lanky uniformed police-man. A young guy who was studying me with an expression that was clearly not meant to convey helpfulness.

"Uh, I'm a friend of Kate's—Mrs. Quinlan. I drove her here from work."

His face remained expressionless, but his cold brown eyes said he knew I was lying, I was probably a criminal and certainly up to no good. "What's your name?" he asked.

I told him. When he asked for identification, I showed him my driver's license.

He also wanted to know where Kate and I worked, what time we had left the center and what Mrs. Quinlan had said about the reason she had to come home.

"She said that Mel, her stepdaughter, had found the housekeeper's body and she needed to go home right away," I said, wishing that I'd had enough sense for once to mind my own business.

The officer jotted this information into a small notebook. He looked up. "She didn't say anything else?"

I shook my head. When we first got into the car, Kate had babbled. She couldn't believe this had happened. Oh, God. Poor Mel, finding the body this way. I asked if she knew how Consuela had died: a heart attack? a gunshot wound? I wasn't sure if we were talking about death from natural causes or a murder. A second murder. "I don't know," Kate had replied, looking startled. "I forgot to ask." After that we drove in silence.

The officer apparently was finished with his notes. "You can't go back there," he said, nodding his head toward the voices. It sounded as if someone—Mel probably—was crying. "I'm going to have to ask you to leave. If we have any more questions for you, we can reach you at this number, right?"

"Yes." I started to leave, then decided what the hell, I'd already been stupid enough to come inside, why not go all the way. "Uh, could you tell me how Consuela died?"

"Shot," he said. Then he reached over and opened the door for me. I took this as a sign he didn't want me to ask if he knew who'd shot her. I left.

I drove back to the center, trying to piece together the little information that I had. Consuela had been shot to death, probably in the kitchen. Mel had found her body around 4:10 P.M., assuming that she had phoned Kate right away. Had Consuela perhaps walked in on a burglary and been shot?

I remembered from last Saturday morning how Consuela had let Bobby Smythe in from the door at the back of the house. Perhaps she'd come in the back door, maybe with an armload of groceries, unaware that someone was in the house. And the burglar, hearing noises from the kitchen, had crept up on her. . . .

I shook my head, trying to rid my mind of the image of Consuela glimpsing the armed intruder in her kitchen. And maybe her death had nothing at all to do with a burglary. Maybe someone had come there intending to shoot Consuela. An ex-husband perhaps or an angry lover. Or perhaps Consuela's death was connected somehow to Roger's murder. Perhaps she knew something or had seen something that someone didn't want her to repeat. The possibilities made my head ache.

By the time I got back to the mental health center everyone else was starting to leave. I was grateful that no one seemed to have noticed my absence, though someone had left a note on my desk asking to move my interview with Dr. Nelson tomorrow to 9:30. I suddenly remembered that a little over an hour ago Kate and I had been discussing her upcoming meeting with Dr. Nelson. It seemed like days ago when we'd talked about that tabloid article. Right now it seemed pretty trivial.

I forced myself to work on a news release I intended to send out the next day, but I found it impossible to concentrate. I tried to return phone calls, but everyone seemed to have left for the day. Finally I decided to give up and try again tomorrow.

I was locking my office door when I heard the phone ring. I briefly considered ignoring it, but I was afraid it might be Nick trying to change our dinner plans.

I picked up the phone on the fourth ring. "Hello?"

"Liz, it's Kate. I'm glad you're still there." She sounded exhausted and maybe depressed.

"Are you okay? And how's Mel? Is there anything I can do?"

"No. I just wanted to thank you for driving me . . . for everything."

I heard the sounds of voices in the background. Lots of voices. "Where are you?"

"Police headquarters. Mel had to come downtown to give her official statement. I don't know why they couldn't wait until tomorrow. The child is practically hysterical, and she's already told them everything she knows at the house."

"Were there any signs of a break-in?" I asked, feeling only a little ashamed of my unseemly curiosity. "Was anything missing?"

"No. It was suicide. Consuela left a note, but . . ." She stopped. "Sorry, I've got to go. Talk to you later, Liz."

I looked at the receiver in my hand, hearing the drone of the dial tone. Consuela had shot herself? Somehow that seemed even more shocking than if she had been murdered. And what had Kate been about to say before she was interrupted?

• • •

"THAT'S FUNNY," Nick said that evening when I told him about Consuela's death.

I peered at him. "Funny?"

We were eating dinner at Ninfa's, one of our favorite Tex-Mex restaurants. Nick took a sip of his frozen margarita before answering.

"Oh, I was just thinking that I ran into Sheila Lemur on the way out of the office. I told her that I thought she'd done a good job on that story about Kate's workshops. Sheila said Kate had just phoned her to say she had a great idea for a follow-up story."

"A follow-up story on the Powerful Woman workshops?"

Nick nodded. "Sheila's going to interview her tomorrow. Apparently Kate was quite vehement that Sheila talk to her right away. Kate convinced her she'd have an exclusive on some juicy revelations."

Revelations? "What kind of revelations? I certainly hope she's not giving an interview about Consuela's death!" I gulped a mouthful of my margarita to take away the bad taste in my mouth.

Nick shrugged. "Sheila didn't really say, but I had the impression she was talking about the seminars. She's a life-style writer, not a police reporter."

The waiter arrived then with our chicken fajitas. I watched him set the platters on the table, thinking about what Nick had said.

"Probably Kate phoned her this morning before she'd heard about Consuela. She was pretty angry about a story that appeared in this new throwaway paper. It was an interview with the guy whose wife ran him over after attending Kate's workshop. He made Kate sound like some anti-male terrorist. I bet she called Sheila to refute John Carter's charges.''

Nick was wrapping strips of grilled chicken and globs of refried beans and guacamole into a flour tortilla. He shook his head. "Kate phoned her tonight. Sheila said she was running late because Kate phoned just as she was leaving.''

I stared at him. Had Kate also phoned Sheila from the police station? Either Kate was one of the most cold-bloodedly ambitious people I'd encountered in a long time, or the reality of Consuela's death had not yet hit her.

Nick's fork stopped midway to his mouth. "Oh, I meant to tell you before. I'm going out of town for a few days, maybe a week.''

"How come? And where are you going?''

"El Paso.'' Nick told me how he needed to track down information on a businessman who'd opened a chain of medical clinics that seemed to specialize in bogus Medicare claims. The home office was in El Paso. "I've been trying to interview people over the phone, but it will be a lot easier to follow up some leads in person.''

"When are you leaving?''

"Tomorrow night.'' He rolled his eyes. "I've been after them for weeks to okay the funds, and this afternoon my editor walks by and says, 'Okay, you can go, but I need the story right away.' ''

"I'll miss you,'' I said. Nick and I were seeing each other almost every night. Even if we were too busy to get together, we at least talked to each other on the phone.

He took my hand. "Me too. But it will only be for a few days.''

I sighed. "I guess I could use the time to get caught up on my work.'' A not especially exciting prospect at the moment.

"Just as long as you don't get involved with those deaths at the Quinlan house."

"How could I get 'involved' with them?" I asked, annoyed by his proprietary tone.

He looked at me, shaking his head. "There's something so bizarre about this whole thing—Roger being murdered, his body sent to the seminar and now the housekeeper committing suicide—that I thought you might decide to solve the crime."

I pulled my hand away. "That's ridiculous!"

"For a mild-mannered PR woman you seem to have been involved with more than your share of murders."

"That's not *my* fault," I sputtered. "You sound as if I go out looking for violence. It's just an unfortunate coincidence—a tragic coincidence—that deaths happened to have occurred when I was around."

Nick raised one eyebrow. "That's probably true about Caroline Marshall's death and then those murders at the center. But you did choose to play amateur detective." He grabbed ahold of the hand I'd just pulled away. "What I'm saying, Liz, is be careful. You're not directly involved in this one—unless you choose to be."

His blue eyes peered intently into mine. "Please steer clear of Kate. There's something about her that doesn't seem right to me. I might be wrong, and I know I didn't think so at first but the more I learn about Kate Quinlan the more I think she might be a very dangerous woman."

Was she? A dangerous woman or the victim of some malicious killer? "I have absolutely no intention of getting involved in any dangerous situations," I said.

For some reason Nick did not look relieved. "You didn't the other times either."

# Chapter Ten

I PHONED KATE'S OFFICE THE NEXT MORNING BUT SHE wasn't in. Missy Gould, the clinic receptionist, told me that Kate had taken the day off but would be back tomorrow. "And of course she wants *me* to cancel all her therapy appointments," Missy groused. "A lot of the other therapists do that kind of thing themselves."

I wished her luck, then tried Kate at home. Only her answering machine answered. I left a message for her to call me.

I wished Kate had consulted me before contacting Sheila, the *Chronicle* reporter. From a purely selfish viewpoint I could not imagine a story about Powerful Woman workshops ("led by Kate Quinlan, a psychotherapist at the Houston Mental Health Center") in any way benefitting the mental health center. But even forgetting about the mental health center's interests, I couldn't envision the story helping Kate either.

Was the woman's judgment so poor that she couldn't foresee that a new boss, who'd reportedly been annoyed by a story in a tabloid that no one read, might be more than a little agitated to read a second story a few days later in the mega-circulated *Houston Chronicle*? Was Kate's need to one-up John Carter, to tell her side of the argument, so strong that she couldn't see the negative consequences of this publicity if she did indeed go on trial? And if Kate thought that Sheila would write only what Kate wanted her to write—to let her dictate the story—she was very trusting and naive indeed.

I tried to tell myself that this was not my problem. I'd done what I could. I still wanted to scream at Kate to cancel the damn interview, but instead I settled for grabbing my steno pad and heading for my own interview with Dr. Nelson.

He was not in his office. I knocked a second time, loudly, on his closed office door. Nobody responded. Just as I glanced at my watch, I heard rapid footsteps behind me. I turned just in time to see a tall, long-legged man bearing down on me. Instinctively I stepped back. The man, loping down the hall, looked as if he needed brakes.

Abruptly he stopped in front of me. "You must be Liz James." Laser-like gray eyes examined my face.

When I nodded, he stuck out a large hand and clasped mine in a firm handshake. "Larry Nelson. Sorry to keep you waiting."

Inside his office he moved a stack of journals off a chair and motioned for me to sit down. "Obviously, I haven't finished moving in yet," he said as he set the stack precariously on a corner of his already crammed desktop. He pulled his leather desk chair so that he sat directly across from me, crossed his long legs, and grinned at me. "I hope you're not one of those journalists who like to do personality assessments based on office furnishings."

I smiled, following his gaze around the large magazine- and book-cluttered office, practically empty except for his desk, desk chair and an extra pair of black leather chairs. "My office is a mess, too, and I don't have the excuse of having just moved in."

"How long have you been in your job?"

"Almost eleven years now." For some reason admitting how long I'd been at the center always embarrassed me, like confessing to a terminal lack of ambition or a fear of moving out of your parents' house. I tried to cover it by adding, "Long enough to get the place cleaned up."

"That's a long time for someone so young—almost your whole career, right?"

I nodded. "I worked for a newspaper for a year, then I came here." I was tempted to point out that my young self was almost exactly his age. His longish light-brown hair and narrow face—with a dimple, no less—made him look rather boyish, but in preparation for my interview I'd read his curriculum vitae. Young Dr. Nelson here was pushing thirty-four.

I decided it was time to get on with the interview, *my* interview of him. I opened my notebook, clicked on my ballpoint. "I guess I need to start asking my questions about you."

He shrugged. "Talking about you seems much more interesting."

Yeah, right. "I understand that your particular interest is in short-term therapy. Is that going to affect the way you run the marriage and family clinic?"

"You mean am I going to make therapists stop seeing their clients after eight or ten sessions?" He shook his head. "Nah. Even I will admit that there are some people—a very few—who require longer-term therapy. I do think, though, that it's important for therapists to be more accountable: setting goals with the clients and regularly assessing whether or not they're making progress in meeting those goals."

He went on to outline his plans for the clinic—increased communication within the department, a greater emphasis on continuing education and learning new therapeutic techniques—while I took notes. "If possible, I'd also like to streamline all the paperwork therapists here have to do. Everybody tells me that's a real pain in the ass."

I noticed that one of Nelson's feet, enclosed in a cordovan-colored loafer, was bouncing up and down. For a shrink, this guy was definitely on the hyper side.

"Any other things you'd like to change?" I asked.

He'd been gazing out the window. Now he turned back to look at me. "Being a full-time therapist, particularly being an attentive and responsive therapist, is an emotionally exhausting job." He ran a large hand through his hair and sighed. "I mean, it wipes you out."

I believed it. I don't think that I myself would be up to listening to hour after hour of tales of misery. Not without becoming either totally callous (and I'd met a few therapists who were) or wanting to run home screaming from my office every night. And for all my grousing about psychotherapists—their ridiculous jargon-talk, their unfortunate tendency to lump everyone into a diagnostic category—I had an enormous respect for the many good therapists I knew who daily did battle with other people's demons.

"I'd like to do something about that," Dr. Nelson said.

"Such as?"

He grinned, his smile rueful. "I'm working on it. When I find some answers, I'll let you know."

I smiled back. "I'd appreciate it." Dr. Larry Nelson, I thought, might end up being a very interesting clinic head, if he managed to circumvent all the administrative red-tape and implement some of his ideas.

"Of course, I'm not naive enough to think that making any changes around here will be easy," he said. "At this point I'm just trying to get to know the staff." He glanced at his watch.

I figured I had another five or ten minutes max. I pulled out my copy of his vita. Just a few background facts and I was out of there. "You came from the Menninger Clinic. What made you want to come to Houston?"

"My folks live here and, now that they're getting older, I'd like to live nearby. And the job seemed challenging. Some of my former colleagues work at the center, and they made the place sound intriguing."

"Oh, who are they?"

There was something in his expression that made me suspect that he wished he hadn't brought up the subject. He paused before answering. "Roger and Kate Quinlan."

I stared at him. When Kate told me about her upcoming meeting with her new boss to discuss the tabloid story about her, why hadn't she mentioned that she already knew him?

"Really? When did you three work together?"

"About six years ago, during my psychiatry residency at the Menninger Clinic. I rotated through Roger's department. In fact, we worked together on several research projects."

I jotted it down. "What kind of projects?"

"Clinical research. I did several studies comparing the effectiveness of various types of therapy in treating depression."

He met my eyes. "Roger published the studies," he said in a flat voice.

It was, unfortunately, done all the time: graduate students or med students did the research and their supervisors took the credit. "He didn't list your name on the article?"

Dr. Nelson shook his head. "Roger even seemed quite offended when I complained about him publishing my work as his own. He seemed to think that I should feel flattered that he thought it was worth stealing. Said if I'd submitted the article on my own, the journal never would have published it."

That sounded like Roger. Guilt apparently had never been a part of his emotional repertoire. Still I wanted to know one thing. "And after that you kept in touch with the Quinlans?" Why bother?

"Oh, we ran into each other from time to time at professional meetings." His tone was mild, but his burning eyes belied his voice. "And Kate and I were once quite close." This time both his expression and his voice were carefully neutral.

"Oh?" I smiled my tell-me-more smile, but he didn't bite.

"I'm sorry, but I have another appointment in a few minutes. If you need any more information for your story, just call." He stood up.

I did the same.

"Oh, by the way," he said, as I started for the door, "have you seen this?" He picked up a tabloid-sized paper from the pile on his desk and handed it to me.

I glanced at it: the *Houston Spectator* story about Kate. "I've read it," I said, handing it back to him. "It's a throwaway rag that nobody reads."

"We did," he pointed out.

I felt the distaste I usually experience when my nephew or one of my nieces came running to me to tattle on a sibling. Except they had the excuse of all being under the age of seven.

"I wouldn't worry about it if I were you," I said coldly. "That piece is so obviously biased that no one will take it seriously. The man, John Carter, comes across as a hate-filled lunatic.''

"Oh, I agree," Nelson said calmly. "And I'm not at all worried about that particular piece."

He walked with me to the door. "What I am worried about is the next article. I know Kate, and she won't shrug this off the way you are. As far as Kate Quinlan is concerned, this Carter guy has just thrown the first punch."

His deep-set gray eyes bore into mine. He spoke so quietly that I had to lean forward to hear his parting words. "Trust me. She is about to come out swinging. And yes, *that* worries me."

AMANDA O'NEIL looked up from the leafy green salad she'd been eating. "Now that," she said, "is very interesting."

Amanda and I had been friends long enough for me to realize that the glint in her hazel eyes meant she knew something. In this case something about Larry Nelson. "What's so interesting about it?"

"I heard that Roger Quinlan tried to convince our esteemed director not to hire young Dr. Nelson."

"Really? Maybe Roger was afraid that if Larry came here it might get out that he'd stolen Larry's work for the journal article."

Amanda shrugged. "That sounds like old news to me. I bet Roger just didn't want to be shown up by one of his former students. From what I've heard, Larry has published a lot, and Roger, despite all his talk about the book he was supposedly working on, hadn't published anything in years. And then, if that wasn't bad enough, both of them were going to be heads of different clinics at the same mental health center. Considering Roger's sorry job performance as an administrator, I could see how he wouldn't welcome the competition in that area either.''

I thought about what she'd said. Granted, Roger Quinlan had seemed a petty, mean-spirited man, as well as a competitive one. But was professional competitiveness really the reason he hadn't wanted Larry Nelson working at the center? ''Maybe,'' I suggested, ''Roger blackballed Larry for more personal reasons.''

Amanda arched her delicate eyebrows. ''I think that envy or professional jealousy is quite personal, actually. And, I'd like to point out, Roger didn't succeed in blackballing Larry. He was hired in spite of Roger's objections, which, I'm sure, raised Roger's hackles.''

I shook my head. ''Lord, I can't imagine how you can do therapy with kids. Do you do all this nitpicking with eight-year-olds? 'Now, Justin, are you sure you mean your little brother is a butthead? Might it not be more accurate to say that he's an annoying pest?' ''

She laughed. ''So tell me,'' she said, ''what personal reason of Roger's are you talking about?''

''I'm not sure. It's just that when Larry talked about Kate I sensed that something had gone on between them once, as if they'd had more than a professional relationship. He said that he and Kate had once been quite close.''

''So you think that Roger didn't want Larry to be around Kate again,'' Amanda guessed. ''Afraid that their romance might be rekindled now that he and Kate were having marital problems.''

''Maybe,'' I admitted. ''Though when he spoke about Kate he did not sound like a man in love. And when Kate mentioned him she didn't even admit that she'd ever met him before. She was just concerned that he wanted to discuss that sleazy tabloid article with her.''

Amanda speared a forkful of spinach. ''Now wouldn't

you love to be a fly on the wall at that meeting?''

"Yes, actually. Very much. Though I guess it's possible that Larry meant he'd been close to Kate in some non-romantic way. Maybe they just worked together and were friends.''

Amanda nodded. "That's possible. Kate told me once that she and Roger met while they were working together in Kansas. So if Roger was Larry's supervisor, maybe the three of them worked in the same department.''

"And now Larry is Kate's boss.'' I wondered how Kate felt about that—a former friend being her boss. Particularly a former friend who hadn't sounded all that friendly toward her when I interviewed him.

I munched on my chicken salad sandwich. It was delicious, chunky with nuts and chopped up apples, spiced with a bit of curry.

Amanda was moving on to new topics, telling me about the child-psychology conference she'd attended and the latest on her two kids: Adam, the perfect son, now excelling in medical school, and Sam, the black sheep, currently contemplating dropping out of college in his senior year. Sam, I'd always suspected, was Amanda's favorite child. Though, even under prolonged torture, she would probably not admit to a preference.

I listened, expressed interest, asked questions about the boys. Amanda then wanted to know when Nick would be back. I said I wished I knew; everything was taking longer than expected in El Paso. She inquired about my fight with Margaret. I said we still hadn't spoken, and no, I didn't much feel like discussing my feelings about the estrangement. Maybe another time . . .

I returned to my own preferred conversational topic: Kate and Larry. Nothing like talking about other people's problems when you want to avoid talking about your own.

"Amanda, there really was an undercurrent of hostility when Larry talked about Kate. Maybe they were romantically involved once, and the affair turned sour. Though I can't imagine Kate picking Roger over Larry. Larry is so much more attractive and appealing than Roger was."

Amanda's large hazel eyes grew larger. "Our young Dr. Nelson seems to have made a big impression on you. Is he married?"

I could feel my face grow hot. "I have no idea. Or interest in the subject, for that matter. If anything, my reaction to the two of them is more a reflection of how repellent I found Roger. He was such a mean-spirited, testy person."

"Yes, he was," Amanda agreed. "The kind of guy a lot of people would have liked to see dead."

The question, of course, was which one of those people was bold enough—or furious enough—to follow through on that wish.

# Chapter Eleven

By late afternoon I still hadn't heard from Kate. I phoned her again at home. At this point it was probably too late to stop her interview, but at least I could be forewarned about what kind of article to expect.

Mel answered the phone. Kate wasn't home, but she'd left a note on the refrigerator saying she'd be back by five. "That's almost forty-five minutes from now," Mel added. She sounded scared.

"Did you just get home from school?" I asked, trying to sound casual.

"Yeah, just a few minutes ago." A pause. "I thought Kate would be here. I know she was taking the day off from work."

Now Mel sounded accusing. I didn't blame her. What kind of person leaves a young girl alone in a house the day after she'd discovered a dead body there? Even taking into account that Kate was not Mel's real mother and was perhaps a bit short on maternal feeling for the child, I'd still think a reasonably sensitive human being would anticipate how Mel would feel walking into that empty house. Es-

pecially when that particular human being was profession-
ally trained to be sensitive to the needs of hurting people.

"You think you might be able to go to a neighbor's
house for awhile or a friend's house?" I asked. "Just until
Kate gets home, I mean."

I could hear Mel's labored breathing on the other end of
the line. "The only person I know around here is Consuela's friend Juanita, the housekeeper next door. But today
is her day off. And I can't think of anyplace else to go."

She sounded on the edge of tears. "What about your
mom?" Hadn't someone told me that Mel's mother lived
nearby? "Maybe you could call her."

"She's out of town." A pause. "Until next month." A
longer pause. "She's getting treatment so she'll be well
enough for me to come live with her again." This time Mel
couldn't hold back the tears.

I listened to her cry. Quiet, gulping sobs. A scared kid
who didn't know what to do.

I glanced at my watch. Oh, what the hell. My newsletter
copy would just have to wait. "Mel, listen to me!" I waited
until the sobbing had subsided a bit. "Would you feel better
if I came over there and stayed with you until Kate got
home?"

The answer was faint but unequivocal. "Yes."

"I'll leave now. I should be there in about fifteen
minutes." I'd drive fast.

Mel took a deep breath. "I'm going to take a walk
around the block. Then I'll wait for you out front."

I told her I'd see her in a few minutes, then headed out
the door.

Mel was sitting on the front steps of her large house
when I pulled into her driveway. She waved and stood up
when she saw me. I waved back, thinking that she looked

very relieved and seemed to be a lot calmer than when we'd talked on the phone.

I got out of the car and walked over to her. Up close, I could see how red and puffy her eyes were, how pale her round face looked. I wanted to give her a hug, but I wasn't sure if she'd appreciate it. Instead I smiled at her. "So what would you like to do now? We could take a drive or go somewhere to get something to eat, if you'd like."

Mel shook her head. Her dark hair looked limp and greasy. "There's food inside." Then, as if she wasn't sure if that sounded rude, she added shyly, "I mean I'd like to go into the house—as long as someone else is with me."

"That's fine," I said, following her around to the back of the house. The door to the back porch was unlocked. I glanced around the screened room, the place where the delivery man said he'd picked up the box containing Roger's body. Was the door to the porch usually left unlocked, I wondered.

"My key is to the back door," Mel was explaining as she hunted in the pocket of her jeans for the key.

"Do most people come and go through your back door?"

"Yeah," Mel said as she unlocked the deadbolt. "Only company ever comes in the front door. Or people who are delivering something."

We walked into a tiled hallway. I could see the sunroom on our right and up ahead, on the left, the kitchen. In front of me, Mel's body stiffened. She took a a nervous step forward, glanced around, then motioned for me to follow her into the kitchen.

"Oh, I'm not really hungry," I said, suddenly realizing that my offer to go out for food had forced Mel, out of a sense of hospitality, to go into the one room in the house she least wanted to enter—the kitchen where yesterday she'd discovered Consuela's body.

She glanced back at me. "It's okay," she said. "I want to get something to drink. And I need to get used to being in there."

I doubted if I would have felt the same way so soon after such a gruesome discovering. Certainly I wouldn't have when I was fifteen or sixteen. While Mel poured two glasses of iced tea from a plastic container, I checked out the kitchen. I wasn't sure what I was expecting—bloodstains on the floor, a police-drawn outline of the body? There was nothing. Or at least nothing obvious. The alcove that looked as if it might have once contained a table and chairs was now empty.

I jumped when Mel set a glass on the kitchen counter, the noise too loud in the silent house.

"Sorry," Mel said. "I didn't mean to startle you."

"It's okay." I smiled sheepishly. "Your house is just so quiet." Some source of reassurance I was.

"Tell me about it." Now that it was clear that she wasn't the jitteriest person in this house, Mel seemed to relax. Leaning on a pale gray Formica countertop, she took a swig of iced tea, then pointed to the breakfast alcove. "That's where I found her—slumped over the table that used to be there. Kate must have got rid of it while I was at school."

"She was sitting at the table when she"—I searched for the right word—"died?"

"Yeah." Mel turned probing brown eyes on me. For the first time I could see her resemblance to Roger. "But I don't think that Consuela killed herself."

"Why not?"

"Because she was Catholic—seriously Catholic—and wouldn't kill herself. And because the note that she left was all wrong."

"Wrong how?"

"She called Roger 'Dr. Quinlan,' and Consuela never

called him that. She always said 'he' or 'mister.' And Consuela never wrote long notes. Her English wasn't good, particularly her written English. Sometimes she'd take phone messages for us, but all it would be was someone's name and phone number, never any message."

"But the note was in her handwriting?"

Mel nodded. "I guess so; it looked like it," she said reluctantly. "But maybe somebody made her write it, to make it look like a suicide."

"What did the note say?"

Color spread across Mel's plump face. Why? A full minute passed and Mel still hadn't answered. Instead she stared, as if suddenly transfixed, at her iced-tea glass.

What could the note have possibly said? And why had Mel, seemingly so forthright only a few minutes ago, suddenly clammed up?

Both of us heard a car door slam, then footsteps on the driveway. Mel hurried to the kitchen window. "It's Kate." Now that she had someone else in the house with her, Mel didn't sound especially happy about her stepmother's arrival.

We waited in silence as Kate's key turned in the back lock, then heard the rapid footsteps moving across the tile floor.

"Liz!" Kate strode into the kitchen. "I thought that was your car in the driveway. I certainly didn't expect to see you here." She didn't sound displeased by my presence, merely surprised.

"I came to stay with Mel until you got home."

Before Kate could respond Mel said, "I've just been telling Liz that Consuela would never have written that fake suicide note." The teenager's voice was cold, her eyes fixed on Kate's face.

Kate set her purse and a manila folder on the countertop.

"You think that because you liked Consuela and you don't want to believe she'd do such a thing. But Mel, the note *was* in her handwriting and her fingerprints were on the gun." Kate sighed. "Sometimes when people are desperate enough they do things that seem totally out of character. I think Consuela might have thought this was the only way out for her."

Mel's face contorted into a grimace. "So you think she killed Roger?"

"What?" I asked. But neither of them seemed to have heard me.

Kate kept her eyes on Mel's face. "I don't know what to think anymore," she said quietly, looking incredibly tired.

"Well *I* do." Mel's eyes blazed her defiance. "And I know that Consuela didn't kill herself and she didn't kill my father either." With a venomous look at her stepmother, Mel turned on her black high-tops and stalked out of the room.

"Oh, Lord." Kate sighed and ran one hand through her hair in a massaging gesture.

"Uh, did Consuela's note say that she killed Roger?" I got back to my as-yet-unanswered question.

"Not in those words." Kate gazed off into the distance, as if she were trying to recall Consuela's exact wording. "She said she was sorry, but she couldn't go on living with what she'd done to Dr. Quinlan. She couldn't live with herself anymore. Something like that."

"That was all she said about Roger? She didn't mention what it was that she'd done to him?"

Kate shook her head. "No, I'm sure that's all she said. The police took the letter, but I read it a couple of times, trying to make sense of it."

I studied her pale, tired face. "So you *do* think that Consuela wrote the note herself?"

Kate nodded. "It was her handwriting and, despite what Mel thinks, the language was not complex and the note was only a few lines. Consuela could manage that."

"What do you think she meant by feeling sorry for what she did to Roger?" The phrase could be interpreted in a lot of ways that had nothing to do with murder.

"You mean do I think she shot Roger?" When I nodded, Kate said, "No. I've been thinking a lot about it, and I don't think she killed him. For one thing, I can't imagine why she would. What's her motive? I don't mean that she liked Roger; he was as demanding and high-handed with her as he was with everybody else. But if she couldn't stand being around him anymore she could have just quit. I can't see any benefit to Consuela in Roger's death. In fact it's just the opposite. Without Roger's salary, I can't afford to keep her or this big house. We had almost nothing in savings. Roger believed in spending every dollar he made."

Still this house and its contents had to be worth a lot. I wondered suddenly if Roger had left a will and, if he had, who had inherited his property. Were he and Kate so estranged that Roger had taken the trouble to write her out of his will—if, of course, she had ever been in it?

"So, in answer to your question," Kate concluded, "what I suspect is that Consuela knew something about Roger's murder, but no, I don't think that she was the one who killed him. She seemed very upset when the police came to search our house after they learned the box with Roger's body was picked up on our porch. At the time I just thought Consuela was so angry because they made such a mess of the house. But now I wonder if she didn't have another reason for being upset."

"You think she was an accomplice?" It made sense. The

complex logistics of the murder—shooting Roger, having a big enough box ready, arranging for the delivery at the appropriate time to Kate's seminar—almost required some kind of inside help.

"That seems more likely. Roger was very stingy with everyone but himself. If somebody paid her enough, I could see Consuela being more than willing to do something like help move the box with Roger's body into a closet to get it out of the way and then later help move it to the back porch for the deliveryman to pick up. One person wouldn't be able to carry that box unless he was exceptionally strong."

"Or had a dolly," I said, remembering the man who'd wheeled in the box to the Powerful Woman seminar.

There was something else that I meant to ask Kate about. "Do you always go in and out the back door?"

Kate nodded.

"So when you left for the workshop that Saturday, was the box sitting on your back porch?"

"No. The police asked me that too. I'm reasonably observant, and I certainly would have noticed a box that size."

"So someone put it there after you'd left for the seminar. Was Consuela here when you left the house?"

"No, she didn't work on weekends unless we had something special going on, like a party. No one was here when I left that morning. Mel was at her mother's. I assumed that Roger was with one of his many female friends," Kate said, her voice surprisingly bitter.

Was she perhaps less blasé about Roger's infidelities than she claimed to be? Certainly most wives found their husband's philandering deeply hurtful and humiliating. Maybe Kate, despite her claims to the contrary, was no exception. And with everyone else in the household gone for the weekend, what better time to get rid of a louse of a husband? Kate could have sent the body to the workshop to divert suspicion from herself—a ploy that didn't work, but nevertheless might have seemed like a good idea at the time.

But if Kate herself killed Roger, did that mean that Consuela had known that Kate was the killer? Perhaps she'd come back to the house unexpectedly and seen Kate with the body. But even with the help of a dolly for moving, could Kate have hoisted Roger's body into the box by herself? Roger had been a fairly slight man, probably no more than 150 or 155 pounds, but that was still a good forty pounds heavier than Kate. Or maybe Consuela had helped Kate move the body. Maybe Consuela had been Kate's accomplice.

I shivered. Which meant that I might now be standing here chatting with a double murderer.

"Is something wrong, Liz?" Kate asked. "You're not looking very well."

"A headache," I lied. "It's nothing. I need to get back to work."

"Well, thanks for coming to hold Mel's hand. I would have gotten here earlier but the interview lasted longer than I expected."

"Oh, how did it go?" For some reason Kate's newspaper interview seemed less important than it had an hour ago.

"Great!" Suddenly the tiredness seemed to leave Kate's face; the memory of her interview apparently energized her. "I really think I told my side of the story."

We'd see what she thought once the story came out. "Did Sheila mention when the story might run?"

"Probably later in the week, she said."

"Did you tell your attorney that you were doing the interview?" I asked, curious. The other question I wanted to know—was the mental health center mentioned—was not one that Kate could answer.

"Are you kidding? Bobby would have told me that only someone with a death wish would talk to a reporter right now."

I could name a few other people who shared that sentiment, I thought as the two of us walked to the back door. Me, for one.

Kate said good-bye on the back porch. I told her to tell Mel good-bye. The teenager had not shown her face again after stomping out of the kitchen.

I was unlocking my car door when I heard a sharp tapping sound. It took me a minute to locate the source of the noise: Mel in an upstairs window. She waved at me and mouthed one word: "Thanks."

My smile felt forced as I waved back at her. I tried hard to convince myself that my suspicions about Kate were probably totally off-base. But what if they weren't? I was leaving a mouthy, obstreperous, and highly curious teenager alone with a possible murderer. A possible murderer who didn't like the kid all that much to start with.

I got into my car, feeling like a jerk.

# Chapter Twelve

"WE MEET AGAIN." ABOVE THE CARDBOARD BOX SHE was carrying down the hall of the mental health center, Kate Quinlan's smile seemed strained.

I peered into the box. It was filled with manila folders, notebooks, a few books, a box of tissue. It looked as if she'd just cleaned out her office. "You moving somewhere?"

The glint in her eyes told me the answer before she opened her mouth. "I just quit."

"You're kidding! Why?" It didn't seem the smartest move in the world for someone who'd just been telling me that she'd have to cut back on her living expenses now that she was single again.

"Larry Nelson." She made the name sound like a curse. Kate glanced toward the back door. "I need to get going."

Tough. And I needed—well, wanted—to hear this story. "Let me walk out with you," I said smoothly, "so you can tell me what happened."

I hurried ahead so I could hold the door to the parking lot open for her. "So what about Larry Nelson?"

A muscle twitched in the corner of Kate's mouth. "The bastard told me to stop talking to the press and quit giving my seminars. I told *him* to go to hell."

We were at her car now: a tan Ford Explorer. Kate unlocked the door and shoved the box into the backseat. She turned back to face me.

"Oh, Kate, I'm sorry."

"Don't be," she said curtly. "This is probably for the best anyway. I knew that Larry and I could never work together, given our past history."

I raised an eyebrow inquiringly. "What history is that?"

"Oh, Larry and I were having an affair when I first met Roger. In fact I was with Larry at a Christmas party when he introduced me to Roger, who was his supervisor. Anyway, Roger and I fell in love—in infatuation, as it turned out—and I dumped Larry. He never forgave either of us, Roger or me."

"But if you think that Nelson is doing this now to punish you because you once jilted him, that is certainly grounds for appeal," I said. "Why don't you take this to the Employee Grievance Committee? I don't think Dr. Nelson has the right either to tell you to stop talking to the press or to stop doing your workshops, as long as you don't hold them during your working hours here."

Kate sighed. "But I don't want to take it to the grievance committee. Larry would undoubtedly point out that he did not fire me; I quit. And he has all these reasons—stupid reasons, granted, but nevertheless reasons—for me stopping the workshops. He says that they hurt my credibility as a therapist. Clients won't perceive me as this dispassionate professional. They'll think I'm this ballbreaking Powerful Woman person."

"He said that?"

"Not in those words, but, yes, he said that. Also he

thinks I'm damaging the mental health center's reputation.''

I looked at her. "You know you're doing exactly what Larry wants you to do: quitting.''

Kate smiled wearily. "No, I know Larry. He would have infinitely preferred a good fight.''

Which, as I recalled, was more or less what Larry had said about her. "So you're saying he wanted you to stay and suffer?'' Wonderful trait for a psychiatrist, sadism.

"I'm sure that Larry would vehemently deny that revenge has anything to do with his actions. He's doing what he thinks is right and if, in the process of doing that, he gets to dictate my behavior, all the better. The man is a bona fide control freak, and there's no way I could work with him.''

"Well, do you think you might be able to be reassigned to another clinic? Maybe you could transfer to the adult clinic.'' Now that Roger was no longer the head of that clinic, I thought but did not say.

"With Tricia Whitmore in the next office?'' Kate rolled her eyes at me. "I know. Maybe Tricia and I could lead a group together. Now wouldn't that be fun!''

She leaned over and patted my hand. "I appreciate your concern, Liz. I really do. But you know that old saying about soldiers fighting their best when there's no escape route, no possibility of retreat? Well, now I have to make a go of Powerful Woman. I have no other job, no safety net to fall back on. Who knows? This might be the best thing that ever happened to me.''

I hoped she believed that. I watched Kate slide into the driver's seat. "Well, good luck,'' I said.

"Thanks. I'll be in touch. I'd appreciate your feedback on the rewrites I've made on the book.''

I tried to smile at her as she turned on the ignition and, waving, drove away.

• • •

THAT NIGHT I lay in a tub full of steaming bathwater, thinking about my day. I felt anxious and strangely out of sorts, and I wasn't entirely sure why. Partly, I guess, I was concerned about Kate. I, who only yesterday had suspected her of being a possible murderer (and I still wasn't entirely sure that she wasn't) tonight felt sorry for the woman. What I was sure of was that Larry Nelson had set her up. From past experience he'd known exactly how Kate would react to his ultimatum: She'd say to hell with him, she wasn't going to play with him anymore, and then snatch up her toys and march home. Sure, she was childish and hot-headed. But Larry Nelson was something worse: a manipulator and a bully. And despite what Kate said about the psychological benefits of having no safety net, I strongly suspect that she was going to regret her decision to quit. Maybe regretted it already.

I added more hot water and reminded myself that I loved soaking in the bathtub. Except tonight I didn't. I, who'd always reveled in my solitary interludes, who savored the silence, the time to unwind without any demands on me, tonight felt lonely. Although he'd only been gone for a few days, I missed Nick. And, much as I hated to admit it, I missed my sister too. Yes, Margaret was pushy, controlling, and intrusive, but I was used to her. I suddenly remembered how during the what-do-you-want-to-change exercise I'd done at the Powerful Woman seminar I'd written, "Divorce my sister." Well, I'd gotten what I wanted. The only problem was that now I knew what I really wanted. I did want Margaret in my life, but our testy, juvenile relationship had to change. I just wasn't sure that it was about to happen in my lifetime.

In my bedroom the phone started to ring. I considered letting the answering machine pick up the message. The phone rang again. I leaped out of the water and, grabbing a towel, ran for the phone.

I got there before the answering tape clicked on. "Hello?"

"You sound out of breath, sweetheart." It was Nick's voice, sounding warm, interested, happy to hear me.

"I was in the tub."

"Oh, I would have called back."

"No, I'd rather talk to you now. How's your story coming? When are you coming home?"

"Well, there's good news and bad news."

I waited.

"The good news is that the story is much bigger than I expected. I picked up some really good stuff, records proving that this scam has been going on for years."

I heard the excitement in his voice, the exhilaration that was always there when he got his teeth into a good story. "And the bad news?" I asked.

"I'm going to be here for longer than I thought. I talked to my editor this morning and the paper has okayed it."

"For how long?"

"I'm really not sure. Maybe a couple of weeks. Maybe longer. It's hard to tell at this point. The worst case scenario is probably a month."

I felt a surge of disappointment, then told myself to snap out of it. A month wasn't that long. I was no dependent parasite. I was a self-sufficient, independent woman—and needed to start acting like one. Preferably immediately.

"Of course, I should be able to get back for at least one weekend," Nick was saying. "Or do you think you could fly down to El Paso for a few days?"

I said sure, that would be fun. But I knew from having been around him before when he was in the middle of a hot story that there would be little time for reunions. The only thing that Nick was really going to be able to focus on for the next few weeks was his story.

"So what's been going on with you?" Nick asked.

I told him about Kate quitting her job.

"It sounds as if she wanted to quit all along," Nick said. "This Nelson guy just gave her an excuse."

"Why do you think that?"

"The comments about soldiers fighting better with no escape route and losing her job might be the best thing that ever happened to her. People don't think things like that minutes after they've told their boss to stuff it. Kate probably has been thinking for awhile that she'd like to concentrate on her book and the seminar, and Nelson just made her do it sooner than she'd planned. She already had her rationalizations ready. She seems more of an entrepreneurial type than a therapist anyway."

"You might be right," I said. When I thought about it, Kate had not seemed very upset this afternoon. Certainly not as upset as I would have been in the same situation.

Nick and I agreed we'd try to get together the weekend after next. We'd decide later whether I'd go to El Paso or he'd come home. "I miss you," he said. "And I love you."

"Me too." I hung up, feeling even more lonely—and now cold and wet to boot.

I returned to my now-chilly bath water. As I added more hot water I realized something else that I missed: the excitement about a work project that I'd heard tonight in Nick's voice. And yes, I'd glimpsed that this afternoon too when Kate talked about making a go of her book and seminar. Once I'd felt that way about my job at the mental health center. I hadn't realized until tonight how very much I wanted to feel that excitement about my work again.

# Chapter Thirteen

THE *CHRONICLE* STORY ABOUT KATE RAN THE NEXT morning. I was in my office, reading it and nursing a cup of coffee, when Larry Nelson marched in the door.

"Have you read this?" he asked, waving a newspaper in front of my face.

I glimpsed the photo of Kate Quinlan, beaming confidently at us from a blurred sea of print. Was the man always so hyper? "I'm reading it now." Hint, hint: And would appreciate your leaving my office so I could continue doing so.

Dr. Nelson chose not to take the hint. Instead he settled his lanky frame into the molded plastic chair next to my desk. "I'll wait while you finish it."

I did. "Okay, I've read it." I glanced over at him, feeling annoyed.

"So what do you think?"

"It wasn't as bad as I expected it to be," I admitted. Sheila Lemur obviously liked Kate, and her story portrayed Kate as a feisty, independent woman besieged by unfortunate events. While at times Kate sounded a bit hot-headed and defensive in the story, she did not—in my mind, at least—sound like a man-hater or a husband-killer.

Larry directed his laser-like eyes in my direction. "Obviously we have different expectations. I thought the story was very damaging to the mental health center."

"The only mention of the center was a few words saying that Kate also works here," I said coldly. "Or should I say 'worked?' " Wasn't it enough for this man that he'd pushed Kate into quitting? What else did he want?

"I didn't fire her, you know. She quit."

Spineless as well as vindictive: what an attractive combination. "Which she would not have done if you hadn't demanded that she give up her workshops and stop talking to the press."

"True. But you're wrong if you think I wanted Kate to quit. Given my choice, I would have preferred that she stay. Despite this workshop foolishness, Kate is a good therapist." The deep-set eyes regarded me levelly.

Okay, so maybe he wasn't spineless. But Dr. Larry Nelson's autocratic manner was annoying. What did he want from me anyway? "Thanks for coming in to show me the article," I said in a cool but civil voice. As in, Now you can leave.

He refused to be dismissed. "Can't you do something about the story?"

"Like what? Demand the paper print a retraction saying Kate is a former employee of the center? At the time she gave the interview she did, in fact, work here."

"I was thinking of something more along the line of having someone from the center, probably a psychiatrist, doing an interview about the potential damage of those one-shot encounter groups."

I stared at him, too angry to even try for tact. "And you're volunteering to be the official spokesman who attacks Kate's workshops? Kate must be right. You really do hate her, don't you?"

He glared at me. "This has nothing to do with any personal feelings about Kate. And, no, I do not hate her."

Yeah, right.

"Actually I'm not talking about singling out Kate's workshops," he said. "I think that all these one-session transformational groups can be potentially very harmful to certain people. For the majority of participants—those with fairly well-integrated personalities—the groups are harmless. Probably a waste of their money, but maybe they pick up a few interesting ideas. A month later they've forgotten all their good intentions about changing their lives, but so what, they had an entertaining day."

I knew where he was going with this and I wanted him to cut to the chase. I did it for him. "But you're concerned about the already unstable people who come to the workshops."

"Precisely. None of these groups have any kind of psychological screening of their participants. Someone who should be in a psychiatric ward could just pay his money and sit back waiting to be transformed. The danger is that some of the more confrontational techniques designed to break down participants' defenses could push an already-unstable person right over the edge. And at the end of the session that person is just sent home. There's no follow-up, no accountability."

But couldn't almost anything—a disturbing movie, an impassioned speaker—push a susceptible mentally ill person over the edge? Did that mean that impassioned speeches and emotionally charged movies should be abolished too? "Do you know of anybody personally who was damaged by an encounter group?"

"Yes," Larry said.

I looked at him questioningly. When he didn't add further details, I asked him the question any reporter would ask. "So what happened?"

He was studying the books on my bookshelf when he answered. "He—a college student, very bright, articulate, very unhappy—went to one of those marathon sessions where you can't eat anything or even leave to go to the bathroom. The workshop leader told him he had to shape up. He was worthless, he was shit. That everything bad in his life was his own fault."

Larry turned to me and I could see the pain in those intense eyes. "Never mind that on some days the chemicals in his brain made it an insurmountable task to even get out of bed. It was all his fault. If he were a worthwhile person, a real man, he wouldn't feel that way."

Larry stopped talking. I sensed he was too absorbed in his own thoughts to continue. But I wanted to know. "So what happened to him?"

The answer was almost a whisper. "He walked out of the group, drove to his apartment and hanged himself. The note he left said he was finally ready to take responsibility for himself."

I could see tears welling in his eyes. "Was he your patient?"

Larry shook his head. "No, he was my brother." He stood up. "So you can see why I feel very strongly about these transform-your-life workshops."

Without another word he walked out the door. Walking more slowly than before, his shoulders stooped slightly forward.

SURPRISINGLY NO one else mentioned Kate's interview to me that day. Even Dr. Cody, the mental health center's director who usually reacted to the newspaper clippings about the center that I sent to his office, didn't find the article worth mentioning in our conversation later that morning. I wondered if he was even aware that Kate no longer worked here.

I had intended to eat my lunch at my desk, but when Lorna spotted me in the hall and asked if I had lunch plans, I jumped at the chance to get out for awhile. We decided to walk to M. D. Anderson Cancer Center. It was close by, fast and, if you didn't mind hospital cafeteria fare, the food was fine.

"Did you hear about Kate quitting?" I asked as we walked through a parking lot to the huge, pink hospital.

"Yeah. She stopped in to say good-bye to me. I was kind of surprised that she quit so abruptly. I would have thought she'd allow more time to break the news to her patients and have them deal with some of the termination issues. Maybe she'll call them from home so they don't feel, you know, abandoned by her. I sure hope she does." Lorna trailed off, looking a bit embarrassed about criticizing her friend.

I wondered if Kate had even considered her patients' welfare when she quit. "So who's taking over her patient load?"

"Larry Nelson, our new clinic head, is reassigning them. He's taking quite a few of the cases himself, I think."

"I just interviewed him for the newsletter. What's Nelson like to work for?" I asked in a carefully neutral voice.

Lorna considered the question as we entered the hospital. "I like him. He's smart and enthusiastic and hardworking. He's trying to get to know everybody and pull us all together as a team. I think he's really going to shake things up."

That I could believe. "And most of the therapists upstairs are happy about that?"

Lorna snorted. "You've got to be kidding. Some of the therapists who've been here forever, particularly the ones who have a private practice on the side, hate Larry's guts. He wants them to try new techniques and be more accountable for what's happening in their therapy, and they want to keep on doing things the way they've always done them. And then Larry's rule about no moonlighting really chaps their butts. Some of these guys are almost doubling their incomes by seeing private patients."

So Nelson wasn't just sticking his nose into Kate's after-work activities. I could imagine that there were a significant number of unhappy campers in Larry Nelson's clinic. "So everybody is just giving up their private practices?"

"Hardly." Lorna shook her head. "Three or four of them went to Dr. Cody to complain about Larry. Said he was violating their rights. But Dr. Cody said there was some rule against therapists in state-funded facilities also working as private therapists. He said Larry had a perfect right to enforce the rule, even if some of the other clinic heads choose to look the other way when their therapists have private practices."

"I'm sure that made Larry's staff very happy."

"Yeah, a few of them are talking about looking for jobs in the other clinics, but right now there aren't any openings. And Larry did tell everybody that he realized it might take a couple of months; he doesn't expect people to just dump their private patients."

"That was big of him."

Lorna lifted an eyebrow. "I sort of like him. I admire his passion. And"—she grinned slyly—"I think he's kind of cute."

A cute pain in the ass, I thought as we entered the huge cafeteria and picked up our metal trays. It was an opinion, however, that I intended to keep to myself.

Over my tuna salad sandwich, apple and bowl of green Jell-O (a childhood passion I only indulged in hospital cafeterias), I turned the conversation away from the wonderful Dr. Nelson to topics I'd rather discuss. What, for instance, did Lorna think about the chances of Kate making Powerful Woman a full-time endeavor? Lorna had been to more of the workshops than I had.

"If anyone can make a success of it, it will be Kate," Lorna pronounced between bites of pasta salad. "She's a dynamic speaker and all the publicity she's been getting lately should help too."

"You mean you think that the stories about Robin running over her husband and Kate going on trial for Roger's death will help the workshops?" I asked. Not *my* idea of good public relations. "I mean I know it drew a bunch of curiosity seekers—the angry woman's group—right after the first story, but I can't imagine those kinds of articles helping in the long run."

Lorna shrugged. "Publicity—any publicity, good or bad—draws people. So maybe they just come out of curiosity or prurient interest—so what?"

But were there enough curiosity-seekers to financially support Kate in the months ahead? That was the pertinent and, as yet, unanswerable question. "So with all these new rules are you going to be able to keep working on the Powerful Woman workshops?" I asked Lorna.

She shook her head. "I was getting kind of tired of it anyway."

I could believe that. I, who'd only attended one and a half workshops, had grown heartily sick of hearing Kate talk about empowerment. I hesitated, then blurted out what I'd been thinking. "Tell me the truth, Lorna. Didn't you think that Kate's workshop was kind of simplistic?"

She smiled. "Sure. But that doesn't mean that it isn't

valuable. You know, when people recall the moment when they decided to change some significant behavior—to stop drinking, stop smoking, finally lose the excess weight—it's usually something personal and emotional that spurred them into action: a wife saying she was leaving the guy if he didn't stop drinking, a doctor telling the woman she was going to die early if she didn't lose weight. Often the incident that triggers change is something very simple but with a lot of personal impact to that individual.''

''And you think that Powerful Woman can have that kind of effect?'' I asked. ''I'm not just talking about a temporary euphoria, this big resolve to change your life that just peters out like a three-month-old New Year's resolution.''

''I wonder about that myself,'' Lorna admitted as we set our trays and dirty dishes on a moving conveyor belt to the dish-washing area. ''Particularly for someone like Robin, who seemed to be trying to justify her acting out with all that now-I'm-empowered talk.''

Outside the air was thick with Houston's familiar humidity. I was surprised when Lorna turned to me and said, ''You know the thing that really bugs me about those workshops?''

I shook my head. ''What?''

''They seem to encourage impulsiveness: Don't think and weigh your options, just act. If it feels good, do it! Run over your husband; he's a bastard anyway. Attack your swinish boss; he deserves it. Don't even think about the consequences. And I'm not even sure how that happened. Kate said—and she's right—that she never advocated violence. But maybe it's because Kate herself is such an impulsive person that that's the message that seeps through.''

I looked at her. ''But you don't think that Kate is capable of violence, do you?'' Lorna, after all, knew Kate a lot better than I did.

Lorna turned her large green eyes on me. She looked uncharacteristically solemn. "Are you asking me if I think Kate killed Roger?"

I shrugged. "Yeah, I guess I am."

"Kate didn't do it," Lorna announced. "She never would have done things that way—sending herself a body and interrupting her workshop. For one thing, Kate is incredibly disorganized. I was always making some last-minute arrangement for the workshop that she totally forgot about. She's not a detail person. If Kate had been in charge of sending Roger's body, the box would probably have arrived two hours after the workshop was over."

"Sending herself Roger's body doesn't sound like something Kate would do," I agreed. "The workshop was also too important to her to disrupt it like that."

"Exactly. Kate is impulsive and she's decisive. She makes up her mind quickly and acts. If she were going to kill Roger, she'd probably just march in and shoot him or give him a shove off a cliff. Whoever killed Roger was an entirely different personality—careful, detail-oriented, secretive. He'd have to do a lot of planning to pull things off. By no stretch of the imagination was this an impulsive crime of passion. And whoever did it was trying to hurt Kate too. He wanted to humiliate her, to rub her nose in the gore. Kind of like a guy killing his ex-wife's lover and then dumping the body in her front yard."

Like Larry Nelson, for instance? Punishing the woman who'd spurned him by killing the man she chose instead of him, then sending her the body. I tried to push that thought aside as Lorna and I walked in the backdoor of the mental health center and headed for our separate offices.

THE REST of the afternoon seemed to go by too fast, filled with too many phone calls and too many meetings. By the end of the day I still hadn't finished writing the last of my stories for the next newsletter and I decided to work late. Without the constant interruptions, I could finally get some work done.

By the time I glanced again at my watch it was almost 7:30. Time to go home. I'd finished my last article, the interview with Larry Nelson, and I was famished. I was pulling my office door closed when I heard the footsteps behind me. I froze.

"Did I startle you?" It was Larry Nelson. "I'm sorry."

"It's okay." I didn't feel like explaining that my fear was a direct result of having been attacked last year in almost this exact spot on another night when I'd worked late.

"You're working late tonight," he observed as we turned and walked together toward the backdoor.

"Yeah, finishing my stories for the newsletter. What about you?"

"Oh, just trying to get caught up on my paperwork. Where are you parked?" he asked as we walked outside.

"Just over there." I pointed at my trusty old Toyota.

He walked with me to my car. Ten years ago I might have found the action sexist. Today—after hearing too many reports of kidnappings, rapes and car thefts in the medical center—I was grateful for the gesture.

I unlocked my car door. "Thanks. Good night, Larry."

He hesitated. "Would you be interested in having dinner with me?"

"Uh, sorry, I can't. But thanks anyway. I have plans for tonight." Plans to settle down with a Lean Cuisine, a glass of wine and the latest Jonathan Kellerman novel, but I wasn't going to go into specifics.

"Well, maybe another time," he said smoothly. Then paused. "You *are* single, aren't you?"

I nodded. "But I'm involved with someone right now."

"Oh, of course." The words kind of hung there awkwardly.

"Well, good night." I tried to smile, but it didn't feel right.

"Good night, Liz."

I turned the radio on loud as I pulled out of the parking lot. "Involved with someone?" Why hadn't I said "engaged"? Granted, Nick and I hadn't done the formal announcement and engagement-ring routine, but we'd agreed we wanted to get married—someday. Involved could mean anything. To some people four dates translated into involved.

And then, as I turned onto Holcombe Boulevard and headed toward home, I thought: It might have been fun to go out to dinner with Larry Nelson. Even engaged persons went out for casual dinners with fellow employees. So how come *my* knee-jerk reaction to his invitation was "absolutely not"?

# Chapter Fourteen

THE PHONE WOKE ME SATURDAY MORNING.

"You were asleep, weren't you?" It was Margaret's voice. She did not sound all that contrite. When motherhood had forced her into becoming an early riser, Margaret decided that the rest of the world should follow suit.

I glanced at my alarm clock through narrowed eyes: 8:15. "It's okay. I was going to get up in a few minutes anyway." Or at least I was going to try.

"Well, I'm sorry."

I opened my eyes wider. Was this truly my sister on the line or some imposter who just happened to sound like her? And was she—Take-No-Prisoners Margaret—actually trying to apologize to me?

An awkward pause followed. "What's up?" I finally asked. "How is everybody?"

"That's why I'm calling," Margaret said. "It's about the kids."

"Is something wrong?" I had a mental image of Maria, the youngest, lying in a hospital bed, her blonde curls spread across the pillow.

"Nothing serious," Margaret said quickly. "It's just that they all miss you. Last night at dinner the twins were asking why you didn't come over anymore. Then Maria said that you'd promised to take her to Baskin-Robbins but you never did. And you always told her that it was very important not to break promises."

It would have been a cheap shot—and one Margaret was totally capable of delivering—except for the fact that I had promised Maria I'd take her out for ice cream, and then I'd forgotten about it. And four-year-old Maria took her ice cream very seriously.

"Oh, hell. Tell her I'm sorry. How about if I pick her up this afternoon? No, listen, I'll take all the kids somewhere. We can go to lunch or to a movie or to the zoo. Tell them they can pick."

"This afternoon isn't good for us," Margaret said. "Maria is going to a birthday party and the twins are going to play at friends' houses. How about Sunday afternoon instead?"

"Fine." I was sitting up in bed now, wishing I had a cup of coffee.

Margaret paused. "The kids really do miss you, you know. You're such a big part of their lives, particularly since they hardly ever see their grandparents."

"I've missed them too," I said truthfully.

"I suppose you and Nick have plans for the weekend," Margaret said, segueing into her nosy sister role.

"No, Nick is in El Paso working on a story."

"So what are you going to do with yourself?" According to Margaret's way of thinking, insufficient busyness was the deadliest of the seven deadly sins.

I yawned. "I haven't decided yet." Now that sleeping late was crossed off my list of possibilities.

"You know," Margaret began slowly in the wheedling

tone that always clued me in that she was about to venture
onto thin ice. "Since you have the time, it would be a
perfect day to visit those caterers I was telling you about.
I could pick you up after I drop Maria off at her party."

I considered slamming the phone down in her ear, but
decided against it. She would only call back.

Margaret must have taken my silence as encouragement
to continue. "If we don't get the arrangements made now—
if *you* don't get them made, I mean—it's going to be too
late to book a first-rate caterer."

And that was her response to my stop-interfering-in-my-
life-or-forget-about-seeing-me ultimatum? Saying "you"
can make the wedding arrangements instead of "we"—
although in fact *we* would still be making them?

I took a deep breath. "You don't have to worry anymore
about the arrangements, Margaret. Nick and I have decided
to elope."

I heard her gasp. "I'll pick up the kids at one tomorrow," I said and hung up.

I WAS sitting at my kitchen table finishing my first cup
of coffee and reading my newspaper when the doorbell
rang. I glanced at the clock on my stove: 8:45. Margaret
must have run for the car the minute she put down the
receiver.

I glanced out the front door's peephole, then unlocked
the door. "Mel?"

She smiled at me, an uncertain, tentative smile. Once
again Roger's daughter was dressed in faded, baggy jeans
and a black T-shirt. "I know I should have called first, but
I was afraid if I did you'd tell me to forget it, so I just
came instead."

*Forget what?* I wondered, motioning for her to come
inside. A conversation with her was still probably an im-

provement over a heart-to-heart with Margaret.

I poured myself another cup of coffee and got Mel the Diet Coke she'd requested. We settled down in my living room.

"Kate told me yesterday about those therapists at the mental health center who got killed last year," she began hesitantly.

I nodded, not knowing what else to do.

"And she said that you caught the killer."

"I don't know if I'd say that I *caught* the killer," I amended. "The killer found me. The best I did was get away."

She sent me an oh-you're-too-modest look. Because she wanted to believe that I'd single-handedly solved the crime, nothing I said (like, for instance, the truth) was going to shake her of that conviction. "Whatever," Mel said, moving on to more current concerns. "I want you to help me solve this case."

Case? I shot her a quizzical look. "Are you talking about your father's death?"

She nodded. "And Consuela's. I already told you that I'm sure Consuela didn't kill herself."

Which, of course, was supposed to be enough reason for everyone else to believe it too. Warnings—in the form of Nick Finley's recent plea to me to back off, stay away, do *not* get involved with the deaths in the Quinlan household— flitted briefly across my consciousness. I ignored them. "So tell me," I asked instead, "what makes you think there is a case to solve? The last time we spoke you seemed convinced that Kate killed your father and maybe Consuela too."

"Oh, I've decided I needed to keep my mind open to other possibilities," Mel said airily.

"Why?" Teenagers, from my own past experience and

current observation, were seldom noted for their open-minded tolerance of the grown-ups sharing their home. "What made you decide that there were other suspects besides Kate?"

"I started talking to people. Juanita—she works next door for the Smythes and was a friend of Consuela's. She told me that she saw a bunch of people come to the house that Friday afternoon when Roger was killed. And Mr. Smythe—you know, Kate's lawyer—said that the autopsy shows that Roger was shot some time between 2:30 and 5 P.M. on Friday. So one of those people who came to the house on Friday afternoon could have been the killer."

I tried to quickly process all the information she'd given me. So if Roger was shot on Friday afternoon or early in the evening and his body was delivered to the workshop shortly before 11:15 on Saturday morning, where had the body been all Friday night? "Uh, did Mr. Smythe happen to tell you if they have any idea where the shooting took place?"

Mel shook her head. Her hair, I noticed, looked as if it had been recently trimmed. And washed. A big improvement from the last time I'd seen her. "But it's pretty obvious, isn't it?" she said.

"Not to me." In fact, to my mind the single most striking fact about Roger's death was that almost nothing was obvious.

Mel looked distinctly disappointed. Maybe I wasn't such a hotshot amateur detective after all. In the voice of one explaining the obvious to a not-very-bright child, she said, "Okay, Roger left his office after lunch, telling his secretary he was going to work at home. Then that afternoon he had all these visitors. Juanita saw two of them, a woman and a man. The woman came first, alone, and the man came later. Juanita wasn't exactly sure of the time the woman came, but she said the guy was at our front door around four because that's when Juanita was going home for the day.''

"Did Juanita also see your father that afternoon?" I asked.

Mel looked puzzled. "She didn't mention seeing him. Why? What difference does that make?"

The kid needed to read some mystery novels. "What if Roger was never at your house? I know he *said* he was going home. But what if he changed his mind—or was shot before he got home? Is there anybody who can verify that your father was actually at the house that afternoon?"

Mel fished in a huge canvas purse and eventually came up with a small spiral notebook and a pen. She made notes before resuming the conversation. "You're right. That's something we'll have to check on."

*We* will have to check on?

Before I could squelch that particular suggestion, Mel quickly added, "I'll need to talk to Juanita again, too, to see if she saw those visitors—the woman and the man—actually go into the house. Maybe all they did was ring the doorbell and then go away."

"Nobody else was at your house for even part of the afternoon? Was Consuela there? Or did you come home after school, before you left for your mother's house?"

Mel shook her head. "My mother picked me up at school on Friday. And Consuela had Friday afternoons off." She guessed what I was going to ask and answered it. "She always left by 12:30."

"Of course, maybe Juanita did see Roger come home and she just didn't mention it to you," I said. In which case who the two visitors were became significantly more important.

Mel jotted more notes in her little notebook. "Okay, I'll

ask Juanita about Roger and try to get a description of the visitors." She looked up at me, her expression expectant. "That could help a lot, couldn't it? I mean, if we had some description of that man and woman."

"Maybe," I said, feeling as if I was breaking the no–Santa Claus news to a six year old. "I guess if someone could identify the people from those descriptions, the police could go talk to the man and woman to see if they heard or saw anything unusual."

"Or if they happened to bring along a .22-caliber pistol for the visit," Mel said grimly.

"You know for sure that he was shot with a .22-caliber pistol?"

"That's what the police told Mr. Smythe."

"Was the gun that Consuela—uh, was killed with also a .22?"

Mel shook her head. "No, Mr. Smythe said she was shot with a Saturday night special, a cheap handgun, and it wasn't a .22."

But if our super-organized killer was trying to make it look as if Consuela was confessing to killing Roger before shooting herself, wouldn't he or she have used the same gun? If that .22-caliber pistol had been discovered with Consuela's body and her fingerprints were on the gun, Consuela would have been inextricably linked to Roger's murder. The fact that a second gun had been used meant that Roger's killer had undoubtedly already gotten rid of the murder weapon by the time Consuela died. Too bad. Or, alternatively, it might mean that Roger's killer still had that weapon, but he'd had nothing to do with Consuela's death.

I was sipping the last of my coffee, considering all the possibilities when Mel looked up from her notes. "I was thinking," she said, "that you and I should divide up the work."

That got my attention. "What work are we talking about?"

Mel looked impatient—an expression she was perfecting. "Interviewing the suspects, gathering information, the whole detective bit. And, by the way, what about your boyfriend? Isn't he an investigative reporter? Maybe he could help us out too."

"Did anyone ever mention your resemblance to your stepmother?" I inquired. "Particularly in the delegating authority area."

Mel glared at me. "No! And what does that have to do with anything anyway?"

Same one-track mind too. I glanced at my watch, suddenly remembering all the errands I needed to run this morning. "Listen, Mel," I said, trying to be nicer, "why don't you just leave this to the police? Tell them about the visitors to your house that Friday afternoon. Or if you don't want to talk to them, tell Mr. Smythe."

Mel's lower lip jutted out stubbornly. "The police already have their version of what happened. They don't want any new information. They think Kate killed Roger, and Consuela killed herself. They did check to see if Kate could have killed Consuela, but she was at her office all day seeing patients: Her alibi checked out. So they brilliantly concluded that if Kate didn't kill Consuela, then Consuela had to have killed herself. I think they think that Consuela helped Kate or knew that Kate shot Roger, but didn't want to tell the police about it. Then Consuela was supposed to feel so bad about everything that she shot herself. Which is a lot of bull. Consuela would never have killed herself and she never would have helped Kate either. She didn't like Roger much, but she hated Kate. Consuela was always telling me how bossy and bitchy Kate was. She probably would have run to the police if she had any evidence that Kate killed Roger.''

"So if you don't want to talk to the police, why don't you go tell this to Mr. Smythe? He's right next door and he wants information that helps Kate's case.''

"Because I don't like him,'' Mel said flatly.

She was starting to irritate me. "You only talk to people you like?''

"Hardly.'' Mel's tone was as cold as my own. "I think that Mr. Smythe is trying to convince the police that Consuela killed Roger and then killed herself. Juanita told me he was asking her a lot of questions about Consuela. So he only wants information if it proves that Kate didn't kill Roger and Consuela did.''

"Maybe that's what he's thinking now because he doesn't have any other evidence that might get Kate off. But if there was some new information showing another person killed Roger I'm sure that Mr. Smythe would be happy to have it. His goal is to get the charges against Kate dropped, not to accuse Consuela.''

"But the easiest way to do that is to make the police think that a dead woman is the killer. She's not around to defend herself, to say where she actually was that day or who she was with.'' Mel's eyes flashed. "She's a real easy target.''

"Yes, she's a convenient scapegoat.''

"So you see why I want to do my own investigation,'' Mel concluded.

Yes, I saw. She wanted to exonerate Consuela. Find her father's murderer. Even get her stepmother off the hook. But I wasn't convinced that Mel could find this clever killer. And at the same time I was afraid that she might find him—and end up as the killer's next victim.

I told Mel how dangerous messing into a murder case

could be, particularly when the killer sounded as cold and calculating as this one. Then, because I was afraid that I'd made the process sound too exciting, I added, "And trying to gather this kind of information isn't like one of those TV detective shows where everything turns into a big adventure. Usually what happens is that the facts you spend so much time getting lead nowhere. Or you get contradictory information or nothing useful at all. Most of the time trying to play detective is incredibly boring."

"I don't care if it's boring," Mel said. "And I'm *not* playing. If you don't want to help me I'll do it by myself."

I could tell by the flinty look in those Roger-like eyes that she meant it. I debated my options. I could refuse to help and hope that Mel ran out of steam before she did too much damage—or encountered a killer. Or I could ask a few questions myself, keep an eye on Mel and hope that the killer didn't decide to come after the two of us.

"Okay," I said finally. "I'll help you out provided that you're careful and keep me informed and don't do anything stupid."

Mel seemed to hear this as unqualified assent. She beamed at me. "That's great!" She picked up her little notebook and peered down at it. "Now I thought it would make the most sense if you were the one who talked to the people at the mental health center, considering you work there and everything."

Five minutes later I was walking her to the door. "I'll call you as soon as I talk to Juanita again. That might not be until Tuesday because she has Mondays off, and I don't want to go over there when Mr. or Mrs. Smythe is around."

I told her I'd let her know what, if anything, I found out at the center. "Be careful," I said again, sounding too much like my sister for my own comfort level.

Mel nodded vaguely, the brushing-you-off look familiar

to all parents. "Say, you forgot to tell me if your hunky boyfriend can help."

"Sorry," I told her, "the hunk is in El Paso." And would be having a stroke if he knew I was getting involved again in another crime.

# Chapter Fifteen

ON MONDAY MORNING I STARTED ASKING QUESTIONS, telling myself that I was merely humoring Mel—my stint as detective would last only half an hour, max.

I began with Missy Gould. I'd known Missy for years. She was friendly, unsuspicious, and a consummate gossip—an ideal combination in this particular situation. As the receptionist for all the adult clinics, she was also in an ideal position to monitor the comings and goings of all the people I was interested in.

But I didn't want to ask my questions at Missy's desk in the middle of the clinic waiting room, where one of the people I was asking about could be walking by. I phoned her. "You have time for a coffee break, Missy?"

"Hold on a sec." I heard her give someone directions to the rest room. "Sure, Liz, I'd love to take a coffee break. It's just going to have to be a short one."

She arrived in my office with her coffee mug. I made a quick trip down the hall to the human resources' coffeepot, then kicked my door shut and told Missy what I wanted to know. I would like to think it was my inherent honesty that made me explain to her why I was asking her to squeal on her coworkers—that and the fact I couldn't think of any other plausible reason why I would be asking these questions.

Missy, who daily dealt with much stranger requests, just nodded calmly and said, "Yeah, I can understand why Mel would want to look into her father's death. I probably would too if something like that happened to my dad."

Missy took a swig of coffee. "But I don't really know very much about Tricia Whitmore. Her office is on the opposite wing from my desk, and she usually uses the front stairs to get to her office. So I don't see much of her. And when I do see her, she barely says a word. She's not a very friendly person, you know."

Yes, I said, I'd noticed that too. I was also thinking that gathering this information was turning out to be a lot harder than I'd anticipated. Particularly since frosty Tricia was unlikely to confide in me what she was doing on the day Roger was killed.

"But I do know about Kate Quinlan," Missy said, looking pleased with herself. "I remember what she was doing the Friday Dr. Quinlan died because a policeman came to interview me about it."

"And?" I prodded. "Did Kate leave the building any time during the afternoon?"

"I don't know that," Missy said. She must have read the disappointment on my face because she quickly added, "But I *do* know that Kate had a cancellation that afternoon: Her four o'clock patient cancelled. I took the message."

I could feel my heart start to pound faster, but I tried to sound nonchalant, "So Kate could have left for the day at four?"

Missy shook her head. "No, she had a five o'clock patient after that. And he didn't cancel."

But Kate could have run to her car, driven home, shot Roger, maybe shoved the body into a closet and got back to the center in time to greet her five o'clock client, if she had been quick about it all. "Uh, did you happen to see Kate at all between four and five? Or maybe talk to her on the phone then?" It was a lot to recall about what you were doing last month, but if the police officer had asked her the same questions, maybe Missy would remember.

She shook her head. "The policeman asked me that too. I was pretty sure that I didn't see Kate then, though she could have walked past me and I might not have seen her if I was busy talking to a patient or something. Kate apparently said she was alone in her office for that hour, catching up on her paperwork."

Which she probably was. It was just too bad that there was no one who could corroborate her alibi.

Missy studied me, her eyes narrowed. "You don't think that Kate shot Roger, do you?"

"No," I said honestly. Kate may have had the opportunity to kill Roger, but I still couldn't see her doing it. It just didn't feel right. The only problem was that sometimes my feelings were wrong.

"Me neither," Missy admitted. "Now that Tricia Whitmore, she seems more of the type to kill him. Underhanded and cold, and I heard that she was screaming at Dr. Quinlan a few days before he died. He even had to throw her out of his office. Everybody was talking about it."

But wouldn't it have been stupid for Tricia to shoot Roger only days after having a very public shouting match with him? And while I was inclined to agree with Missy that Tricia was frosty, duplicitous and vengeful (let us not forget Tricia's "I just want to make sure the bastard is dead" crack at Roger's funeral), I didn't think Tricia was stupid. On the other hand, passion made a lot of smart people behave stupidly.

Missy glanced at her watch. "I need to get back to the clinic." She stood up. "You know the person you should ask about Tricia is Elaine Robertson, Dr. Quinlan's old secretary. Elaine was the one who told me about Tricia's little hissy fit. Elaine thinks Tricia is a Class-A bitch."

Which did not, I reminded myself, mean that Tricia had murdered anyone. I thanked Missy for the information and said I appreciated the tip about Elaine. I'd probably go talk to her that afternoon.

The only problem was that I couldn't think of any excuse for asking Elaine my questions about Roger and Tricia. I'd known Missy for years. After last year's poison-pen letter deaths at the center, she was used to me asking intrusive questions about coworkers. But I barely knew Elaine. I'd interviewed her once about a year ago and she'd seemed a pleasant enough young woman in her early twenties, shy and very conscientious. To work with Roger Quinlan for the past year, she had also needed to be competent and tolerant of temper tantrums. But I had the sinking suspicion that Roger might have drilled into Elaine that a psychiatrist's secretary needed to be extremely discreet about her boss and his work, which might not bode well for my information gathering.

After prolonged deliberation, the only reason I could find for asking Elaine my questions was that I wanted to interview her again for our newsletter. I phoned her. Elaine pointed out that I'd already interviewed her. I said yes, but since she now worked for someone else—Dr. Jane Ross, the new head of the adult clinic—I thought a second, updated profile was in order.

"Okay," Elaine said, not sounding very enthusiastic about it. "When do you want to do it?"

"How about in half an hour?"

Elaine agreed. She'd come to my office. "It's not going to take very long, is it?" she asked, sounding like someone trying to psych herself up for an impending root canal.

"No," I assured her, "it will be short and painless." I just hoped it would be worth my time.

Elaine arrived precisely on time, looking miserable. She was short and stocky, about twenty pounds overweight, with long brown hair that hung stick-straight to her shoulders. "If I knew you were going to be taking my picture, I would have worn something else," she began, gesturing at her faded print shirtwaist dress.

"I can take your photo another day this week," I said, feeling sorry for her. It was not, in fact, a very flattering dress. I wouldn't have wanted to be photographed in it either.

She perked up a bit at that news, but not much. I'd forgotten how nervous Elaine had been when I'd interviewed her before. She'd acted as if I'd been trying to extract classified information from her, rather than innocuous personal tidbits.

"Tell me what you do in your new job," I said, smiling reassuringly at her.

"Basically the same things I did for Dr. Quinlan," Elaine said. "Except now I do them for Dr. Ross."

Uh-huh. I took notes on what she'd done for each of her employers; enquired about her two cats, Gabby and Garfield (I had reread my previous interview of Elaine.); asked if she'd recently gone camping. Oh, really, where did you go?

The official interview was over in ten minutes. "So tell me," I said, smiling at her, glad that she looked at least a bit more relaxed now. "Off the record,"—I laid my pen on my desk for emphasis—"isn't Dr. Ross a lot easier to work for than Dr. Quinlan?"

"Maybe in some ways." Elaine's eyes darted nervously around the room, as if the ghost of Roger Quinlan was lurking behind my file cabinet.

I took a deep breath. "I always thought of Dr. Quinlan as being a rather difficult and demanding person," I said. "Very bright and certainly very competent, but, you know, definitely temperamental too."

She nodded. "Yes, a lot of people thought that about him—that he was difficult, I mean."

"But you didn't?"

Elaine considered the question. "No. He *was* a perfectionist, but if you did things the way he wanted them done, he was very appreciative. Even"—she looked embarrassed—"rather sweet."

Sweet? I briefly considered the possibility that Elaine had been one of Roger's multitude of girlfriends, then dismissed it. Roger had fired four secretaries in rapid succession before he found Elaine. He would have had enough sense not to mess up a good boss-secretary relationship when he finally had one. He could find another girlfriend, but a good secretary was hard to come by. Besides he already had one lover working in the clinic.

"You must have been very upset when Dr. Quinlan died so unexpectedly," I said.

"Yes, it was awful."

I tried to look as if I was trying to remember the details. "It happened on a Friday, right?" When she nodded I added, "And Dr. Quinlan left work early that day."

Elaine nodded again. "He always worked at home on Friday afternoons. He never wanted me to schedule meetings or patients after eleven o'clock on Friday mornings."

"So he left when? At noon?"

"Usually. He left a little later than usual that last day, about 12:15 or 12:20." Elaine looked as if she was fighting back tears.

It was not a graceful segue, but I was afraid she'd be sobbing too hard in a few seconds to even hear what I was asking. "Didn't Dr. Quinlan have some big fight with Tricia Whitmore right before that?"

Elaine stiffened. "Not *that* day," she said primly. "It was earlier in the week, Monday morning, when Tricia—well, Dr. Quinlan called it 'acted out.' "

He would. "Really?" I leaned forward, looking (I hoped) fascinated. "What was she so upset about?"

"I have no idea," Elaine said. An obvious lie. "But she certainly was yelling a lot. You wouldn't believe the language she used."

I shook my head disapprovingly. "And she's the one who's always talking at meetings about the need for more professional behavior."

"That's what *I* said to—" Elaine stopped herself in time. She glanced at her watch. "I'd better get back to my office. I told Dr. Ross that I'd only be gone twenty minutes."

I tried my best to look puzzled, acting as if I hadn't heard her. "I don't know why I thought I'd heard that Tricia had done *something* that day with Dr. Quinlan." I took a stab in the dark. "She didn't leave early with him or take a message to his house?" I hoped that Elaine hated Tricia as much as I thought she did. She was certainly smart enough to realize that whatever I was accusing Tricia of was at the least unsavory—and at the worst criminal.

"Tricia was *not* with Dr. Quinlan when he left for home." Elaine stood up, ending our interview. "But she came looking for him shortly after he'd gone. And about half an hour after that she left for the day. She said she wasn't feeling well." Elaine's expression was so carefully neutral that I had no idea if she bought Tricia's story of illness.

"Did you by any chance happen to phone Dr. Quinlan at home that afternoon?" I asked.

Elaine shook her head. "He didn't like to be bothered at home." She moved toward my office door and then turned back to me. "You certainly ask a lot of strange questions," she said, her expression considerably less friendly than it had been a few minutes earlier.

"Yes," I said. "Everybody tells me that."

# Chapter Sixteen

TUESDAY NIGHT I WAS HOME FROM WORK ABOUT TEN minutes when my doorbell rang. Puzzled, I padded in stocking feet to my door to peer out the peephole. Mel was standing outside, a big grin on her face.

I unlocked the door. "Hi, this is a surprise."

"A good surprise, I hope." Her rather cocky smile said, Of course, you're delighted to see me. A big change from her previous unannounced appearance at my apartment last Saturday morning.

I asked her to come in, finally noticing the cardboard pizza box she was carrying. So maybe her visit wasn't such a bad surprise after all.

Mel marched into my living room. "Hope you haven't eaten yet. I ordered the Pizza Supreme—everything except anchovies—'cause I wasn't sure what you liked."

"I like anything except anchovies. And your timing is great; I was just starting to think about what I could make for dinner."

I set out plates and poured Diet Cokes into two glasses. "Uh, Kate *does* know that you're here, doesn't she?" I asked as Mel set out my stainless steel silverware and paper napkins.

She shrugged. "I left a note on the refrigerator. Not that she cares where I am. Kate gave me money to buy take-out food for the entire week. Said she was going to be working late trying to make arrangements for her seminars and I should just eat without her. I'll probably get home before she does."

I tried to tell myself that my attitudes about parents'— or in this case, stepparents'—responsibilities toward their children were hopelessly old-fashioned. That Mel was six-teen—old enough to drive and old enough to be home alone at night. But I didn't convince myself. "What's Kate doing with the workshops?" I asked, trying not to sound disapproving.

"Who knows? I think she's trying to make them bigger and better, but she doesn't really talk to me about it."

I wondered what the two of them did talk about. Or if they talked at all. "Isn't your mother coming back to town soon?" I asked as we sat down to eat, hoping I wasn't venturing onto a touchy topic.

Mel held up her palm as she swallowed a mouthful of pizza. "Two more weeks, if everything goes okay." She smiled a shyer, more private smile than before. "Then I'm going to move in with her. Mom said when she gets back we'll go out together to look at town houses. The apartment she's been living in is really too small for the two of us."

I wondered suddenly where Mel's mother was getting all the money. Residential alcohol treatment programs and town houses, even rental ones, were not cheap. Could Roger have left his ex-wife money in his will? Although Kate had claimed she and Roger had no savings, maybe there were some other assets that Sissy had inherited.

"The pizza is delicious," I told Mel. She smiled, but after that we ate in silence.

"I'm stuffed," Mel announced finally, eyeing the empty pizza box. She had reason to be.

"Me too." I'd eaten about five slices less than Mel had, but the waistband of my skirt definitely felt tight. I smiled at the teenager. "Maybe the next time you come over I'll nuke us some Lean Cuisines."

"Yuck."

"Oh, they're better than you think." Not to mention about one-fifth of the fat and calories.

Mel looked unconvinced, also uninterested. "I came here to tell you what I found out this afternoon from Juanita."

I stopped wiping off the table and sat down.

Mel smiled the cocky grin she'd worn at the doorway. I've got something *good*, it said. "Juanita saw the woman visitor go inside our house the Friday afternoon Roger died. It was around 1:45, she said. While she works in the kitchen, Juanita always watches this soap that starts at one, and the show was almost over when the woman arrived."

"Did she see when the woman came out of your house?"

Mel shook her head. "She hadn't come out by two o'clock. After that Juanita started cleaning another room, so she couldn't see our front porch."

Which, unfortunately, meant some additional visitors may also have appeared at the Quinlan house when Juanita was not in viewing distance of the porch. "Did she say what this woman looked like?"

"Yeah. She was probably in her twenties, Juanita said. Medium height and thin and wearing some boring navy blue suit. Short straight blonde hair."

Tricia Whitmore right down to the boring professional suit! So she had roused herself sufficiently from her illness to drive over to her lover's house. Ex-lover, from all accounts.

Mel was watching my face for a reaction. "Doesn't that sound a lot like that Tricia Whitmore, the woman who wore the pink dress to Roger's funeral? I know that he worked with her a lot. She came to the house one time when I was there."

"Sure sounds like her," I said, wondering just how much Mel knew about Roger's relationship with Tricia. "Did Juanita say anything else about the woman, like if she seemed angry or sad or anxious?"

"I don't think so. You know, she was watching TV too. I thought that under the circumstances Juanita noticed a lot."

"She did. I just meant if Roger and the woman had had some big screaming argument on the front porch, Juanita would have noticed that. So probably Roger just invited the woman inside right away." Which he probably would not have done if he thought he had reason to be afraid of her.

I remembered what else I wanted to find out. "So Juanita did see your dad that afternoon?"

"No. I asked her that. She said she was sure he was there—Roger came home early every Friday afternoon—but she never actually saw him. She saw someone let the woman in the house, and she just assumed it was Roger. From the Smythes' kitchen window she could see our front porch, but not into the house itself."

Too bad. Still it was extremely probable that it was Roger who'd let Tricia Whitmore—if the woman visitor actually was Tricia and not just another thin blonde in a navy suit—into his house. Kate was at work, Mel at school, and Consuela supposedly gone for the day. "By the way, did Juanita happen to see Consuela leave?"

"I asked her that too." Mel was starting to look a bit

deflated. "She said she didn't see Consuela go, but she knew Consuela always left around noon. Juanita said Consuela liked to get out of the house before Roger got home because he'd always think of something he wanted her to do before she left."

"What about the man who came to visit? What did Juanita say about him?"

"She said he was very tall, probably in his late twenties, and he was wearing a dark suit. The only other thing I remember was that she said he was real nervous."

"Nervous how?" Nervous from the situation, as in I'm-about-to-shoot-this-guy-the-minute-he-opens-the-door? Or congenitally high-strung nervous? Though, come to think of it, it might be hard to make the distinction from a casual glance out the window.

"Juanita said the guy looked like one of those little boys with too much energy. He kept moving around the porch."

"Hyper," I said. Tall, hyper, boyish-looking Larry Nelson? I made myself a mental note to find out if he'd been in Houston that day interviewing for the new job. "Did she say anything else about this guy: If he was heavy or thin, what his hair looked like?"

Mel narrowed her eyes, trying to remember. "Brown hair, nothing special. I think she said thin too, but I'm not sure. Maybe I just pictured him thin when she said he was pacing around the porch."

"Did she see him go inside?"

"No." Mel looked disgusted. "Isn't that a pisser? Juanita was going home then. The man was standing outside when she was getting into her car. So she didn't see if someone let him in the house or if he just walked away when no one answered."

"She didn't have any idea if he'd been on the porch for awhile or if he'd just got there?"

Mel shook her head. "So we don't know if the woman was still in the house with Roger or if the man ever even saw Roger. Maybe the woman shot him and left, and he was dead by the time the man even started knocking."

"But what would she have done with the body?" I asked, as much to myself as to Mel. Granted, Tricia Whitmore was a fit, athletic woman and Roger was not a large man. But could she have single-handedly moved Roger's body out of the house? If the woman indeed was Tricia, she wouldn't have been able to shove Roger's lifeless body into some closet, and then come back later with a packing box, tape and label. Unless Tricia had a key to the house and knew exactly when Kate would be away from home. Tricia would have had to make all the arrangements—shooting, cleaning up, then packing, addressing, and moving the box out for pickup—at the time of the shooting. And that took one very cool-headed murderer indeed.

"Maybe Tricia shot Roger that afternoon and took his body to her car," Mel said. "Then she could have brought the box back the next morning after Kate left for her workshop. The door to the back porch is almost always unlocked, so she wouldn't have had any trouble getting inside. Or maybe Tricia just left the box on the back porch Friday afternoon and never came back at all."

"Except Kate said she walked through the back porch on Saturday morning on her way to the workshop, and the box wasn't there."

"Maybe it was behind some of that junky lawn furniture sitting out there," Mel said.

"It was a pretty large box," I pointed out. "Hard to hide behind a few chairs." Though actually, now that I tried to picture it, it was a possibility. If Kate had come home around eight-thirty Friday night, she likely wouldn't have noticed a box sitting behind the familiar old lawn chairs in the dark. And if she was in enough of a hurry on Saturday morning, and if the box was lying on its side rather than standing upright behind the grouped chairs, she might not have noticed then either. Of course if that were the case, the killer would probably have had to return on Saturday morning, after Kate left, to shove the box out in the open for the deliveryman to see it. The killer would have had to work fast and be aware of Kate's schedule in order to get to the Quinlan house after she'd left and before the deliveryeryman arrived, but it could have been done.

"You know what we don't know—or at least I don't know—is when the call to the delivery service was made," I said to Mel. "Did the killer shoot Roger on Friday and then phone the delivery service? Or were the arrangements made days in advance?" The thought of that—the killer calmly making the arrangements for the body of a then-living, breathing person to be picked up dead a few days later—made me shudder.

"I'll try to check that out tomorrow," Mel said, making notes.

"The thing that keeps bugging me is all the logistics involved in this thing," I said. "I mean did the killer walk up to Roger carrying a huge, already labeled box and a supply of masking tape? And how did the killer manage to move this big, heavy box? Did she—or he—bring a dolly along with the other supplies?"

I looked at Mel. "You didn't have all that stuff—big boxes and a dolly—at your house, did you?"

Mel shook her head. "Roger was this neatness freak who thought all boxes, and almost everything else that other people saved, should be thrown out. And I'm pretty sure we didn't have a dolly either. Roger didn't do much work around the house himself. He hired other people to do it."

"Do you know of anybody besides your family who had keys to the house?"

"Consuela did. I think Juanita did too; Consuela gave them to her after she got locked out once. And my mother had one."

Consuela I expected, and a neighbor having an extra key made sense. But Mel's mother? Roger Quinlan did not look like the kind of man who'd give his ex-wife a key to his house. "Why did your mother have a key?"

Mel's plump face reddened. "I made a copy of my key and gave it to her. Sometimes she needed to pick up stuff for me when I was in school, like clothes for the weekend, and Consuela wasn't always there to let her in the house."

It sounded pretty feeble to me. I could also imagine how pleased Roger or Kate would have been to know that the first Mrs. Quinlan was snooping around their house while they were gone.

"Did your mother and Roger get along fairly well?" I asked.

"No, but she didn't kill him, if that's what you mean."

I sighed. Of course Mel would think that—most daughters would be unwilling to suspect their mother of murder. But with a key to the house and an in-house (though unsuspecting), teenaged informant around to feed her information about Kate and Roger's schedules, committing this complicated crime would have been made a whole lot easier. "What time did you say your mother picked you up at school that Friday afternoon?" I asked, knowing Mel wouldn't like the question.

She didn't, but she answered anyway. "Three-thirty. But she got to school earlier than that. She was waiting when I got out of school."

Which gave her more than enough time to drive to her ex-husband's house, shoot him, hide the body and get to

Mel's school—about a fifteen or twenty minute drive from the Quinlan house—in enough time to be parked and calmly listening to the radio when Mel trotted to the car. According to the coroner's report, Roger could have died as early as 2:30 Friday afternoon.

I glanced at Mel, seeing the stubborn set to her square jaw. If Juanita had seen a third visitor that afternoon, a tiny, blonde woman, would Mel tell me about it? Or if her mother had suddenly started asking a lot of questions about when and where Kate's workshop was going to be held or was Roger still working at home on Friday afternoons, would Mel share that information with me? Somehow I doubted it.

"My mother couldn't have killed Roger," Mel said, her eyes flashing angrily. "Not because she didn't hate him. She did. He treated her like shit when they were married, cheated on her all the time and taunted her about her drinking problem—which she didn't have before she married him. Then he dumped her. A few years later he moved back here with his new wife—the independent, successful professional woman he'd wanted my mother to be, even though she never wanted that for herself—to rub Mom's nose in his new life."

I tried to get the chronology straight. "Roger and your mother lived together in Houston, but he moved to Kansas after they were divorced?" She nodded. "Maybe," I suggested, "he moved back to Houston to be closer to you."

Mel snorted. "Yeah, right. Roger's idea of perfect visitation rights were about two weekends a year, one of them on Father's Day. No matter where he lived, even when I was little and living in the same house, Roger was *always* too busy to bother with me. I never called him Daddy the way most little kids do. Roger wasn't anything special to me—just another acquaintance."

She sounded angry, not sad. I remembered the first time I'd met Mel, at Roger and Kate's symposium party. I recalled the hostile way she'd talked about Roger—sneering I'd just written off as typical teenage cynicism but today it sounded like more than that. "But Roger must have wanted to have you around if he had you come live with him and Kate."

Mel shook her head. "Roger was only interested in punishing my mother for her drinking, not in having me around. I think he thought that the shock of having her only child taken away from her might make her shape up. Except it didn't. It only made her feel more helpless, more depressed."

I could see the sadness now in Mel's eyes. Clearly it was her father, not her mother, she was angry with.

"When I lived with Mom, she had to at least cook meals and get me ready for school and see that I had clean clothes and got my homework done," Mel explained quietly. "She didn't usually drink much until at night when I went to bed. And she was never a mean drunk, just kind of sleepy and out of it. But when Roger took her to court and got custody of me—saving himself a bundle in child support, too—Mom no longer had anything that she really had to do. She had enough money, from a trust fund from her mother, so she didn't really have to work if she lived modestly. And so she started drinking earlier in the day, except for the weekends when I was there with her. Then she just drank at night."

I wanted desperately to do something to register my sympathy for this child who'd had such pathetically poor parents: hug her or even just pat her arm. But sympathy was not what Mel wanted. I could see that in the fierce glint of her eyes, in the way she'd unconsciously pushed her chair away from me when she told me the story.

"So you see," she concluded coolly, "my mother was in no shape to plan that murder. If she had shot Roger she would have left his body and probably the gun with her fingerprints on it and just walked away. Or more likely, knowing Mom, she would have called 911 right away and confessed everything."

"I'm glad she's getting help for her drinking problem now," I said softly.

"Me too." Mel's eyes suddenly welled with tears. "And that goes to show you how much Dr. Roger knew about treating alcoholism. It was only when Mom was sure that I was going to come live with her again that she had a reason to stop drinking. She told me that when she was getting on the plane to go to the Betty Ford Clinic."

But might not Sissy Quinlan have managed to pull it together long enough to arrange her despised ex-husband's murder? If she was able to curtail her drinking during the weekends with her daughter, couldn't she have sobered up long enough to plan a murder that would wreak Sissy's revenge on both her sadistic husband and on his successful second wife? And in the process she'd also regain custody of her daughter, the only person Sissy seemed to care about. Many people had killed for a lot less than that.

MY PHONE was ringing as Mel walked out the door. I got it on the sixth ring.

"Liz? Hi, it's Kate. Is Mel at your place?"

"She just left. Do you want me to try to catch her?"

"No, don't bother. I've just got some exciting news I want to share with you."

"What?" I asked when she volunteered no further information.

She laughed a teasing little laugh. "Come to breakfast Saturday and I'll tell you."

I sighed. "Why don't you just tell me now?" I had never, not even as a child, liked secrets or the people who wanted you to plead with them to *p-le-e-ase* tell you theirs. "I might be going out of town this weekend." Then again I might not. Nick and I had planned on getting together this weekend, but last night when we'd talked on the phone, he'd sounded too wrapped up in tracking down some new sources to really want to take a break.

"No, I'd rather tell you in person, and all the details aren't worked out yet. Anyway I'd like to see you, and I know Mel would too. If you can't come Saturday, then we can make it for dinner instead. Pick a night later in the week that's convenient for you," Kate said. "I'll order in some take-out food."

Before I could voice any further objections she said, "I'll call you tomorrow. Need to go now."

Only after I'd hung up the phone did it occur to me that Kate had not expressed one iota of interest in what Mel was doing at my apartment.

# Chapter Seventeen

WHEN I WALKED INTO MY OFFICE WEDNESDAY, CARRY-
ing the morning's first cup of coffee, Tricia Whitmore was
waiting for me. She sat in the chair next to my desk, looking distinctly unfriendly. "I understand that you've been
asking a lot of questions about me," she said in a quiet
voice. Her eyes, however, were venomous.

I took a sip of coffee as I sat down at my desk. Maybe
the caffeine might shove my sluggish morning brain into
gear. There was no point denying that I'd been asking about
her. Elaine Robertson must have gone running to Tricia to
report that I'd been inquiring about her. I wondered why
Elaine, who seemed to dislike Tricia so much, had squealed
on me.

"So what?" I said.

"So why don't you mind your own fucking business,"
Tricia said.

I almost laughed. Was this an example of the high-level
confrontational skills they'd taught her in graduate psychology classes? Maybe Tricia was going to stick her
tongue out at me next. Or maybe moon me.

"I can't imagine why you're getting so upset about a few innocuous questions," I said blandly. "After your well-publicized screaming match with Roger Quinlan a few days before Roger died, a lot of people are probably wondering what you were doing on that particular Friday afternoon."

"You bitch!"

For a moment I thought Tricia was about to leap up and hit me. She settled for shooting looks-that-could-kill in my direction. For a therapist, the woman had very poor impulse control.

"I'm warning you—" she began.

I interrupted, pretending I hadn't heard her. "You know, it does seem very strange that Roger died on the same afternoon that you had to go home early because of a sudden illness."

"How do you know he died that afternoon?" Tricia asked sharply.

"Autopsy results," I said, stretching the truth only a tad. Roger could have died in the afternoon. Or in the early evening. Was Tricia pretending for my benefit not to know when Roger had died? Or was she afraid that the police might make an unfortunate connection between Tricia's early departure from work and Roger's time of death?

"I wasn't feeling well," Tricia said. "I was sick all weekend with a stomach virus."

"Oh, it wasn't you then who stopped at the Quinlan house around 1:45?"

Tricia stared at me. "Who told you that?"

"An eyewitness."

She looked as if she didn't believe me. As if she suspected that I was bluffing. Tricia showed me her inscrutable-shrink expression, saying nothing.

I took a long shot. "You *were* wearing a navy suit Friday

afternoon, weren't you?" If she hadn't been, I'd lost.

She blanched. I could see it. Tricia's thin, horsey face had grown a shade paler. "I-I don't remember what I was wearing that day," she lied.

I felt a surge of excitement. "You know you're right. This *is* none of my business. The only people who have a right to know where you were and what you were doing that afternoon are the police."

She studied me through narrowed eyes, looking as if she was trying hard to control her fury—but not quite succeeding. "Actually," she said, "I only stopped at Roger's house for a few minutes. I needed to return some things of his that had been at my apartment." Her eyes darted to my face, assessing my reaction.

When I didn't say anything, she added, "I also wanted to apologize to him for my outburst in his office earlier in the week. I needed to keep my job. I told him that. Our affair had ended, but we could still behave civilly to each other. After all we were both professionals."

"And what did Roger say about that?"

"He said fine. It was certainly to his advantage that the two of us got along with each other at the center. I think he was relieved that I was willing to be reasonable about it."

I didn't believe her. I wasn't entirely sure why I didn't, but I didn't. I did believe that Tricia had apologized, and I certainly believed that she needed the job. Brand-new Ph.D.s were almost always saddled with big grad-school debts, and Tricia would be hard-pressed to find another job right away. From everything I'd heard, there was currently a glut of clinical psychologists in Houston.

What I didn't believe was Roger's reaction. Kate had said that Roger was trying to get Tricia fired. Amanda had mentioned that Roger had tried to prevent Larry Nelson from being hired at the center. Clearly this was a man who wanted no reminders of old relationships-turned-sour walking past his office. I could easily imagine Roger, after having enjoyed watching his old girlfriend grovel, saying, "Get real, Tricia. We can't work together, particularly after your little scene in my office broadcast our affair to the entire mental health center. If I were you, dear, I'd start searching for another position. Because, if I have anything at all to say about it, your unprofessional demeanor is going to have you out on your ass by the end of the month."

That was the way I suspected Roger had responded, but I had no way of proving it. Certainly Tricia was not about to admit that her old lover had sneered at her apology. Of course, the more interesting question was whether Roger's supposed rejection and verbal pink slip would have pushed Tricia into killing him. Could she have brought along a gun in her purse, just in case Roger didn't want to make up?

"From what I heard, you stayed more than a few minutes," I told her. Which was more or less true. Fifteen minutes after Tricia's arrival, when Juanita's soap was over and she moved to another room, Tricia had still not left the Quinlan house.

Tricia's eyes swiveled to the side, as she thought about that one. "I was out of there by 2:08. I remember that time on my car clock when I turned on the ignition." Her watery eyes blazed at me. "And when I left, Roger was very much alive. He said he planned to spend the afternoon at home getting caught up on his work."

So had Tricia driven home to pick up her gun and an oversized packing box and then returned to share her feelings with Roger about his tacky treatment of her? If Tricia actually had left the Quinlan home at 2:08—and probably she had; a good liar always kept to the truth as much as possible—she could have returned any time before four without Juanita, who by then was busy cleaning other parts of the Smythe house, witnessing her arrival. It was certainly possible that by the time the nervous male visitor arrived on the front porch Tricia had already returned to the house, shot Roger, pushed the box with his body onto the back porch, then gotten the hell out. She even could have phoned the delivery company on the way home.

Tricia stood up. Her face was rigid with barely controlled anger. "I hope that I've answered all your questions, Liz." She stalked out of my office without waiting for an answer.

KATE QUINLAN'S voice on the phone sounded much too perky. Could I come tonight for the dinner she'd promised me? All the details of her surprise had been finalized this morning, she said with obvious excitement in her voice.

"Great," I said. Tricia had just stormed out of my office. Why not begin and end the day focused on the Quinlans?

"What are you in the mood to eat?" Kate inquired.

"Oh, I like almost everything. I'll eat whatever you normally eat."

"We ate whatever Consuela decided to make. Now we eat take-out. You want Chinese, Mexican, Thai, or burgers?"

"Mexican."

"You got it. Dinner's at seven-thirty. Come prepared to be stunned."

I arrived at 7:25, wearing slacks and a silk T-shirt and what I hoped was a suitably anticipatory expression. Kate told me that Mel had gone to pick up our dinner and then ushered me into the kitchen. She handed me a frozen margarita in a big crystal goblet. "I don't cook, but I am capable of making simple blender drinks."

"If I drink all of this I'll be to drunk to even hear your good news."

"In that case maybe I'd better tell you right away." Kate tasted her own margarita, nodded her approval. She motioned for me to come sit with her at a small butcher-block table in the breakfast nook.

Wasn't this the table where Consuela's body had been discovered? I gulped a mouthful of margarita, hoping it would calm my suddenly queasy stomach.

"It's a new table," Kate said quietly. "I got rid of the old one."

I sat. "So tell me your news," I said, trying to smile.

"I have a contract for my book!" Kate looked as if she was on the verge of bouncing up and down in her chair, the way my four-year-old niece did when she was excited.

"That's wonderful. Tell me all about it."

"Well, I found a literary agent who helped me write a great proposal for the book. The first publisher who Olga, my agent, submitted the book to snapped it right up."

"Wow," I said. "She sounds like some agent." Particularly since I had seen the original book and knew what Olga had to work with.

"Yes, she is. I showed her the chapter I'd already written, which she liked, but said needed work. We kind of changed the original focus of the book a bit. We're thinking of another title too. Instead of *You Deserve Better*, maybe *It's Your Life, Lady—So Start Acting Like a CEO*."

"Is that what you meant by changing the focus—making the book more upbeat?" I asked.

"Well, that's part of it: more of a cheerleading, you-can-do-it tone with lots of specific advice that readers can use. I'll have the exercises from the workshop along with some new ones. And Olga definitely agreed with you that the book needs more case histories, more examples of women who've managed to change their lives."

Sipping my surprisingly good margarita, I tried not to

look smug. Olga sounded like an astute woman.

"When I told her about you, told her what a genius interviewer and writer you are, Olga also agreed that it would be best if you were the one who wrote the case histories."

The margarita suddenly went down the wrong way. I was getting less fond of Olga by the minute.

Kate waited for me to stop coughing. "I can pay you whatever you want. I got a humongous advance." When I didn't respond immediately, she added, "Just name a figure."

"One hundred dollars an hour," I said, choosing the first outrageous number that came to mind. I still didn't want to be Kate's ghostwriter.

"Fine," she said, not even blinking. "Can you get on it right away? I have a really tight deadline."

"How tight?"

"I told Olga I could get them a complete manuscript in six weeks." Kate smiled at me. "We're going to have to work our asses off."

I took a big gulp of margarita. Maybe it wasn't going to be so bad after all—getting rich while I did Kate's scut work. "You said," I reminded her, "that being more upbeat was part of this new change in focus for your book. What's the other part?"

"Oh, Olga thought there should be more of an emphasis on male-female conflicts. She said that was why the publisher leaped on my book proposal. With all the publicity about the women who attacked men after attending my workshop, the publisher thought this could be a really hot book."

I felt as if I was missing some crucial information. "Isn't your publisher in New York? How did he know about the news stories about your workshop? Did one of the wire services pick it up?"

"Oh, no, we sent all the *Chronicle* stories as part of the proposal."

So much for my outdated ideas on negative publicity. Apparently taking out your aggression on the pesky male in your life sold books. "You're not planning on condoning what Robin did, are you?" Maybe I was going to have to forgo a bundle of money.

"No, of course not. I certainly want you to interview Robin—it *is* an interesting story—but I intend to really emphasize that it's not always wise to act out your anger."

"Particularly," I said, "when you get arrested for it."

"Yes," Kate said absently. "I'm working now on my chapter on anger against men: getting in touch with your anger, harnessing it in a positive way, that kind of thing. And Olga and I decided I also should have chapters on 'Prince Charming Is Only in Fairy Tales,' 'Why Women Still Stay with the Frogs,' and 'Only You Can Give Your Story a Happy Ending.'"

"Catchy," I said. I wondered when Mel was going to get back with the food.

Fortunately, right at that moment, I heard a car door slam in the driveway. A moment later, Mel was standing in the kitchen, carrying two large take-out sacks from Los Tios.

"Hi," she said, setting the bags on the butcher-block island in the middle of the kitchen. "We weren't sure what you liked so we got a little of everything."

"Except anchovies?" I smiled at her. "Didn't you say the same thing when you brought over the pizza?"

Mel smiled back, but she seemed subdued. Not sullen, as I'd seen her before when she was around Kate, but muted somehow. Or maybe just preoccupied.

She continued to act that way—physically present, but mentally somewhere else—throughout dinner. She'd been accurate in saying they'd ordered a little of everything: enchiladas, fajitas (chicken *and* beef), tacos, chalupas, refried beans, along with a large supply of guacamole, sour cream and flour tortillas. Kate spread the food across the kitchen counters in a makeshift buffet line. We served ourselves, poured our drinks (I switched to iced tea in concession to my upcoming drive home) and brought it all to the little butcher-block table. While Mel ate silently, Kate chattered about her new plans for her workshop, and I tried to act interested.

"I'm trying to talk Mel into helping me organize the workshops better," Kate told me. "She's much more de-tail-oriented than I am."

Mel looked at me. "And Mel told her that she isn't in-terested."

That's what I'd told Kate too, and look how much good it did me.

The phone rang then, and Kate got up to answer it on the kitchen extension. We heard her say, "Hi, Bobby. I really can't talk now. I have company."

She listened for a moment, then rolled her eyes. "Okay, five minutes, but that's it." She covered the mouthpiece. "Sorry, Liz, apparently there's something I have to hear right this minute." Then, speaking into the phone again, "So tell me, Bobby."

As Kate turned her back to us to listen to her attorney, Mel leaned across the table and whispered to me, "Come with me. There's something I want to show you."

Kate glanced at us when we left, then turned back to the phone. "He said *what*?" she was saying as we walked out of the room.

I followed Mel to the staircase at the front of the house. "It's upstairs," she whispered.

"What is?" I whispered back.

"You'll see," she said, starting up the stairs. She led me

into a small room near the front of the house. A study. The room held a large mahogany desk and chair, several file cabinets, a black leather Eames chair next to a glass-topped end table holding a reading lamp. Two of the walls held bookcases crammed with books.

"This was Roger's study," Mel explained, though I'd already figured that one out with a quick glance at all the psychiatry texts on the bookshelves. Mel walked closer to the desk. "Look at this," she said, pointing.

I squinted at a spot on the tan carpet, then kneeled to better study the dark reddish-brown stain.

Mel kneeled beside me. "It's blood. And I bet it's Roger's blood."

"Maybe it's something else," I said unconvincingly. "Like red wine."

"Looks like blood to me. And the men from the carpet-cleaning company who were here this afternoon told me they thought it looked like blood too."

Mel glanced behind her at the open door to make sure that Kate was not standing in the doorway. "The stain was under the desk, the men said. They didn't even see it until they moved the desk. That's why the police didn't notice the stain when they searched our house.

"I bet Roger was in here sitting at his desk when he was shot. After the killer moved Roger's body, she—or he—must have come back to clean up. Whoever killed Roger shoved the desk forward about a foot to cover up the blood-stain."

I stared at her, not knowing what to say. The sudden sound of Kate's voice, calling from the staircase—"Hey, what are you guys doing up there?"—made me jump.

# Chapter Eighteen

THE DAY WAS NOT STARTING OUT WELL AT ALL. RIGHT as I was about to leave for work, my phone rang. It was Nick, sounding rushed and apologetic. He'd discovered some new leads for his story that he wanted to follow up, before he came back to Houston. He knew that we'd planned to spend the weekend together, and he certainly wanted to see me. . . .

"You want to cancel so you can work on the story," I finished for him. "It's okay. I understand." I did understand, but I was disappointed too. I missed him, and I really had been looking forward to flying down to El Paso on Friday night to spend the weekend with him. The fact that I couldn't think of anything else I felt like doing this weekend made me feel doubly irritable, particularly when I recalled the undercurrent of excitement I'd heard in Nick's voice when he talked about his story.

Needless to say, I was not wearing my smiley face when I encountered Larry Nelson in the hallway outside my office. "Just the woman I'm looking for," he said, grinning down at me.

"What can I do for you?"

"I wanted to tell you how much I liked your story about me in the newsletter."

"I'm glad. Thanks." Something about his expression told me that was not the only reason he'd come to talk to me. I waited.

"Uh, could we step into your office?"

"Sure." Maybe it was the pissy mood I was in, but I had the strong impression that whatever Larry wanted to talk about was something I did not want to hear.

We sat down, me at my desk and Larry in the only other available chair. "This *is* a bit awkward," he began, "but I felt I really wanted to discuss this with you to make sure that I was reading the situation correctly."

That sounded ominous, even though I didn't have a clue what he was getting at. I smiled encouragingly at him, thinking how boyishly vulnerable he looked. "Go ahead and tell me. I can take it."

"Remember the night that we were both working late and I asked you to go to dinner with me?" When I nodded yes, I remembered, he continued, "I realize you said that you were involved with someone right now, but I was thinking the other night that of all the people I've met so far at the center you're one of only a handful who I'd really like to get to know."

I smiled. "I'm flattered." Also not at all sure how I felt about this.

He turned those laser-like eyes on my face. "So I decided I was going to ask again. I enjoyed talking to you, and I'd like to do it some more. If dinner is a problem for you, we could go to lunch instead."

If my significant other wouldn't mind, he meant. Well, my significant other was currently so preoccupied with his work that he probably wouldn't even notice even if we were both in the same city. And, in any case, I didn't need Nick's permission to go out to eat with another man. "Dinner would be nice," I said.

He beamed at me, showing his dimple. "That's great. How about Monday night?"

"Monday would be fine." A nice, safe time for colleagues to get acquainted, not like a real date on the weekend.

"Terrific. Why don't you pick a restaurant you like and we'll work out the time on Monday." He turned his dazzling smile once more in my direction. "I'm really looking forward to it."

"Me too." The smile on my face made me feel dumb the second Larry was out of my office. While I watched his long-legged stride as he disappeared down the hallway, I told myself that this dinner would be the perfect opportunity for me to discover if Larry had been the nervous man pacing around Roger Quinlan's front porch on the day Roger was murdered. That certainly was one of the major reasons I'd agreed so readily to Larry's invitation.

THE REST of the day was one of those back-to-back meetings days that I despise. I wish I could convince the rest of the world of what I long ago concluded: Anything that is accomplished in a committee can be finished in half the time—and with ninety percent less tedium—outside the group. Unfortunately, mine seems to be the minority view on the subject. Every year I become an unwilling member of more and more inane committees.

When I got back from the last of the meetings, it was four-thirty and there was a small pile of pink While You Were Out messages waiting on my desk to be answered. I scanned them, enjoying the notes that Jessie, the secretary next door who takes my phone messages when I'm out, had attached to the ones she felt were worthy. There was a call from my six-year-old nephew Will: "He's mad at his mom and wants to know if he can come live with you. You're supposed to phone him IMMEDIATELY." A half dozen more or less routine calls I could put off until tomorrow morning. And one from Robin: "Yes, she will let you interview her. If possible, tonight at her house. Please call to confirm."

Mentally asking Will's forgiveness, I phoned Robin first.

"Oh, yeah. Hi!" Robin said in her perky cheerleader's voice. "I got your message on my machine. Now, can you tell me what kind of book you're writing?"

I explained that it was Kate's book, that I was only doing some of the interviews of women who had benefitted from Kate's workshops.

"Oh," Robin said, sounding considerably less upbeat. "Well, there might be a problem then."

"What kind of problem?"

"I didn't realize that this was Kate's book. I thought it was yours."

But Robin didn't even know me. I'd heard her speak at the Powerful Woman workshops, but we'd never met. "Your problem is with Kate?" I cleverly guessed.

"Well, yeah. I don't think she'd want to print what I have to say about her workshops."

"Really?" Less than a month ago Robin had been a walking, talking advertisement for Powerful Woman. "I hope you don't mind me asking, but I heard you talk at your second Powerful Woman seminar. And at that point— you know right after the, uh, car accident—you were saying how much you'd gotten out of the workshop, how empowered you felt."

"Things change," Robin said in a stony voice. "It took me a while to come to my senses. John said that workshop was a form of mind control, just like those people who are manipulated by some cult leader and then have to be deprogrammed before they get back to normal."

"Did someone deprogram you?"

"Well, not exactly deprogramming like those guys who hold a cult member prisoner in a motel while they try to talk sense into him. Nobody kidnapped me or coerced me or anything."

When she didn't continue, I asked, "So what happened to make you change your mind about Kate?"

"Oh, John and I went away for a long weekend together, and we talked things out. Told each other how we really felt about things. Got in touch with our feelings."

I tried not to gag. "So you and John are together again?"

"Oh, yes. I moved back into the house last week."

"And John dropped the assault charges against you?"

"Of course," she said, sounding annoyed that I would even ask such a thing.

A moment of silence followed while I considered if there was any way Robin's slant on the workshop could prove helpful. On the one hand, she seemed to be a certifiable flake. I'd thought that even before she went back to John. On the other hand, her story was interesting. And maybe Robin could provide a cautionary tale about impulsive changes—especially violent ones. I also would be paid one hundred dollars an hour to interview her.

"I was thinking, Robin, that it might be valuable to tell different women's experiences of the Powerful Woman workshop in the book," I said. "The negative experiences as well as the positive. I'd like to show the reader what different participants got out of the workshop."

Robin snorted into the receiver. "Well, I sure could give you an earful about that."

"So you're willing to talk to me? Tonight," I added

quickly, thinking that once she discussed this with John she might get cold feet.

"Oh, sure, why not?" Robin gave me directions to her house. "Is seven okay? John is working tonight. He won't be home until after nine."

I told her I'd be there at seven. And, I told myself, I'd be sure to be long gone before nine.

Next I phoned my nephew. My sister answered the phone. I told her that Will had phoned me and I was returning the call.

"Oh, is he after you to let him come live with you again?" Margaret asked. "I don't know what I did to deserve such a pigheaded kid."

I managed, with some effort, not to point out that little Will was a virtual clone of his pigheaded mother. At this point, the one topic Margaret and I seemed capable of discussing without rancor was her children. If I shared my opinion about the stubbornness gene she'd passed on to her son, even that subject would probably be taboo.

Will got on the phone. "Aunt Liz, can I move in with you tonight?"

"Not tonight, honey. I'm not going to be home until late. I have an appointment."

"Why don't you pick me up after the appointment?"

"I won't be back until after your bedtime. You have school tomorrow."

He sighed. "How about if I move in tomorrow night then? I could sleep in your extra bedroom."

"What are you and your mom fighting about this time?" I enquired.

"She's always bossing me around. Every minute she has to tell me what to do."

Yes, that was Margaret all right. "Mothers are like that."

"Yeah," Will said. "That's why I want to move out."

"But if you moved out Maria and Lisa would miss you terribly."

"Yeah, right. They're another reason I want to move out."

"You'd also be very bored at my apartment," I pointed out. "There are no kids around here to play with. No Nintendo either. And the only game on my computer is that jigsaw puzzle, which you've already told me is not your idea of a cool game."

"I can live with it," Will insisted. "It will be fun. You'll see. We can go out for ice cream like we did that one Sunday."

I sighed. My hope for the child was that someday his dig-in-his-heels determination—perversity, his mother said—would be put to good use in fighting corruption, perhaps holding out against bribes and temptations that a more flexible man would have fallen for. "I'll talk to you tomorrow, Will." He would not be moving in with me, but maybe I'd take him out for pizza and a heart-to-heart talk about his family problems.

"Okay, bye." He hung up.

I had barely put down the receiver when my phone rang. "You didn't tell the child that he could come spend the night with you, did you?" Margaret asked in a tight, angry voice.

"No, of course not. Is that what he said?"

"No, he's not talking to me."

Despite myself, I felt a stirring of sympathy for my sister. If this was the way her son was acting at six, what was he going to be pulling at sixteen? "Why don't you go talk to him? He's basically a sweet boy. I think his feelings are just hurt."

"Is that what he told you?"

"No, he didn't give me any details. I just inferred it."

Margaret was silent. "You know," she finally said, "it's a lot easier being a part-time aunt than a full-time mother. You always get to be the good guy."

"I realize that."

"Did he tell you I was mean and bossy?"

"You're not mean," I said.

"Thanks," she said, as if she meant it, and then hung up.

IT WAS almost seven by the time I found Robin Carter's home, on a tree-lined cul-de-sac in the affluent Memorial area. I parked on the street, thinking that there was one question I could cross off my list of interview topics. Just one look at her striking three-story cedar and glass house gave me a pretty good idea why Robin had decided to go back to the loutish John. Even if the oversized garage at the side of the house looked as if it could hold a great many classic cars.

Robin answered the door at my first knock, as if she'd been waiting for me. She smiled broadly at me, unleashing a torrent of words. "Hi! You're Liz, right? I remember seeing you at the workshop. Didn't you sit in the back row?"

"Yes," I said. To both the questions. I followed her inside, thinking that she seemed thinner than the last time I'd seen her and, despite a great deal of carefully applied makeup, she looked tired.

Robin beamed when I told her how spectacular her house was. "It's won architectural awards," she confided in a hushed voice. She nodded at the stark, totally white living room with its high, vaulted ceilings. "And I decorated it myself. John's first wife always hired decorators, but I'm a more hands-on kind of person."

I took in the two facing white couches, the white textured

rug under the round glass coffee table which held a vase of white lilies. "It's very contemporary looking," I said.

"That's what I was shooting for," Robin said, taking it as a compliment.

She followed me to a longer glass-topped table behind one of the couches, where I stooped to inspect the group of white-framed photographs: John and Robin's wedding photo (Robin smiling broadly, wearing a lacy white wedding gown; and John, in a black tux, smiling tightly like a man who didn't smile much but had just been asked to by the photographer). John with two sullen-looking teenaged boys, who had his same square jaw and steely blue eyes. John standing in front of a classic Corvette. John in front of an older-model Porsche. John in front of a Jaguar. John standing in front of his car dealership, holding a big, gold trophy.

If it wasn't a cardinal rule of journalism to ask the toughest question last, I would immediately have blurted out, "So Robin, have you managed to reconcile yourself to a love-me-love-my-car kind of marriage?" Still I would have loved to know what Robin told herself every morning when she spotted this little photo collection.

"Maybe we'd better get on with the interview," Robin said with a tad more coolness in her voice than had been there a minute ago. She eyed the portable tape recorder I was carrying with obvious alarm. "You're not going to tape everything I say, are you?"

"Not if you don't want me to. If you'd prefer I'll only take notes. It's just that having a tape of our conversation assures that you're quoted accurately."

"Well, I don't know. It kind of makes me nervous thinking that every word I say is being recorded."

She hadn't looked very nervous when she was telling all those TV reporters how empowered she felt after running over her husband with his car. "Why don't we try it and if it bothers you I'll turn it off?" I suggested. "A lot of people forget that the recorder is there once we get talking."

"I guess I could try it." Robin did not look thrilled at the prospect. "By the way, would you like a glass of wine? I've got a nice bottle of Chardonnay."

"Sure," I said, "that would be great." Even though I didn't really want one. When I was working I prefered caffeine, but maybe a glass of wine would make Robin less nervous. And, I hoped, more revealing.

Robin suggested that we sit outside on the deck. While she went to get the wine, I walked outside. It was a lovely night, less muggy than usual, and the view from the back of Robin's house was spectacular. Her perfectly manicured backyard sloped down into the bayou, and the weeping willows on the edge of the property blocked any view of neighbors' houses.

"This is wonderful," I said when she returned with two glasses and a half-filled bottle of wine. "It's so serene, as if you're out in the country somewhere, not in the middle of Houston."

"Yes, the backyard is the best thing about the house," Robin agreed. "I sit out here a lot by myself. It's like my own private world."

She seemed more relaxed now. After pouring our wine, she curled up in one of the long cushioned lounging chairs, not even seeming to notice when I switched on the tape recorder.

"Let's talk about the first Powerful Woman workshop you attended," I began. "Why don't you tell me what you expected to get out of the workshop, why you decided to go to it."

"Well, I didn't really know what to expect," Robin said.

"I saw a brochure about the workshop somewhere and it sounded kind of interesting. And I didn't have anything else to do that Saturday."

"So you didn't have any goal for the workshop—say, for instance, to work on your marriage problems?"

Robin shook her head. "No, I knew I was feeling bored and restless and I hoped that the workshop could make me feel better. But I didn't go there thinking, 'Oh, I'm going to work out my problems with John.' I went there thinking, 'Let's go see what this is about.' "

"So when you arrived at the workshop, would you say you were still feeling bored and restless?"

"No, I would say I was pissed off. I'd just had a big fight with John. When I told him I was going to the workshop he said I was just throwing away his money. We'd gone out for breakfast and he started shouting at me in the restaurant. I just walked out on him. I took a taxi to the workshop."

"What was your first reaction to the workshop?"

"I loved it. Of course I loved it. There I was, furious with my husband, and this beautiful, confident woman walks onto the stage and says, 'You don't have to take shit from anyone. I dumped this jerk I was living with, found myself a wonderful job. You can too—if you have enough guts to just do it. You can have anything you want, create exactly the kind of life you've always dreamed of, if you're brave enough to go for it.' "

I nodded. "So what did you think when you heard that?"

"I thought about how mad I was at John. How he was always at work or else out in the garage fiddling around with his damn cars. He didn't have any time for me anymore."

"Okay. Besides being angry with him, did you think

about changing your life—how you wanted your life to be?''

"I thought I did." Robin finished her wine and poured herself another glass. I shook my head when she offered to refill my glass.

"But all I really did," she continued, "was think how perfect everything was going to be once I didn't have to listen to John complain about how much money I spent on clothes and how wonderful it would be to never have to attend another boring classic car rally."

Robin finished her second glass of wine, then leaned toward me. "You see, it was like a little kid's fantasy. A fairy tale where the fairy godmother waves the magic wand and everything is totally wonderful. The marriage counselor John and I are seeing says that's magical thinking. Real marriages involve compromise and communicating with each other and working out the problems."

She sounded as if she had lifted the last line from her marriage counselor. I watched as Robin poured herself a third glass of wine, wondering if she always drank this much.

"And that," she said, slurring the words a little, "is the trouble with the Powerful Woman workshop. It sells women a bunch of bull. Even our marriage counselor said that: Kate tries to make women believe in this magic thinking—just wave your wand and everything in your life is suddenly terrific."

I could have argued the point, citing Kate's brainstorming with Annette at the second workshop about the necessary steps for starting her dressmaking business and Kate's spiel to the group about planning how to reach your goals. In one sense, Robin had heard what she'd wanted to hear of Kate's message and had filtered out the rest. But there was also an element of truth in what Robin was complaining about. Kate had urged the Powerful Woman participants to push aside their fears, envision the life they wanted, and then go for it. She'd told Robin to stop making excuses for John's selfish behavior and to start forging a new and more fulfilling life for herself. The fact that running over John Carter was clearly not the kind of forging that Kate had had in mind did not absolve her of all blame. Robin had heard Kate's message and then "just did it."

"So you're saying that Kate telling you that you could make your life better made you want to kill your husband?" I asked.

Robin set her empty wineglass on the wood deck. The look she sent my way was definitely unfriendly, as if here I was trying to trip her up with a trick question after she'd been so sweet to me. "I'm saying," she said sternly, "that the thought never once crossed my mind until I got into that workshop. And I never, ever would have done something like that if everybody hadn't been saying, 'Oh, you deserve better, Robin. Go for it, Robin!' After hearing that over and over again I walked out the door and saw John waiting for me, wearing this big scowl on his face. Something inside me just *snapped*! It was as if I was hearing all those women shouting, 'You *don't* have to take it anymore, Robin!' "

"You mean it was kind of like temporary insanity?" I wondered if this was the explanation Robin had intended to use in court if John hadn't dropped the assault charge.

"Yes," Robin said coolly, "exactly like that."

I had the suspicion that at any second she was going to ask me to leave, so I quickly added, "Could you tell me a little about how you and John got back together again?"

"Oh, sure." This apparently was the part she liked to talk about. "I'd moved out and was living in my own place when John called me one Saturday morning. He was just so sweet on the phone. Told me how much he'd missed me, how empty the house seemed without me. He said he really wanted us to get back together, and this time we'd work out our problems instead of just sweeping them under the rug. John said he'd thought a lot about it and he finally realized that the car accident was just a big misunderstanding.''

A big misunderstanding. I jotted the words in my steno notebook, nodding at Robin to keep talking.

"John came over that evening, bringing me these gorgeous roses. We went out to dinner and talked for a long time, really hashed things out. The next weekend we went away for this *very* romantic weekend in Acapulco. When we got back we started seeing a marriage counselor. He's helped us a lot. John was saying just last night how our marriage is better than it has ever been.''

Just like in the fairy tale. "I'm glad that things worked out for you,'' I said. "But you know when I was listening to you talk about what happened it does seem as if, in a circuitous kind of way, that Powerful Woman *did* help you. I mean if you hadn't left John, do you think he would have been willing to go into marriage counseling and work on your marriage?''

"It certainly did *not* help!'' Robin's tiny heart-shaped face rapidly registered disbelief, horror, and finally seemed to settle on revulsion. "Kate Quinlan and her sicko, irresponsible seminar almost ruined my marriage. I might have killed my husband—something I never, ever would have done, wouldn't have even thought of doing, if I hadn't been manipulated by Kate Quinlan.''

"So both you and your husband think Kate is responsible for your hitting him with the car?''

I thought she was going to say, "You'd better believe it!'' but she didn't. Instead she gazed at her backyard, down the grassy slope to the murky water of the bayou below. "Of course I have to accept some responsibility for my own actions," she said quietly. "Kate didn't hold a gun to my head."

I agreed with the sentiment, but I didn't believe that Robin did. Instead she sounded as if she was mouthing the words that her marriage counselor had told her she should feel. The right words for the courts, the media, maybe even for her husband.

Robin turned back to me, her eyes hard and unflinching. "But I can tell you that while I accept responsibility for my terrible mistake, my husband lays all the blame on Kate Quinlan. And I wish I'd never laid eyes on that awful woman."

I was in my car, driving myself home, five minutes later. Robin had said all she had to say. I'd noticed her glance nervously at her watch. It was almost time for the love of her life to get home, and she wanted me out of there.

I was happy to oblige.

THE PHONE was ringing as I unlocked the door to my apartment. Was Robin having cold feet already, I wondered, while half hoping the phone would stop ringing by the time I got inside. Let whoever it was leave a message that I could choose to answer—or not—tonight.

As I entered my living room, my answering tape was informing my caller that I couldn't come to the phone right now. I locked the door after me and waited for the message.

"Liz, it's Mel. *Please* call me tonight. It's important." She hung up before I could get to the phone.

I kicked off my shoes and dialed the Quinlans' number. Mel picked up on the first ring.

"Hi, this is Liz. I was just getting home when you called. What's up?"

"I called the police today about the bloodstain on the rug," she said, then stopped, apparently waiting for me to react to the news.

"And what did the police say?"

"They came over and cut off a piece of the carpet so they could analyze the blood."

"So it *is* blood for sure?"

"Yeah, that's about all the guy who came would tell me: It *is* blood. The question is whether it's Roger's blood. That's what they're going to test for."

I had a sense that there was something else Mel wanted to tell me. "You're not home alone again, are you?" I asked, envisioning her sitting by herself in the big, silent house.

"No, Kate is here. Actually she's in the shower right now. She's upset and hardly talking to me, though."

So that was it: my second Mom-is-being-mean-to-me call of the day. What was it my sister had said this afternoon? We part-time aunts got to always be the good guys. While the full-time mother/custodial stepparent was left with the role of Wicked Witch of the West.

"Did Kate say what she was upset about?" I asked in a carefully neutral voice.

"Well she wasn't really mad at me, though Mr. Smythe was. *He* said I should have called him instead of the police. That by my phoning the police myself I'd made things look even worse for Kate, like I'd discovered evidence that she'd been trying to hide."

Had Kate been trying to hide the bloodstain under the desk? If that had been her intention, I would have thought she'd do something more effective—replace the carpet, for instance, when Mel was away at school. Eventually, someone was going to move that desk and see the bloodstain. Surely Kate, who planned to move out of the house as soon as it was sold, would have realized that. Maybe she'd assumed that the carpet cleaners would remove the entire stain—a pretty naive assumption, but no one had ever said Kate was much of a homemaker.

I forced myself to focus on what Mel was saying: Bobby Smythe was furious with her. In a way I could see his point, but I also doubted that the bloody carpet would have been significantly less incriminating if Bobby, rather than Mel, had pointed it out to the police. Unless Smythe would have decided not to share this particular piece of information with the Houston Police Department.

"So did Kate tell you why she was so upset?" I was more interested in Kate's reaction than in her attorney's.

"She said she never thought that Roger was killed here, at the house. She'd always assumed that he was shot somewhere else, and the killer just dropped off the box on the back porch after she'd left for her workshop on that Saturday morning."

"It is creepy to think that he was shot there," I agreed, then instantly wished I'd kept my opinion to myself.

It didn't seem to bother Mel. Or, more accurately, she'd already realized on her own how creepy it was to be living in the same house where her father had very likely been murdered. "But the thing that really bothered Kate," Mel continued, "was who moved the desk over the bloodstain."

"Probably the killer."

"But why bother?" Mel said. "Why did the killer not want us to know that Roger was shot there?"

Because the killer was very likely someone who lived in the house or had easy access to it, and she or he didn't want the police to narrow the search down to that small group of people? It was the conclusion that the police would probably jump to. Bobby Smythe was right. It certainly did not bode well for Kate Quinlan.

This time I tried for diplomacy. "I think the killer didn't want to leave any clues that could help identify him later. If the police knew right away that Roger had been shot in his study, the first thing they'd do was try to figure out who was at your house that afternoon and evening."

"Okay, I get it. Like the woman and man who came here that day could say their visit was unimportant if the police thought that Roger was killed somewhere else. The only problem with your theory is that when I called about the bloodstain, I told the detective about the man and woman who Juanita saw at our house on the afternoon that Roger died—and the detective couldn't have cared less."

"What did he say?"

"He said he'd look into it, but I don't believe him. He made it real clear that he's sure they've already got Roger's killer, and he's not interested in investigating any other possible suspects."

I heard a noise in the background, then Mel calling, "I'm down here in the kitchen, Kate."

To me Mel said, "I'm going to make this up to Kate. I didn't know . . . Gotta go, she's coming."

I was left holding a receiver that droned the dial tone into my ear, filled with questions I hadn't had the time to ask.

# Chapter Nineteen

"So," LARRY NELSON SAID, LEANING FORWARD IN OUR booth in the dark, wood-paneled Italian restaurant. "Tell me about yourself."

I laughed. "That's a very shrink-like question." Particularly since only minutes before he'd been asking innocuous, chatty questions about a newspaper story he'd read recently about the mental health center. Had I placed the story? What reporters did I usually work with? Now he was switching to tell-me-your-life-story.

Larry grinned. A nice, self-deprecating smile that transformed his tired eyes, his solemn face. "Gee, it always worked like a charm before. Would you prefer that I ask specific, probing questions like you do? The journalistic rather than the psychiatric approach?"

Touché. "Yeah, I guess I am more comfortable with specific questions. So what do you want to know?"

"You're single now. Have you been married?"

I nodded. "I've been divorced two years. Max and I were married for seven years."

He waited patiently for more details, another shrink-like

mannerism—therapeutic silence—that I found annoying. A few days ago I'd been looking forward to this dinner, but from the moment we'd met at the restaurant tonight, I'd sensed that both of us were either tired or out of sorts—not in the mood to be sparkling dinner companions.

"How about you?" I asked. "Have you ever been married?"

"Yeah. Not for as long as you, though. Linda and I were married for only thirteen months—a great record for two psychiatrists, right?"

"How long have you been divorced?" It wasn't the question I was really interested in—So what's the story? What went wrong in only thirteen months?—but since I didn't feel like revealing the gory details of my marriage, I figured I'd better stick with the polite questions.

"Not quite a year."

I inspected him. "You know you don't have that crazed, newly divorced look." Abandoning the idea of tact at the first opportunity.

"Thanks, I think." He took a sip of his red wine. "Sometimes I think I'm just good at hiding it."

"I guess I wasn't—good at hiding it, I mean. I was terribly depressed before and after my divorce. I can remember people at work being very solicitous, very tender." I shook my head, remembering all my colleagues' invitations for lunch or weekend outings, the casual visits to my office just to see how I was doing that day. "In fact, looking back, I must have been a real basket case."

"It's very helpful to have a strong support system like you had."

I thought he sounded wistful. "Yes, it was. I really thought of the people I worked with as being a kind of second family for me."

"And do you still feel that way?"

I thought about it. "Sometimes. I mean I have a real affection for a lot of my coworkers, but right now I don't really need a second family. I'm not depressed or feeling terribly vulnerable. If anything, I feel as if I'm in a career rut, as if I've been doing the same thing too long, and it's time to move on."

"So why don't you move on?"

"I guess I still have to figure out what I want to move on to."

The waiter arrived then with our dinners—veal piccata for me, spaghetti carbonara for Larry—and I assumed we'd finished with that topic. Larry, however, apparently felt otherwise. The minute the waiter left, he inquired, "What do you enjoy doing the most?"

I shrugged. "I really like to interview people, to ask questions. I like to write, though I'd like to try doing some other kinds of writing—maybe a nonfiction book or even a novel. I like to solve puzzles, to put together pieces of information in a new way that makes me go 'Aha!' "

He smiled. "That's one of the things I enjoy about doing therapy, trying to help a patient unravel his problem, to see what's causing it and maybe finding a different way of dealing with it. Each case is a mystery that needs to be solved."

I smiled, liking the analogy, wondering how many patients seeing therapists at the mental health center viewed their problems as mysteries to be solved.

Larry maneuvered his fork and pasta spoon to twirl his spaghetti around the fork. Before raising the food to his mouth he looked me in the eye and said, "You *do* have an idea of what kind of work you'd like. The pertinent question is why are you staying in your rut?"

I set down my fork. "You know, you have a lot more in common with Kate Quinlan than you think."

He laughed, almost choking on his food. Then, sipping water and shaking his head, he added, "And here I always thought I was much more subtle than Kate."

I raised my eyebrows. "I wouldn't say that."

He smiled, letting it go. It was a trait I'd often noticed in therapists—the ability to move on, to accept what the other person was saying and not get their feelings hurt: Oh, you feel that way; that's interesting. It was a trait I wished I had.

"If it isn't too intrusive," he said, his smile mocking, "do you think you might tell me a little about your current relationship? Like how serious is it and anything else you might want to throw in."

"Nick and I are engaged," I said stiffly. For someone who liked asking questions so much, I certainly did not enjoy answering them. "He's out of town right now." What did *that* mean? I wouldn't be sitting here with you if my honey Nick was in Houston? I quickly added, "He's an investigative reporter working on a story in El Paso."

"So the two of you both like to ask questions and solve puzzles and write?"

I nodded. "Our approaches are different, but yes, basically we both do like a lot of the same things."

"That's nice," Larry said. Surprising me because he looked as if he meant it. "I thought that Linda and I had a lot in common: the same profession, the same kind of background—both of our dads are doctors. But the similarities were actually quite superficial. What we wanted from life was very different. Linda wanted a flashier life than I did. I wanted kids; she told me after we were married that she'd decided she didn't. I think we both ended up feeling as if we'd been duped by the other. You know: 'How come you didn't *tell* me that you felt like that?' "

He sipped his wine, then sent me that now-familiar probing look. "Which, considering our professions, is pretty pitiful. I don't expect psychiatrists to have exemplary personal lives, but I do expect them to have a bit of insight into what's messing things up."

I nodded sympathetically. "It's awfully hard to know what's going on when you're in the middle of the action. And it sounds as if you do have insight now."

"A bit late, I'd say." His smile was bitter. "The ironic thing—and I just realized this a few weeks ago—is that Linda was actually quite a bit like Kate. Two take-charge women, both risk takers, impulsive, exciting. Both in mental health professions." He glanced away. "And both of them, it turns out, walked out on me."

Oh, God. I leaned forward to pat his hand, then decided not to. I didn't want to send out messages that could be misinterpreted. "You know I think Max, my ex-husband, left me emotionally years before he ever moved out of the house. But I was still so hurt and angry when he physically left. Even though at the same time I was kind of relieved to have it all over with."

It crossed my mind that it was easy now to talk about that post-divorce roller-coaster ride of emotions. Easy now that I was over Max, over my depression, my sour sense of failure, my middle-of-the-night fear and loneliness. But it certainly had not been easy when I was at the place, only a few months out of the divorce, where Larry Nelson was now.

"Do you see much of your ex-husband?" Larry asked. "That's something I'm always curious about. Some people tell me they end up having a better relationship after they're divorced than they ever had when they were married. Other people always hate each other's guts."

I swallowed a mouthful of veal. "I wouldn't say that Max and I are great friends, but we don't hate each other either. Occasionally we talk on the phone, but not very often.''

''Sometimes I wonder what kind of relationship I would eventually have had with Linda,'' Larry said.

''What do you mean—would have had?''

''Linda is dead.'' Larry glanced up from the spaghetti he was twirling around his fork. ''She and her new husband— they got married two months after our divorce was final— died on their honeymoon. A scuba diving accident.''

I grabbed my wineglass and pretended to be absorbed in drinking my wine. The look I'd just glimpsed in those intense gray eyes sent a shiver down my spine.

I told myself that I had imagined the look. Or rather misinterpreted grief or pain for the raw fury I thought I'd seen. Psychiatrists, I reminded myself, were extremely adept at *not* revealing their emotions. They were trained to hide their reactions behind a mask of neutrality. To conduct therapy like an emotional chess game. In short, if an experienced psychiatrist had killed his ex-wife and her new husband, he would probably be terrific at hiding the fact.

Larry also was not acting like someone who'd inadvertently revealed a secret. He added that Linda and her new husband, Todd, a thoracic surgeon, had been in Cozumel when the accident happened. ''Apparently there was something wrong with Todd's air tank. Linda died trying to save him. At least, that's what Linda's mother said that the Mexican authorities told her.''

''Oh, that's horrible,'' I said, envisioning Linda's frantic, underwater attempt to rescue her struggling husband.

''Yes, it is,'' he said solemnly, his eyes now devoid of all emotion.

Over coffee I remembered what I had intended to ask him. I pushed aside a sliver of misgiving and inquired, ''How long have you been in Houston now, Larry?''

"A little over two weeks. I'm just starting to get acclimated."

"Is this the first time you've been here?" I asked. "I mean did you come here before to check out the city? Oh, of course, you *had* to come to interview for the job, didn't you?"

I was babbling away like an idiot! Why didn't I just blurt it all out: I was just curious, Larry. Did you happen to kill Roger Quinlan on the day you came to interview for your job?

"I flew down twice, once in January and then again in March."

"Oh, when were you here in March?" Seeing the puzzled expression on his face, I added, "I just wondered if you were here when the azaleas start to bloom. That's usually in the first two weeks of March. The River Oaks Garden Club holds a tour of homes and gardens, the Azalea Trail, then." It was lame, but it was the best I could do.

"Let me think. It was the first Thursday and Friday in March. Unfortunately, I didn't notice the azaleas."

"Oh, they bloomed later this year." Roger Quinlan had died on the first Friday in March.

Larry Nelson has said that he admired risk-taking women. I wished now that I was better at crawling out on a limb. I smiled what I hoped was a wide-eyed smile of friendly interest. "Did you get to see Roger or Kate when you were here?"

He shook his head. "I tried to, but when I stopped by Kate's office, she was with a patient. I tried to see Roger too, but I never could catch him."

From above the rim of his coffee cup Larry Nelson's laser-eyes studied me.

I'd asked enough questions for one night, I decided. We finished our coffee in silence.

# Chapter Twenty

THE VOICE BEHIND ME STARTLED ME. I HADN'T REALized that anyone else was in the office.

"Liz, you won't *believe* what I just found out!"

I abandoned the news release I'd been working on and swiveled to face my visitor. "Mel." I glanced at my watch: 1:30. "Aren't you supposed to be in school?"

"It's an early dismissal day," she said breezily.

I'd bet twenty dollars that she was lying, but I let it pass. "So what are you doing here?"

She plopped down into my extra chair, a big grin on her face. "Talking to Dr. Nelson and Tricia Whitmore."

"Dr. Whitmore," I corrected. It irritated me that people so often called male physicians and Ph.D.s "Doctor" but wouldn't use the title with the female counterparts.

"She's not a psychiatrist, is she?" Mel asked.

Oh, okay, the kid was just a medical snob, not sexist. "No, she's a clinical psychologist, a Ph.D."

Mel, the physician's daughter, shrugged. "Whatever. My point is that I talked to both of them about being at our house the day Roger was killed."

She looked so excited, so un-Mel-like, that I didn't have the heart to point out that I'd already talked to both of her suspects about their activities that day. "And what did they tell you?"

"Dr. Nelson said he *was* the guy who was pacing around the front porch that afternoon. But nobody ever answered the door. He rang the bell five or six times, then left. He said he hadn't phoned to tell Roger he was coming, so he just figured that no one was home."

She'd gotten more information from Larry than I had in all my circuitous questions about his job interviewing visits to Houston. "Just out of curiosity," I said, "did you ever tell Dr. Nelson why you were asking all of these questions?"

"I told him the truth," Mel said, sending me an isn't-this-obvious look. "That the police have already decided that Kate murdered Roger and won't investigate anyone else. That I don't think Kate did it, and I want to find out who did."

"And what did Dr. Nelson say to that?"

"He said he could understand me wanting to clear Kate. He said that Kate was a lot of things, but a murderer was not one of them. And he wished me good luck."

Such an affable man, that Dr. Nelson. "It's too bad that Juanita didn't see him leave the porch." Because at this point we only had Larry's word that no one had answered the door.

"Oh, but I believed him," Mel said earnestly. "And not just because he was nice to me either," she added, her face reddening slightly. "He had to catch a plane out of Intercontinental at six o'clock. It takes about forty-five minutes to drive to the airport, and then he had to return his rental car and get his luggage checked in. Even if Roger was home, Dr. Nelson didn't have time to kill him, do all the stuff with the box, make arrangements with the delivery service, and still catch his plane.''

"Probably not," I agreed. "If he actually was on the six o'clock flight.''

"I'm sure he was," Mel said tartly. "But I'll check it out anyway.'' She pulled the little notebook out of her mammoth canvas purse and jotted something down. "But this is what I really wanted you to hear.'' She dug through her purse and pulled out a small tape recorder. "I recorded my conversation with *Dr.* Whitmore.''

She rewound the tape, then pushed the play button. I heard Tricia's voice, muffled but definitely Tricia. Had Mel kept the recorder in her purse? Tricia was telling Mel that she could only give her five minutes; she had a patient coming at 1:00.

"Oh, what I want to know won't take long," Mel's voice spoke from the tape. "A witness saw you enter my house on the afternoon my father died.'' Mel paused, apparently waiting for Tricia to say something. Tricia didn't, so Mel went on. "Did you know that your fingerprints have been found in my father's study?''

"They have?" I blurted out.

Mel clicked off the recorder. She shook her head, looking sheepish. "I just wanted to hear how she'd respond.'' She clicked the recorder back on for Tricia's answer.

"That's absurd!" Tricia said in a louder voice than before. "I've never been inside Roger's study. We talked in the sunroom. Briefly. Then I left.'' She did not sound scared or defensive, merely annoyed. A common Tricia Whitmore reaction.

"What did you and Roger talk about?" Mel asked.

"What business is it of yours?" Tricia answered.

"I want to find my father's killer.''

"Try looking in your own house. Your stepmother hated your father."

"But Kate doesn't have any motive to kill Roger. She was probably better off financially with him alive. Roger told both Kate and me that he'd changed his will so that I'd inherit everything—not that there's much to inherit except the house. And if Kate wanted to get rid of Roger all she had to do was divorce him. So the way I see it, *you're* the one with the best motive for killing my father. He had just broke up with you, and he was going to fire you."

Who had told Mel that, I wondered? Kate?

"You sick bitch!" On the tape Tricia had passed the point of annoyance. Her voice now was easy to hear; she was yelling. "You think you know so much. You don't know shit. Yes, your precious father planned on firing me. But you know where I went after I left your house? No, not to a gun shop. To the EEOC office. The woman I talked to said she thought I had an excellent case."

I let out a breath. I hadn't realized that I'd been holding it.

"Someone who'd just murdered your father wouldn't drive straight to the EEOC office would she?" Tricia, sounding smug, asked Mel.

"If she wanted a good alibi she would," Mel answered.

"Get out of my office! And if you ever repeat these ridiculous accusations to anyone I'll sue you for every penny your sorry father left you."

Mel said something else on the tape, but whatever it was was obscured by the sound of a door slamming. Loudly.

In my office Mel clicked off the tape recorder.

"Some tape," I told her.

"Yeah," Mel said, looking proud.

• • •

I THOUGHT about Mel that evening as I drove to Annette Turner's apartment for my interview with her. In my office Mel had seemed so agitated, so stubbornly determined that she was going to find Roger's killer, that I was worried about her. "Don't you see?" she'd pleaded, on the verge of tears. "The police tests proved that the blood on the carpet is Roger's. I gave the police evidence that they're using against Kate. So I *have* to find the real killer."

I'd tried to reason with her, tried to reassure her that she had nothing to feel guilty about, that she'd done the right thing by reporting the stain on the carpet to the police. But I could tell from the way her eyes darted around the room, avoiding eye contact, that she intended to keep meddling. I didn't want to think what might happen if, during her investigations, In-Your-Face Mel happened to confront Roger's murderer—if she hadn't already.

I was glad when I reached Annette's apartment in a small, nicely maintained complex in Bellaire. I needed to stop worrying about Mel. I'd already phoned Kate, but she hadn't been in. I'd try again later. Together we'd work out something to keep Mel safe.

I parked in the visitor's parking slot and found apartment 96 on the west side of a neat courtyard with a small fountain.

When I rang the doorbell, Annette answered immediately. "So you're Liz! I remember you from our small group at the first workshop." She waved me into her apartment. "You're the one with the pushy sister, right?"

Yes, I said, I certainly was. It appeared that she was making more progress with her business than I was with my sister.

Annette laughed. "You have to excuse the mess," she said, pointing at the sewing machine and pieces of material that covered her dining-room table. Half-finished garments—colorful cotton sundresses, a bright yellow linen suit—were draped over every available piece of furniture.

Annette picked up a pink jumpsuit and three appliqued beach coverups that had been piled on two upholstered chairs. "We can sit here. I've given up on trying to keep the place picked up. It will be a long time before I can afford a real office, so I figure I might as well learn to live with the clutter. Who has time to clean anyway? As it is I'm working two jobs. Two and a half jobs if you count all the time I spend trying to convince store owners to take my clothes."

"Have you had any luck with the stores?"

"A few boutiques took my stuff on consignment. A buyer at one of them told me she has a friend who's a buyer for a chain of resorts in Florida. Said she thought her friend would like my sundresses and beach coverups, so I've been trying to concentrate on those."

Annette, who was dressed in jeans and an oversized Houston Rockets T-shirt, stretched out her thin legs and yawned. "Sorry. I haven't been getting much sleep lately. When you said you wanted to interview me for Kate's book, my first thought was that it's too early for that. I don't know yet whether I'm going to be able to make a go of this business."

"What I'm more interested in is what impact you think the Powerful Woman workshop had on you. Are you glad you took it? Do you think you'd have started your designing business if you hadn't gone to Kate's seminar?"

"No, probably I wouldn't have," Annette said after thinking about it for a minute. "I was always sewing for myself and my family, but I never really was ready to take the next step, to try to sell my designs. If I hadn't gone to Powerful Woman I'd probably still be in my old secretarial job—which, incidentally, paid better and had a hell of a lot better benefits than my sales job in this trendy little boutique.''

I scanned her angular face, noticing the dark circles under her eyes, the paleness of her skin. She'd stopped dying her hair. I thought her natural color, light brown, was an improvement over the almost-white blonde hair she'd had when I first saw her. Annette looked as if she'd lost weight too, slipping from fashionably slender into outright skinniness. "Do you wish you were still back in your old job?''

"Never!'' The vehemence of her response wiped out the exhaustion in her eyes. "My life would probably be easier, but some things are more important than money or sleep. I'm doing what I want to do now, and that's worth a lot.''

I jotted a few notes while the tape recorder caught the rest of Annette's answers. Yes, Kate's workshop had helped her to finally get off her butt and start the business she'd always dreamed about. "But it was the second workshop that really helped me. Remember when Kate had me stand up, and we went through all the steps that might be necessary to start my business?''

I remembered. Remembered too how bored the quick-fix members of the audience were by Kate's speech on realistic goal setting and taking responsibility for your life—the sections she'd added after witnessing all the commando raids spawned by her earlier workshop. The memorable workshop which had inspired Annette to march into her boss's office and pinch his posterior.

I asked her the two questions I was dying to know: Did she now regret her counter-chauvinist attack on her boss? And would she have done that if she'd never attended Powerful Woman?

"Yes to the first question and no, probably not, to the second. I'm glad I'm not in that job anymore. And my boss *was* a real asshole. But pinching him was juvenile—he didn't get it. It sure as hell didn't change his behavior. And it didn't help me either.''

"What was it about that first workshop that pushed you into doing something you wouldn't normally have done?"

"I've been thinking about that," Annette said, pushing a strand of brown hair off her face. "In fact Robin and I—remember her, the woman who ran over her husband?—talked about that when we went to lunch once. She and I both felt that there was this current of emotion—almost hysterical emotion—in that workshop. Sort of like those old tent-revival meetings where everybody leaps up, yelling that they're healed. Except, at Powerful Woman you were supposed to act, to do it, to make your life better. But the problem was that nobody talked much about *how* we were going to accomplish that."

"So you would have preferred that the first workshop be more practical—how to set goals, that kind of thing?"

Annette shrugged, smiling ruefully. "I'm not sure. It's possible that I wouldn't have responded at all to the practical stuff if I hadn't been roused by the first workshop. I don't know if I was ready then to hear how hard starting my business was going to be: the long hours, the rejections, the pitiful money. It was only when I realized how crappy my life really was, how much I hated my old job and the way my boss treated me, that I was even willing to think about the next steps. And, of course, once I was fired, I *had* to think about what I was going to do next."

"That's interesting." I wondered why I hadn't picked up on this surge of group emotion at that first workshop. All I'd wanted to do at the end of that first seminar was go home.

"But you know Robin didn't have the same reaction to the second workshop as I did," Annette said. "I think she got off on all the publicity she received after mowing down her husband. That was what she liked about the second workshop—the attention she got. But once that stopped, when no one wanted to interview her anymore, Robin thought the whole Powerful Woman experience was a bust.''

I nodded. ''Yeah, I interviewed Robin. I got the idea that she blames Kate for the car incident. Robin says she never would have considered doing such a thing if she hadn't gone to the workshop.''

Annette snorted. ''Bullshit. I probably wouldn't have actually gone and pinched my boss' ass if I hadn't attended the workshop, but I certainly had thought of it before. And Robin had to have thought about striking back at this jerk who spent his every spare minute with his cars. Kate didn't tell her to run the guy down.

''What the workshop did was encourage us to act on our fantasies. Go ahead, do it, you don't deserve to be treated this way. No one was saying, 'Hey, think about the consequences before you act.' And that probably was irresponsible. So sure, Robin did regret running over her husband. Once she left John she was broke, with no real job skills. The reporters stopped calling and there was a good chance she was going to end up in jail. All of a sudden her old life didn't look so bad. Maybe her husband didn't pay a lot of attention to her, but she had a great house, nice clothes and a lot of free time to go shopping.''

''So she decided to go back to John,'' I said.

Annette's expression suddenly turned grim. ''Robin decided to go back to John at the second workshop. She decided the minute she saw Kate's husband's body roll out of that box.''

''What do you mean? Why would that influence her to reconcile with her husband?''

"Because," Annette said in a hard, tight voice, "she was sure that John was sending her a message."

"Wait a minute. Robin thought that John had Roger killed to send *her* a message?" I asked, certain that I had misunderstood her.

"That's right. I thought it sounded crazy too. That's why I didn't call the police. Robin said that John was saying, 'Look, this is what happens to people who mess with me.' He knew Robin was going to be at the workshop and that she'd see firsthand what happened to John's enemies."

It seemed far-fetched to me. More than far-fetched—the fantasy of a not-too-bright woman who thought the world revolved around her. "That," I said, "is a very bizarre interpretation of Roger Quinlan's death. If the killing was meant to teach anyone a lesson I would bet it was directed at Kate, not Robin."

"Oh, Robin thought that too. Kate was the enemy, the woman who'd turned John's wife against him. Robin said that John was a real eye-for-an-eye kind of guy. So if Kate took John's wife from him, he'd take her husband. And he'd send his wife a warning at the same time."

"A warning she took very seriously," I said, half to myself.

"You bet she did," Annette said. "The next morning she phoned John to say she'd been thinking that maybe they could work things out after all. She moved back in with him that afternoon."

"Robin told me that John called her, saying that he was willing to do anything—marriage counseling, spending less time on his cars, dropping the assault charges—if only she'd come back," I said.

Annette shrugged. "Think about it. Everybody in Houston with a TV set or newspaper has heard Robin spout off about how empowered she's feeling, a transformed woman.

After all that, would *you* tell a reporter that you went back to your asshole husband because he scared you? And, oh yes, you missed his money too.''

"I see your point." The problem was that Robin seemed like such a liar that I wasn't sure that I believed any of her stories: empowered car warrior, contented reconciled spouse or cowering wife.

"I can tell you this," Annette said. "I don't know if John Carter killed Kate's husband. But I do know that Robin Carter *believed* he did. I saw her face when she caught sight of that body. And that woman wasn't just shocked. She was scared shitless.''

# Chapter Twenty-one

I GLANCED BEHIND ME TO MAKE SURE THAT NO ONE WAS eavesdropping, then felt ridiculous when a bald jogger with headphones sent me a blank stare before passing Kate and me on the park jogging trail. So what was I expecting? Mel running up to us, eyes filled with accusations, screaming, "Why are you two talking about me behind my back?"

I sucked in air. Kate's idea of walking was my idea of a slow jog. "Kate, I'm worried about Mel. All of a sudden she seems obsessed with finding Roger's murderer. And I'm afraid that she might be putting herself in danger too."

Kate nodded, but didn't say anything. We passed two overweight women who seemed to be even more breathless than I, then we moved to the left so a lean, white-haired woman in nylon jogging shorts and a Tenneco Marathon T-shirt could pass us. That was the only problem with using Memorial Park's tree-shaded jogging trail. On a nice Saturday morning about a quarter of the population of Houston seemed to have the same idea.

"You need to take this seriously, Kate," I added, my voice sounding shrill.

"I *do* take it seriously," she said, turning appraising eyes on me. "Especially after Tricia Whitmore and John Carter phoned me to complain about Mel. I hung up on Tricia, but I heard Carter out."

I stopped in the middle of the trail. "John Carter?" Mel hadn't told me about visiting him.

"Yes, unfortunately." She motioned for me to get moving. Coming to the park had been Kate's idea. When I called to say I needed to talk to her privately, she'd said she was about to go out walking, so why didn't I join her and get some exercise while we talked. At the time it had seemed like a good idea.

I started walking again. "Mel went to John Carter's office?"

"No, she phoned Robin at their home. Pretended she was doing a phone survey about which banks people use. Unfortunately for Mel, the Carters have one of those caller–I.D. systems on their phone. It listed Roger's name and our phone number. So Robin hung up and phoned John right away, saying someone at my house was probably getting ready to steal money from their bank account."

"What?" Mel trying to steal money from the Carters?

Kate shook her head in disgust. "Robin is not the brightest person in the world. John, however, apparently could figure out other reasons why someone from my family might want information about their bank account." Seeing the look of total incomprehension on my face, Kate added, "Mel was hoping—very naively, I might add—to be able to call the bank and find out if John had written a check to Consuela. Consuela's daughter told Mel that Consuela said some rich man had given her a lot of money. The daughter didn't know the rich man's name or why he'd given Consuela the money. But shortly after Roger's death Consuela was suddenly about five thousand dollars richer."

I finished the thought. "So Mel figured that John Carter was the rich man who'd given Consuela the money for helping him kill Roger."

"Or for not telling the police what she knew. Mel refuses to believe that Consuela would have any part in helping with the murder. About the only thing she's willing to believe Consuela did was move Roger's desk over the blood-stain and maybe get rid of some other evidence."

A jogger whizzed by so close that I almost lost my footing. It was like the Southwest Freeway at rush hour out here. In comparison to Houston drivers, the joggers were slightly more sanctimonious and almost as aggressive.

But I wasn't the only one who was getting sidetracked. "Wait a minute," I told Kate. "You never told me what John Carter said to you."

"He told me that he wasn't sure what I was trying to pull, but if I or anyone in my family ever attempted to contact him or his wife again he'd call the police." Beneath her little lavender visor, Kate's face turned grim. "And then Carter laughed. A mean, scary laugh like you hear from kids who enjoy torturing animals. He said that the number of people in my household seemed to be dwindling rapidly. If I didn't watch out my lovely River Oaks home was going to be unoccupied."

I stopped again. "He said that?"

This time Kate didn't prod me to get moving. "Yes. And you know something? I believed him."

SUNDAY MORNING I was drinking coffee and scanning the *Chronicle* when a familiar-looking photo caught my eye. Dr. Larry Nelson sat behind his desk at the mental health center, looking solemn. The headline explained it all: PSYCHIATRIST CLAIMS POWERFUL WOMAN WORKSHOPS DANGEROUS.

Shit! I skimmed the article, then read it more slowly so I didn't miss any of Larry's barely veiled barbs. The article repeated the objections to self-help groups that Larry had already told me. The groups didn't screen for unstable participants; they were potentially dangerous to susceptible individuals and a waste of time and money for everyone else. Larry had also revealed his brother's story in (according to the reporter) a "choked, emotional voice."

This time I wasn't touched by the disclosure. Holding the newspaper in my clenched fist, I marched to the phone. Larry had given me his new home phone number. I dialed it.

His answering machine came on. Larry's taped voice, calm and mellifluous, informed me that he wasn't at home right now, but he was eager to talk to me.

"Larry, this is Liz James." I tried, not very successfully, to keep my voice neutral. No point in preparing him for an attack. "Could you call me when you get in?"

I hung up, feeling more annoyed than ever. He'd used me. All of his oh-so-interested questions over dinner about my media contacts and how I went about pitching story ideas to a reporter were aimed at getting this article published. I'd vetoed the idea when he originally suggested it, asking me to contact the reporter. The story sounded petty and vindictive to me, as if the mental health center, through a spokesman, was officially attacking Kate. So Larry, undeterred, had contacted the reporter on his own.

My phone rang. I grabbed it. "Hello?" Expecting to hear Larry Nelson's voice.

"Have you by any chance read the *Chronicle* this morning?" It was Kate, sounding testy.

"I just read the story." No need to say which story.

"Did you notice that although Larry's brother killed himself after attending a weekend-long encounter group totally unlike my workshops, that Larry's only other example of a harmful self-help group is Powerful Woman?''

''I noticed,'' I said. It had almost seemed, in fact, as if Larry had reserved his most barbed remarks—his professional dismissal, his surges of ironic wit—for Kate's workshops. ''He arranged this story on his own, by the way.'' The minute the words were out of my mouth I felt like a kid making excuses for a misdeed: Johnny threw the ball that went through your window, Mrs. Brown. I was just playing catch with him.

But Kate apparently had other things on her mind. ''He is such an asshole. You know Larry likes to think that it was Roger who broke the two of us up. But if Roger had never come along, I still would have dumped him. Larry had this pattern of treating women like dirt, then being mortally offended when they walked out on him.''

''He did tell me that his wife left him for another man,'' I said.

''That's right. And do you know what Dr. Larry did when she left him? He slashed up all the clothes she'd left in the closet. A friend from Topeka told me the wife came back to pick up the rest of her stuff and found only shreds of cloth on the floor. He even hacked up her shoes.''

I shivered. At the end of my marriage I could remember being strongly tempted to dump my husband's belongings onto the street. I wanted them out of my house, out of my life. But slashing your ex's clothes and shoes to bits with a razor-sharp blade? That was something else. Something scary.

''His ex-wife died,'' I said. ''On her honeymoon. Did you know that?''

''Yeah, I heard. I bet Larry bought a bottle of champagne when he heard the news.''

"You don't mean that you think he had anything to do with her death, do you?"

A pause, as if Kate was considering her answer. "No. I think Larry is perfectly capable of a lot of disgusting things—I know he was spreading ugly rumors about his ex all over Topeka. But I don't think he's a murderer."

Larry had said basically the same thing about Kate when he'd talked to Mel. I wondered how accurate their assessments were.

"I phoned Larry this morning to tell him what I thought of the story," I said. "But he wasn't at home."

"Oh, I bet he was. Sitting right next to the phone, drinking coffee and rereading his newspaper interview. Chuckling while he listened to the angry messages."

I envisioned Larry listening to my message and snickering. "I guess I'll let you go now," I said. My genteel Southern way of saying, "I want to get off the phone."

"Just one more thing. The reason I called, aside from bitching about Larry, was to see if you'd like to go out for dinner with Mel and me tonight. I'm making an effort to be a more attentive parent-substitute."

I didn't really want to go, but I felt as if I should: frequently my response to Kate Quinlan's invitations. "Sure," I said. "Where do you want to go?"

We decided to meet at Ninfa's at seven o'clock. I suggested the restaurant because it was nearby, and it was the noisy, upbeat kind of place where I hoped we could have a quick, pleasant meal and then go home to our separate residences.

I arrived first and let a hostess seat me at a table for four in a corner of the larger room. The place reminded me of Nick. This restaurant was one of our favorite places for Tex-Mex food. On the phone last night Nick had assured me that he would be coming home any day now. Which was also what he'd told me the week before. I alternated between wanting to believe him and feeling annoyed with him for not being able to cut himself loose from his story.

The waiter was putting a basket of tostados on the table when I spotted Mel and Kate walking toward me. Kate was smiling. Mel was not.

"Sorry we're late," Kate said. "Mel and I have been out shopping this afternoon and I guess we just lost track of time."

"Did you buy anything?" I asked Mel, who had already sat down and was busy shoveling tostados into her mouth.

She nodded and swallowed. "Some jeans and high-tops. And Kate made me buy a dress."

"It looked so darling on her," Kate interjected. "I told her she had to get it."

Darling? It was a word I wouldn't have thought Kate even knew—at least not when used as a modifier. I looked from Mel to Kate, trying to imagine the shopping trip.

When the waiter came to take our orders, Kate picked a taco salad and "your largest size margarita." Mel ordered one of the hefty multiple-entree platters and a Coke. "And could you bring some more of those chips?" I ordered my standard: chicken fajitas and a frozen margarita, without salt, the small size.

When Kate excused herself to go to the rest room, Mel turned to me. "She is driving me crazy! She won't leave me alone for a minute. She's talking to me all the time, following me around, wanting to take me shopping or 'do something together.' I just want her to leave me alone."

I patted her hand. "I think Kate feels as if she's been neglecting you and she's trying to make it up to you."

"I like being neglected better," Mel said, looking sullen.

"Kate is worried about you. I am too. I mean John Carter is not exactly the kind of man you want to mess with, Mel.

Nick told me he'd heard that Carter had some thugs break the leg of some guy who wasn't making his car payments."

"Oh, is Nick back now?"

I shook my head. "Still in El Paso."

"Do you miss him?"

"Yes. And as I was saying about you possibly endangering your life when you pull these detective stunts—"

"I *know*," she interrupted. "Kate has covered this. Okay?"

"Okay."

"She keeps telling me how touched she is that I'm doing all this for her." Mel glanced in the direction of the restrooms to see if Kate was coming back yet. "She doesn't seem to get it. I mean I thought about it a lot and I am totally convinced that Kate didn't murder Roger. I don't want her to go to prison for something she didn't do. But that doesn't mean that I *like* her."

This time I glanced up to see if Kate was coming. "Isn't your mother coming home soon?"

"In a week," Mel said. "And I am counting the days."

We both spotted Kate at the same time. "Nice weather we're having, don't you think?" I asked Mel.

Kate sat down and gulped her margarita. She turned to me. "Did I tell you that I read Mel's English paper on Jane Austen? You have to read it, Liz. Mel is a wonderful writer."

When Kate took another swig, Mel rolled her eyes at me.

It was Mel who noticed Larry and Tricia walking to a table on the opposite side of the restaurant. "Isn't that Dr. Nelson and Tricia"—she looked at me—"Dr. Whitmore?"

"It certainly is." I turned for a closer inspection of Drs. Tricia and Larry. Dr. Larry still had not returned my phone call.

Kate stared at them. "The two of them. Who could believe it?'' She shook her head, then grinned. ''I couldn't dream up any better revenge. They really do deserve each other.''

Kate stood up. ''Excuse me for a minute, won't you?''

''What is she doing?'' Mel asked as Kate strolled, margarita in hand, to Tricia's and Larry's table.

''Who knows?''

We both watched, fascinated, as the couple caught sight of Kate. Tricia stiffened, her mouth open. Larry smiled at Kate.

I wish I could have heard what they were saying. Kate talking and gesturing. Larry nodding and talking back. Tricia sitting there with her mouth open, looking as if she were playing a game of Statues.

Then Kate dumped her mega-sized margarita on Larry's head.

That snapped Tricia out of her stupor. She frantically blotted Larry's head with her napkin as he scanned the restaurant, checking out who'd witnessed the scene.

I waved at him. He didn't wave back.

Kate was smiling as she sauntered back to our table.

''Now that,'' Mel said when Kate sat down, ''was cool.''

# Chapter Twenty-two

TRICIA WHITMORE WALKED OUT OF THE CONFERENCE room ahead of me. During the meeting we'd both attended she'd avoided eye contact. Abruptly she stopped, blocking my path. Turned to face me. "I need to tell you something, Liz. There's nothing going on between Larry Nelson and me."

"Okay." Why was she telling me this?

"It was just a simple get-acquainted dinner between colleagues." When I didn't say anything, she added, "Or at least that's what it would have been if Kate Quinlan hadn't shown up."

I shrugged. "I guess being publicly attacked in the media brings out Kate's aggressiveness."

"From what I've heard, everything brings out her aggressiveness."

I turned to walk away. "I've got work I need to do."

She grabbed my arm. I swiveled back to face her, surprised. Shook my arm free.

"I wanted to warn you about the Quinlans," she said. "You don't know what you're getting into, Liz."

"*You* are warning me?" Who the hell did she think she was?

Tricia, as Mel would have put it, didn't seem to get it. "Yes," she said earnestly. "There are things you don't know about them." She checked out the hallway for eavesdroppers, then spoke again in a lower voice. "Mel is a very disturbed young woman. Roger told me that, and I saw it for myself when Mel came to my office. But what else could you expect from a kid with an alcoholic mother and an emotionally absent, neglectful father? The girl probably had to act out to get attention."

"Now you're a child psychologist too?" I enquired sarcastically. "Another way of looking at this is the old commonsense approach. The girl's father was murdered, Tricia. She wants to find out who killed him. Yes, she's being a bit reckless and intense. But it's surprising how many teenagers are."

"Maybe she just doesn't want to face up to who the killer is," Tricia said in a snotty voice.

I assumed she meant Kate. But Tricia added, "Mel is running around in circles trying to convince herself that her own mother isn't a murderer."

"You mean Sissy?" I asked, incredulous.

Tricia nodded, looking smug. "Roger told me that Sissy was enraged that he'd taken Mel from her. It was like a paranoid delusion with her. Everything that had gone wrong with Sissy's life—her drinking, the breakup of their marriage, her losing custody of Mel—was Roger's fault. Not her fault at all."

"A lot of people were angry at Roger," I pointed out. "You, for example. That didn't mean they killed him."

"But Sissy was threatening Roger. And she was becoming increasingly irrational. She'd call him at work, ranting that she wanted her daughter back. Said he didn't love Mel and he was just keeping her to punish Sissy. She even broke into Roger's house once—she must have got the key from Mel—and left dog shit in Roger's study. She told Roger that if he didn't let Mel come back to live with her, she'd hire someone who'd persuade him to see things her way.''

"It's hard to be persuaded with a bullet in your head," I said. "It sounds as if she was threatening to have Roger beaten up, not killed.''

"Maybe when Roger refused to be persuaded the thug killed him.''

"Maybe somebody else shot him before Sissy even got around to looking for her thug. From what I heard she was in pretty bad shape by the time she finally went into treatment.''

Tricia scowled at me. "I'm not here to prove the case against Sissy.''

I really did not like this woman. "Just out of curiosity, Tricia, why are we having this conversation?''

"I wanted to warn you about the Quinlans. But maybe I was wrong about you, Liz. On second thought, you seem like the classic co-dependent, someone who is enabling Kate and Mel to be as destructive as they want. You might benefit a lot from some psychotherapy.''

"Oh, spare me!'' What was it with these shrinks with their diagnostic insults? "If you're so interested in analysis, Tricia, I'd suggest a little self scrutiny. If I were you I'd spend some time pondering why you have so little self-esteem that you'd get involved with a notorious Don Juan who also happened to be your boss? Maybe you should take that issue up with *your* therapist.''

From the corner of my eye I could see that a couple of women from the business office had come out into the hall to find out what was going on. About the same time I could see Tricia noticing them too. She opened her mouth to get in her parting shot, then apparently reconsidered. Without another word, she turned on the heels of her beige pumps and stalked away.

My day did not pick up a lot after that. After the tedious meeting and my acrimonious conversation with Tricia I spent a couple of hours writing a boring brochure that was too much like all the other brochures I'd written over the years. I needed to get out of this job, find someplace to work with new challenges and people who didn't toss around words like co-dependent. About the only high point in my day was when Amanda stopped by to tell me how much she hated the newspaper interview of Larry Nelson. ''Everyone is asking, what made him think that he's the resident expert on self-help groups? It's not as if he's done any research on this. And he looked awfully petty taking those potshots at Kate.''

''I wish someone would tell him that,'' I said morosely. When I phoned him at his office to voice my opinion, his secretary had said nervously that Dr. Nelson was not in.

''Oh, someone will,'' Amanda said cheerfully. She waved as she backed out my door. ''How about lunch tomorrow?''

''Great. You pick the place.''

I WAS fantasizing about chocolate brownies—lots of them—as I drove home from work. Not a good sign. Feeling tired, frustrated and lonely while also harboring mental images of chocolate could easily trigger a major binge, something I didn't need right now.

I didn't notice the Thunderbird convertible in the apartment complex's visitors' parking until its occupant got out of the car. It took me a minute to figure out why the man limping toward me looked so familiar. He was the man who'd talked to me after the Powerful Woman workshop: John Carter, Robin's husband.

"Liz James, right?" He offered me his hand. "I'm John Carter."

His handshake was too firm, like a grade-school bully who tries to mash your hand. "What can I do for you, Mr. Carter?" I asked coolly.

He moved a little closer, too close. The movement and the handshake seemed incongruous. He was a lean, balding man, a bit stooped, only a few inches taller than I. I wondered if he was imitating some thugs he'd seen in the movies.

"I understand you talked to my wife Robin," he said quietly. "An interview for a book that Quinlan woman is writing." When I nodded he said, "That was unfortunate."

"Why unfortunate?" I was suddenly remembering what Nick had said about this guy hiring people to break legs. I scanned the parking lot, looking for someone who might hear me yell, but no one was around.

"Because I don't trust Kate Quinlan to present Robin's experience the way it happened."

The way *he* thought it happened, Carter meant. "I tape recorded the interview," I said, "so I could be totally accurate in reporting what Robin said to me. And she certainly wasn't complimentary about the Powerful Woman workshop."

Carter eyed me, all pretense of friendliness now gone. "You don't seem to understand. I don't care how you write it. I'm telling you not to write it at all. I don't want Robin's story in Quinlan's book. In any form."

"Is that what Robin wants too?" I asked, wondering if I had a hidden death wish.

"Now she does. She realizes that talking to you was a mistake." He inched a bit closer, keeping his eyes on my face. "Look, Robin told me that you were okay. That you were nice to her, respectful. 'Liz is just the paid writer, John,' she said. So I'm not blaming you."

Who was he blaming then? Robin? Or was everything bad that had happened still all Kate's fault?

Carter seemed to be trying on a new role now: beleaguered man appealing for my sympathy. His voice more genial, his body less tense, taking a step backward so he wasn't right in my face. "I'm not saying that you were going to lie about what Robin told you, Liz. It's just that the whole incident is a segment of my life that I'd like to forget. I guess, as our marriage counselor says, I need to tell Mrs. Quinlan how I feel. I'm not real good about sharing my feelings and communicating, but I'm working on it." He smiled at me. I had the sense that he expected me to congratulate him.

I nodded, the best I could do at the moment.

Carter looked disappointed. "I'm hoping I can persuade Mrs. Quinlan to forget about her book. I mean I'd like to put the incident behind me, to move on with my life. That would be hard to do if a year from now I'm reading a book about my own wife running me over with my car. You can understand that, can't you, Liz?"

"Sure," I said, feeling my hands start to sweat. There was something about Carter's reasonable pose that was almost more disturbing than his earlier surliness. Maybe it was the fact that his cold blue eyes belied his genial tone. Or maybe that he was now inching into my space again.

"I'm glad that you can, Liz." Moving even closer so I could smell the stale cigarettes on his breath. "Because Robin and I don't want to see you hurt. And Robin said I needed to warn you."

Warn me about what? I wanted to know but was afraid to ask. Afraid that I wouldn't like the answer.

"I understand that you're getting quite close to Mrs. Quinlan and her stepdaughter," John said in what he probably assumed was a chatty voice. "Melanie, isn't that her name?"

I nodded, feeling as if I might throw up. How did he know Mel's name? How did he know that I was getting close to them?

"Well, if I were you I'd stop hanging out with them. Things might get ugly and I wouldn't want to see you hurt. Robin said I needed to warn you. I'm working on listening to her more."

"I'm sure Robin appreciates that," I said.

He studied me through slitted eyes, as if he was trying to figure out if I was making fun of him. Moved an inch closer.

Behind me I heard the sound of a car pulling into the parking lot.

"So consider yourself warned," John Carter said. He slapped my face lightly with his palm, his eyes mocking me. His touch as intimidating, as obscene, as a real slap.

He turned and limped rapidly to his car. I was still glued to the same spot, my hand clutching my cheek, when he sped out of the parking lot.

I made it to my apartment before the feelings rushed over me: fear mainly, but anger too. I checked and rechecked the dead bolt, wondering if the door was flimsy enough to be kicked in. Twice I went to peek out the mini-blinds, searching for signs of John Carter. Maybe he hadn't finished what he wanted to tell me when the car drove into the parking lot. Maybe Carter would come back to make sure that he'd convinced me.

He knew where I lived. Knew what time I'd be home, the kind of car I was driving, what I looked like. He knew that I'd been spending time with Kate and Mel. That, more than anything else, was the scariest thing: the thought of John Carter watching me, those searing eyes lighting up with amusement. "He's like one of those kids who enjoy torturing animals," Kate had said, and I could see that too.

I circled my apartment, feeling edgy. Poured myself a glass of wine and drank it, while I continued walking. "Robin said you were okay. Just a hired writer. Not your fault. She wanted me to warn you." I remembered what Annette had said about Robin: "I don't know if John Carter actually killed Roger, but she sure as hell believed he did." Robin Carter knew what her husband was like, knew what he was capable of.

I stopped in front of the phone, trying to decide if I should call someone. The police? They would probably say that there was no overt threat, call them again when the man broke a law. Kate? She already knew that the man was dangerous. Probably I needed to talk to her, but right now I wasn't up to it. Amanda then? Amanda, who was a wonderful, empathetic listener, who would rush over here if I asked her. But no, I didn't feel like talking about what had happened. Not even to Amanda.

I fixed myself hot cocoa and scrambled some eggs. Made myself toast with lots of butter and jelly. Comfort foods that reminded me of my childhood.

Eating helped, but not much.

I stopped myself from pacing again. I allowed myself to peer out the window one more time and recheck the dead bolt. Then I moved on to the bathroom.

I filled the tub with hot water and dumped in the rest of a big container of bubblebath that my nieces and nephew had given me for Christmas. Found a big yellow legal pad and a couple of pens. I locked the bathroom door and was about to step into the steaming water when I remembered that I'd once read that Agatha Christie got ideas for her novels while lying in the bath, eating apples and drinking tea, and scribbling her ideas on scraps of paper. I wasn't much of a tea drinker, but the apples didn't sound bad. Grabbing a robe, I headed for the kitchen and came back with a handful of apples and a Diet Coke. If it had worked for Christie (with only a different form of caffeine), I was willing to give it a try.

I lay down in the warm, soothing water, allowing my mind to wander. I'd been telling myself for years that I wanted to write a novel. I'd even started a few, then abandoned them after a few desultory chapters. So if I was writing a novel now, what would I write about? A little coming-of-age novel, told from the female point of view? A nasty roman à clef describing the breakup of my marriage to Max?

No. What I wanted to do—passionately wanted to do— was kill off John Carter. Slowly. Painfully. *Death of A Car Salesman.* I liked the sound of it. Maybe the sinister and totally disgusting salesman dies of botulism at a classic-car meeting and picnic in the country. Unfortunately the victim's car won't start soon enough to get him to the hospital in time to take the antitoxin. And the grieving widow is left to explain to the police that she'd never thought that the mayonnaise would go bad so quickly. No, of course, she never ate potato salad herself; she was on a diet.

Or maybe arsenic in the brownies? I jotted down the ideas on my yellow legal pad. I'd have to research the arsenic and botulism, of course. Pick the form of death that was more painful.

I added more hot water. Smiled. This was fun.

I chomped on an apple, wondering if Agatha felt this sense of exhilaration when planning her characters' deaths. So what next? Who else deserved to die? Aha! The thought rose like an untethered helium balloon. *A Therapeutic Kind of Death.* An uptight blonde psychologist—let's call her Tricia—and a tall, hyper, shifty-eyed psychiatrist—Larry, let's say—are co-therapists of a group of some type. (Details I could get later.) Tricia notices that the clients in their group seem to be becoming increasingly hostile to her and to Larry. Even when she tells each of them in great clinicial detail what is wrong with him or her, they refuse to believe that their lack of progress in the group is entirely their own fault. Larry sides with Tricia, even going so far as to give a newspaper interview describing typical neurotic excuses therapy patients make to themselves for not liking their therapists.

Then the death threats start. A whispered message on an answering machine: "I know you'll be eager to get this message, Larry. Your days on earth are numbered." An anonymous note in Tricia's mail: "I was just curious. In what diagnostic category would you put a dead female psychologist?"

I could hear my own phone ringing in the bedroom. I ignored it. The machine would pick up any message. I didn't feel like talking to anybody right then.

Got back to my legal pad. Flipped to a new page. Sitting up in the tub, I scrawled Chapter One at the top of the page.

# Chapter Twenty-three

THE RING OF MY OFFICE PHONE WAS A WELCOME INTER-
ruption. I'd stayed up fooling around with ideas for a novel
until almost two o'clock. This afternoon I was exhausted
and more convinced than ever that writing brochures about
the mental health center was not the kind of writing I
wanted to be doing right now.

I picked up the phone. "Liz James."

"Liz? Oh, I was so afraid you wouldn't be there."

"Mel, what's wrong?"

She started to cry.

Oh, Lord. Had she found another body at her house?
"Mel," I said, a little too sharply. "You have to tell me
what happened."

I heard her take big, gasping breaths. Finally she tried to
speak. "I got home from school and went to check the mail
the way I always do. There was a package addressed to
me." She stopped, sounding as if she was taking more deep
breaths.

"What was in the box, Mel?"

"A doll." More deep breaths. "A Barbie doll, dressed

just like me, jeans and a big black T-shirt. She had a hole drilled through one eye, Liz! Like someone shot her in the head. Like someone shot *me*!"

Oh, God. I started to shiver the way I had last night. After John Carter left me. "You're not alone, are you, honey?" Trying to sound calmer than I felt, in control. "Is Kate there?"

"No, I don't know where she is," she said, sounding scared.

I had a mental image of someone hiding in the bushes outside the Quinlan house, watching through the window as Mel opened the package. Remembered John Carter's words: You're getting close to Mrs. Quinlan and her step-daughter . . . We don't want you to be hurt . . . Stay away from them . . . I plan to convince Mrs. Quinlan to give up on her book. "Do you want me to come to your house?" I asked.

"I-I don't know." The words came out sounding like a whimper. "No, I want you to stay on the phone. There was a note that came with the box. It said: People who stick their noses in other people's business end up dead in a box."

"Shit," I said, giving up on calm and control. That bastard. I could just picture Carter's mocking eyes, enjoying himself as he issued his warnings.

"Someone doesn't want me investigating Roger's death," Mel said in a high, scared voice.

"That's right. It's a warning to back off."

"So I must be getting close to finding the killer." This time she didn't sound so scared. There was a definite note of triumph in Mel's voice.

"Close enough to get yourself killed," I said angrily. What would it take to convince this child that she was in danger? "This isn't a game of Clue, Mel. If you pick the wrong person to accuse you don't just lose your turn. You're out of the game permanently. And don't fool yourself that driving around accusing people of killing your father is helping anybody. A killer as smart as this one is very unlikely to cave in and say, 'Oh, Mel, you're right, I admit it. I did shoot Roger and Consuela.' The only thing you're doing is setting yourself up as victim number three.''

I heard a door slam in the background. ''It's Kate,'' Mel said, sounding relieved.

Had the girl heard anything that I'd said? Or did she, like a number of other teenagers I knew, just tune out when she didn't like the message?

In the background I heard Kate greet Mel. ''What's up?''

''I've got to go now,'' Mel told me.

Translation: I'm sick of hearing your lecture. ''Wait, Mel, just one more thing,'' I said, before she hung up. ''Who was the package addressed to?''

''To me,'' Mel said, sounding impatient.

''I know. I mean how exactly was it worded?''

''Hold on.'' A pause. ''It was addressed to Miss Melanie Quinlan.''

That was what I was afraid of.

''Talk to you later, Liz,'' Mel said and hung up.

Kate phoned me twenty minutes later. ''The killer sent her that doll, Liz,'' she said without any preamble. ''It has to be the same person. The doll didn't have any shoes on.''

''So?'' I didn't get the significance of no shoes. ''Maybe whoever sent it couldn't find doll-sized high tops.''

''No!'' Sounding vehement. ''When I opened the box with Roger's body in it he wasn't wearing any shoes. I remember thinking how strange it was that he was fully dressed except for his shoes. He only had socks on his feet. And that was what the doll had too, socks but no shoes.''

Why would anyone take off Roger's shoes? Strangely,

my mind focused on the question. Because they were heavy and the killer wanted to make the box he had to transport as light as possible? Because the shoes had fallen off when the killer was trying to get Roger's body in the box, and he or she didn't want to bother with putting them back on? Or maybe there was another reason altogether, a reason that was somehow significant, but now totally escaped me.

"So the person who sent Mel the doll wants me to know that he's the same one who killed Roger," Kate was saying. "A lot of people knew that Roger was shot in the eye the way the doll was, but almost no one was aware that his shoes were missing."

"I think you need to call the police."

"I did." Kate sighed. "I talked to the detective who'd been here before. He listened and asked a few questions, but no one is exactly rushing over here the way they did when Mel found the bloodstain on the carpet. In fact, I had the definite impression that he thought I probably sent Mel the doll. He also wanted to know who else but me knew about Roger wearing no shoes."

It was a pertinent question, but I didn't know how Kate would know the answer. "Did you tell anybody about Roger's stocking feet? Before today, I mean."

"No, not that I can remember. But when I started to think about it, there were a lot of women at my workshop who could have seen the body. Anybody who was sitting near the front of the room could have seen it quite well. He was just lying on the stage until the police got there. Though I don't know how many people would have even noticed his feet."

"You did," I pointed out. "Others could have too." Robin Carter, for instance, who was sitting in the front row. Did Robin, who supposedly had urged John to warn me because what had happened to them wasn't my fault, decide

that Mel needed to be warned too? Maybe Robin had concluded that Mel was another blameless onlooker who
needed protection from John's vengeance; she could have
told herself she was doing Mel a big favor. And wasn't
dressing up a doll more of a woman thing? I knew it was
a sexist generalization, but somehow I couldn't see John
Carter shopping for Barbie's blue jeans and T-shirt. Though
I had no problem at all envisioning him drilling a hole
through the doll's eye.

But when had Robin seen Mel? Whoever had sent the
doll had to have been around Mel enough to realize that
jeans and a solid black T-shirt were her uniform. On the
other hand, John Carter knew an awful lot about me, and
I'd only seen him once before, when he'd waited for Robin
after the first Powerful Woman workshop. It sounded like
someone was spying on Mel and Kate and me.

"... we'll talk about it when you come over tonight,"
Kate was saying.

"I'm sorry," I said. "I didn't catch what you were saying."

"I said we can discuss all of this when you come over
tonight. Remember? You were going to bring over the interviews you've written for the book."

I had forgotten. Fortunately I'd already written the interviews of the participants I'd talked to. "Sure you don't
want to postpone this for another day?" A day when no
one in the family receives a death threat.

"No, I need to get moving with the book. My agent is
breathing down my neck. And having you here will be a
diversion for us."

I told her that I'd be there by seven-thirty. I hung up,
trying to figure out a way to convince Kate that it might
not be a bad idea to postpone the book for awhile. If, that
is, Roger's killer was who I thought it was.

• • • •

MEL OPENED the door when I knocked. She was wearing
a bright yellow Mexican peasant dress with lots of multicolored embroidery on the yoke. I wondered if this was the
dress that Kate had insisted she buy. If it was Kate had
been right; the dress was very flattering on her.

"You look nice," I said, giving her a hug that she didn't
return.

"Thanks. I figured maybe the killer won't recognize me
if I'm not wearing jeans and a black T-shirt." She motioned
for me to come inside. "But I have to warn you, Bobby
Boy is here."

"Who?"

"Bobby Smythe, J. D. Kate's defender."

I remembered that Mel had said that Smythe was angry
with her for phoning the police about the bloodstained carpet without first consulting him. Was he still angry with
her, or was Mel just nursing an old grudge?

"They're in the kitchen," Mel said, leading me down
the hall.

I could hear the voices before we entered the room. "Oh,
whatever you think, Bobby," Kate was saying in a sly
voice. Was she flirting with him?

When I walked into the kitchen, Kate looked up and
smiled at me. Smythe glanced in my direction, too, looking
less pleased to see me. I noticed his hand moving from
where it had been resting—on Kate's arm.

"Oh, Liz, Bobby has some great ideas about expanding
the Powerful Woman workshops," Kate said, her face animated. "Let me try them out on you. Mel hasn't been
much of a sounding board tonight."

I glanced at Mel. Her expression was stony, but I saw
unmistakable hostility in her eyes. Who could blame her?

"Oh, I guess when you have death threats sent to you

in the mail you sort of lose your objectivity about things like other people's workshops," I said, glaring at Kate.

She blushed. The first time I'd seen that happen.

"We have reported the incident to the police," Bobby said quickly. "They assured me they'd check the doll and the note for fingerprints or any other information that could identify the sender."

"And we all know how much good that will do," Mel said, her voice hard. "The only way the police would take this seriously was if the killer signed the note and hand-delivered the box in front of witnesses."

"How was the package sent?" I asked Mel.

"Regular mail, postmarked Houston." She turned to me. "Want to see it?"

"You need to preserve the evidence, Mel," Bobby objected.

"I've already touched it, remember?" Mel sent him a challenging stare. "I promise not to let Liz touch it."

I saw Smythe's jaw tighten. He glanced at Kate, apparently expecting her to reprimand her mouthy stepdaughter.

Kate nodded at Mel. "Okay, show it to her, then bring Liz back so we can get on with our business. I'll finish up with Bobby."

Bobby, I noticed, did not look at all pleased. Because he'd been enjoying Kate's company, I wondered. Or because he wasn't used to being dismissed so casually, particularly by a client whose fate was more or less in his hands.

"He is such a dickhead," Mel said as soon as we were out of earshot.

"Why? What has he done to upset you?"

"He just fired Juanita, for one thing. He and Allison are going to get a divorce, and he told Juanita that he needed to cut his expenses."

"Most people have to cut back after a divorce," I said. And with the absence of the income from Allison Smythe's lucrative child-psychiatry practice, Bobby Smythe might very well have to alter his lavish lifestyle.

"And now," Mel added, "he's hitting on Kate."

So I'd been right about the look that I'd seen Bobby send Kate. "And how does Kate feel about that?"

"She *says* she's not interested," Mel said with disgust. "But that's not the way she acts."

"Has he been over here a lot?"

"Lately he has. It's like he wants to become Kate's advisor on everything: the trial, her workshops and even her book."

He could take over my role as book advisor, I thought as we entered the sunroom. He was welcome to it. The only extra writing that I felt like doing right now involved mystery fiction. I was surprised how much I wanted to get back to the manuscript I'd started last night. Kate Quinlan could finish her book without any more help from me.

Mel led me to a wicker table in a corner of the room. She picked up the brown cardboard box, enclosed in a Ziploc plastic bag. "Here's the evidence." Holding it up for me to see, trying to pretend that she felt dispassionate about it.

I peered at it, remembering the terror of being the recipient of vicious threats from an anonymous correspondent last year. "You don't have to show me this if you don't want to, Mel."

She looked at me. "I want to." Gingerly she opened the bag, then pulled out the doll.

"That's horrible!" The doll's blonde hair had been colored with some kind of marker so that it looked a mousy brown—Mel's hair color. The doll's black T-shirt hung on her—the way that Mel wore her clothes. And the blue jeans completed the doll's look.

And then there was the hole through the doll's left eye. Neatly drilled, a precise round little hole. Obscene.

"Oh, Mel!" I grasped her arm.

"You haven't seen the note." Mel pulled a tissue from her dress pocket and used it to pull out the paper. She held it up so I could see it. A piece of typing paper with a hodgepodge of letters cut out from magazines. Incongruous cut-out letters with their vile message: People who stick their noses in other people's business end up dead in a box.

"He even cut out the apostrophe," I said. Mel sent me a puzzled look. "In people's. And there's a period at the end."

"We'll give him an A in English," Mel said.

"No, think of how much time that must have taken to cut out all those letters," I said. "Paste them down. It almost sounds like something out of a movie, doesn't it? Most people wouldn't have gone to that much effort."

"Most people wouldn't put a dead body in a box and then send it to Kate's seminar," Mel said.

She had a point. I watched Mel drop everything back in the plastic bag, her mouth curled in distaste. When she was through, she returned the bag to the table. "Kate and Bobby"—the sudden venom in her voice saying: Who asked *him*?—"say I shouldn't even talk to anybody else about Roger's murder. They say the killer was giving me a break, warning me. And if I'm smart, I'll take the warning. They're both pissed off that I don't want to take their stupid advice."

"I agree with them." I watched her scowl. This was not what she wanted from me. Tough. "If you are getting close to the killer—and probably you are or he wouldn't be sending you doll corpses—any more investigating you do could cost you your life. I don't see this guy giving you lots of extra chances.''

I could see the stubborn set to Mel's jaw, the flinty look in her eyes. She was more Roger's daughter than she realized. ''But the police aren't doing anything. They figure that they have the murderer—Kate. And they won't even consider any other possibilites.''

''But it's not your job to exonerate Kate. She has a high-priced lawyer to do that, someone who is extremely competent. You may think he's a jerk, Mel, but Bobby Smythe is certainly giving Kate's case a lot of his attention. Besides that, it sounds as if the evidence against Kate is entirely circumstantial. No murder weapon has been found. There are no witnesses, no one who even saw Kate enter the house during the hours when Roger could have been killed. I'm no attorney, but even if Kate does go to trial, I don't think she'll be convicted. I think Kate is going to be fine—without your help.'' I sure as hell hoped I was right.

''That's what Bobby Boy told me,'' Mel said. ''I think he's full of shit.''

So much for my skills of persuasion.

We walked together to the kitchen. When Mel saw that Bobby was still there, her face hardened. ''I'm going to do my homework,'' she said and left the room.

When I'd first come in, I'd placed a manila folder containing my interviews on the kitchen counter. Kate, still sitting at the kitchen table, was now reading what I'd written. ''Could you give me a few minutes to finish reading this, Liz?'' she asked without glancing up.

Bobby stood up. ''I'll guess I'll be going then.'' He glanced at me, smiling. ''Will you walk out with me, Liz? Kate can finish her reading, and it will give us a chance to visit.''

I wasn't sure how much I wanted to visit with Bobby,

but I followed him to the back porch anyway. Kate, I hoped, was a fast reader.

"Kate has been saying how much she likes what you've written," Bobby said. "She's always said what a talented writer you are."

I didn't say anything. I could see why Mel found his proprietorial tone so irritating.

"Mel showed you the package?" Bobby continued. When I nodded, he asked, "Do you have any idea who sent it?"

I looked at him, surprised. "Do you mean do I *know* who sent it?"

"No. I'm not trying to put you on the stand here. Just asking for educated guesses. Brainstorming." He grinned at me, trying to be ingratiating. "I, for instance, would have guessed that the package came from Mel's mother, Sissy, until I heard that the box was sent from Houston. And Sissy is still at the Betty Ford Center—I checked."

I stared at him. "You certainly can't think that Sissy would send her own daughter a death threat?"

"I don't think that Sissy would actually harm Mel. But I do think that if someone informed Sissy that her daughter was snooping around asking a lot of unfortunate questions, Sissy might send Mel a warning to get her to back off. Sissy could have seen sending that doll as protection: protecting herself, of course, but also protecting her relationship with her daughter. Sissy would not want Mel to realize that she murdered the girl's father."

"You think that Sissy murdered Roger?"

Smythe shrugged. "I don't have any proof of it. I do know that shortly before Roger died Sissy threatened to take him to court to regain custody of Mel. Roger consulted me about it. I told him that her chances of getting custody again were miniscule. Sissy was drinking heavily, she didn't have a job and the trust fund she was living on was barely enough to support her. While I don't doubt that she cares very much for her daughter, I know the court would not consider her a fit mother. Apparently another attorney told Sissy the same thing. She was devastated and began to threaten Roger. Told him that if she couldn't get custody of Mel through the courts, she'd find another way.''

"And that's why you think she killed him?" I asked, not bothering to keep the skepticism out of my voice.

He shook his head impatiently. "Sissy was very unstable and very bitter. She blamed Roger for all the misfortunes of her life. In addition she had become friendly with Consuela when she came to the house to pick up Mel. Consuela had motherly feelings towards Mel. I could see Sissy convincing Consuela that it would be in Mel's best interest for her to live with Sissy. Consuela didn't have much use for Roger, who admittedly was not much of a father to Mel. If Consuela helped Sissy—let her into the house Friday morning, helped her move Roger's body and clean up the mess—Sissy could have managed Roger's killing.''

Maybe. But a lot of other people had wanted to get rid of Roger too. And some of them seemed better qualified than Sissy in arranging such an intricate murder. "I thought that Consuela had already left by the time Roger got home on that Friday afternoon," I said. "Tricia Whitmore, who admits to being in the house with Roger early in the afternoon, certainly assumed that the two of them were alone.''

"I'm sure that Roger assumed they were alone too. But it's a big house, and I'm sure that Roger didn't check every room to see if Consuela was hiding there. Or maybe she did leave before he got there and then came back later with Sissy. Consuela had her own key.''

It was too many maybes for me. Particularly when one of the persons accused of the crime was no longer available to give her version of events. I wondered if Bobby even believed the scenario he'd been creating, or if he was just trying out different versions of Roger's murder—versions that didn't involve Kate.

"If I had to guess who sent Mel that doll I would have to pick John Carter." I described Carter's visit to my apartment complex last night, his warning me to stay away from the Quinlans. "The doll could have been his warning to Mel."

Smythe cocked an eyebrow, looking interested. "Did you tell the police about his threats?"

I shook my head. "I figured they'd tell me to call back when he did something besides talk."

Kate's voice right behind me made me jump. "Carter is who I thought sent it." She stood in the doorway to the porch, her hands on her hips. "Yesterday—the same day that he went to visit Liz—Carter threatened me too. He phoned to say that if I didn't stop the publication of my book, it could be a fatal mistake."

"Why didn't you tell me this before?" Bobby said, looking agitated.

"What did you tell Carter?" I asked at the same time.

"I told him that I'd take his views under consideration," she said to me. "Of course, I have no intention of stopping the book."

"Kate, this is a serious matter," Bobby said. "I think we need to contact the police."

Kate shrugged. "They've been so much help to me in the past," she said sardonically. "Remember, I reported Carter's first threat to the detective on the case. Carter told the police that he'd just been angry and didn't mean any real harm. I'm sure he'd find some similar explanation this time. Maybe saying that 'fatal mistake' was just a figure of speech."

"Maybe you could take out the part of the book about Robin," I suggested. "When I talked to her I didn't think she was exactly a ringing endorsement for Powerful Woman."

"She didn't have much to say, did she?" Kate agreed. "Though *I* have quite a lot I'd like to say about her."

Bobby began, "Kate, libel laws are very—"

Kate cut him off. "I've heard it before, Bobby. From you, in fact."

Bobby, looking annoyed, said he was leaving. "By the way, Kate, I'm going to be out of town for a few days. I need to check on my daddy. If you need to get hold of me, call me at the ranch."

"Fine," Kate said. "Give your father my best. Good night, Bobby." She turned to me. "I like what I've read so far of your interviews, particularly the stuff from Annette. Remember what she said about how helpful it was to attend the two workshops? It made me wonder if I shouldn't make the standard workshop two sessions long to include some follow-up."

Mel joined us on the back porch. Had she been watching for Smythe to leave, I wondered. She waited for Kate to finish, then said, "I've been thinking I'd like to go pick up some ice cream, Kate."

"Fine," Kate said, looking distracted.

"Why doesn't Liz drive with me?" Mel said. "We'll only be gone for ten minutes or so."

Kate looked at me. "It's okay with me if you want to go, Liz. It will give me time to finish reading your interviews."

"Sure, I'll go," I said. What I really wanted to do was go home and work on my mystery, but I didn't like the idea of Mel driving alone at night. Particularly not tonight.

"Take my car," Kate called as we headed out the door. "And get me something with chocolate."

Outside Mel headed for her car. Roger's car, a black BMW sedan. "I don't have Kate's keys, and anyway this car is a hundred times better than her boring old Explorer."

She waited until we'd slid into the car to tell me her news. "I meant to tell you before, but when the doll came I forgot about everything else. You won't believe what I found out this afternoon!"

I felt suddenly exhausted. So much for all the lectures—mine, Kate's, Bobby's—about giving up on her detective schemes. "I don't even know if I want to hear it."

"Yes, you do. And don't worry, the person I was talking to was perfectly safe. She's our neighbor who's about eighty years old and is in a wheelchair. Her nurse was pushing her around the block this afternoon when I was coming home from school. It was one of the first times that I'd really talked to her."

"So what did you find out?"

"On the day that Roger died, Mrs. Hellman and her nurse were taking a walk. Apparently they always take a walk from three to three-thirty, unless the weather is too bad. But that day they saw a black sports car parking in front of our house. The driver was a tall, young, blonde woman, Mrs. Hellman said. She saw the woman get out of the car."

"That was at the start of their walk, at three?" I asked. Mel nodded. So this was after Tricia's visit but before Larry's. Presumably Juanita hadn't been near a window to see this arrival.

"But get this," Mel said, her voice loud with excitement. "I called the mental health center to check on what kind of car Tricia Whitmore has. Do you know what it is?"

I shook my head. I couldn't remember ever seeing Tricia's car.

"A black Miata!" Mel announced triumphantly. "A black sports car."

Despite myself, I was interested. "Did this Mrs. Hellman actually see the woman enter the house?"

"No, Tricia was just getting out of the car when they walked by. And by the time they came back from their walk, the car was gone. Mrs. Hellman said she didn't think much about it until she heard that Roger had died that night." Mel shook her head in disgust as she turned the key in the ignition. "I don't know why she didn't mention it before now, but she did say something about having been sick recently."

Had Tricia come back a second time to see Roger? After he'd informed her that he intended to fire her, maybe Tricia had decided to take matters into her own hands, coming back with a gun and a big packing box. But would half an hour be enough time to shoot Roger, shove his body into a box, label the whole thing and get out? Maybe. If you were a strong and efficient woman who knew what she had to do.

Mel pulled out of the driveway and turned right. "So what do you think?" she asked as we approached an intersection.

She was driving too fast for my taste. Did she even see that we had a stop sign? "Mel, watch out!" I cried as I saw a car on our left speeding toward our intersecting street.

Mel slammed on the brakes. Nothing happened. "They don't work!" Mel yelled, grabbing for the hand brake.

Our car sped into the intersection.

The last thing I heard was a scream before the other car slammed into Mel's door.

# Chapter Twenty-four

I WALKED INTO MEL'S HOSPITAL ROOM. SHE WAS LYING in bed, her face pale except for an ugly purplish bruise on her forehead. The cast on her left arm looked thick and ungainly.

"How are you feeling today?" I asked when I got next to her bed. Close enough to see the tight lines around her mouth, the dullness in her eyes.

"Okay," she said, trying to smile. "The nurse said I could have some pain medication soon. They figured out that I don't have a concussion. Just a broken arm and some cracked ribs."

"That's enough," I said. I'd been to the doctor myself this morning. All I had was a case of whiplash and some bruises. I felt achy, but, considering the speed of the car that hit us, I could have felt a whole lot worse.

"What happened to the driver of the other car?" Mel asked. Last night, waiting for the ambulance, she'd been in too much pain to care.

"He's okay." An arrogant, red-faced oil executive who was furious that Mel had run through a stop sign and dented his new Land Rover. "Bruised a bit by the air bag, but that's about it."

"He's the guy you were yelling at, right?"

I blushed. "*He* was yelling. I just pointed out that his time would be better spent calling for an ambulance instead of worrying about his stupid car."

"Gee, stupid is not the word I remember you using," Mel said with a grin. "And trust me, *he* was not the only one who was yelling."

"Did they tell you how soon it will be before you can go home?" I asked in a changing-the-subject voice.

"Tomorrow morning, probably. They wanted to do some other tests this afternoon or else I could have gone home today." Mel's eyes moved to something behind me, someone coming in the doorway.

I saw the big smile on her face before I saw her visitor.

"Mom!" she cried as the diminutive blonde woman I'd seen at Roger's funeral rushed to her bed.

"Baby, how are you?" The woman leaned down to kiss her daughter. Sitting on the bed, she held Mel's face gently in her hands, as she checked out her daughter's injuries. I saw her eyes linger on the cast on Mel's arm.

"I'm okay, Mom. Really. Broken arm and cracked ribs, that's it." Mel made her injuries sound like a minor cold. "Did you just get back? How did you know I was here?"

"Kate phoned me last night. I came as soon as I could get a flight. You're *sure* that you're all right? Kate said there was a possibility of a concussion."

"No concussion—they checked." Mel sounded tired of the topic. She had other things on her mind. "So can I come live with you now?"

Sissy smiled, a smile that transformed her gaunt, well-lined face. "Certainly. You can move in tomorrow."

"Great!" It was the most enthusiasm I'd ever seen from Mel.

It was time for me to leave. "Think I need to get going, Mel," I said, waving at her as I backed to the door.

"No, wait, Liz!" Mel waved me back. "I want you to meet my mother. Mom, this is Liz James, the woman I wrote you about."

Sissy stood up, smiling uncertainly at me. "I'm sorry to be so rude. I was just so worried about Mel . . ."

"You weren't rude, just acting like a mother." I offered her my hand, which Sissy shook with a surprisingly firm grip for such a tiny woman. "I'm glad to meet you, Mrs. Quinlan."

"Sissy," she corrected. "I'm thinking about dropping the Quinlan part and using my maiden name, Alexander, again." She kept hold of my hand. "I'm glad to meet you, Liz. Mel says you've been a good friend to her."

"She's a terrific girl," I said, "and I know how much she's been looking forward to living with you." I studied her face, wondering if Sissy was up to the responsibility. Would she be any better than Kate or I at keeping Mel out of danger?

As if she knew what I was thinking, Sissy said, "Kate mentioned that you were in the car with Mel when she had the accident. What happened?"

"There seemed to be something wrong with the brakes. She tried to stop at a stop sign, but the car didn't even slow down. Another car going through the intersection slammed into Mel's side of the car."

"Somebody tampered with the brakes!" Mel said, sitting up in bed, wincing. "Probably the same person who sent me a doll with a bullet hole in the eye, warning me to stop looking for Roger's killer or I'd end up dead too."

"What?" Sissy's face grew pale. She sank down onto

Mel's bed, looking as if she was going to faint. "Someone is threatening you?"

No one seeing this woman's anguished face could suggest that she might have been the sender. Not even Bobby Smythe. I patted her shoulder, offering what little reassurance that I could muster. "The doll and the car brakes are not necessarily connected. Maybe the brakes just gave out without anybody tampering with them."

"But they were fine that afternoon when I drove home from school," Mel said.

I shrugged. "I had to have the brake linings on my car replaced, and it seemed as if I didn't have a whole lot of forewarning that something was going wrong. And if your car was sitting in the driveway all evening, it would have been hard to tamper with it without anyone noticing." And it didn't make sense for the killer to warn Mel to back off then not wait to see if she was following his orders before proceeding to a more serious warning. Unless, of course, he'd intended to harm Mel no matter what she did.

Neither Sissy nor Mel looked reassured by my car problems. Sissy made Mel repeat every detail about the package and its contents. Her face grim, she added, "Now tell me everything you did to find Roger's killer."

Mel told her, brushing over the more embarrassing details, but giving her mother the essential facts.

When she was done, Sissy stared off into space, thinking. "Maybe I should take you somewhere out of town for awhile. We'll tell your school that you're recuperating from your injuries, and you can do the work at home."

"I don't want to go out of town," Mel said in a whiny voice.

The fierceness in the small woman's face surprised me. "I don't care what you want. It's my job to take care of you now—to keep you alive. And I intend to do that."

Mel opened her mouth to protest, but Sissy cut her off. "You've done more than enough to help Kate Quinlan. Let Kate prove her own innocence." She glanced at me, her face hard. "If she can."

"I UNDERSTAND you visited Mel at the hospital today," Kate said shortly after she'd ushered me into her house. "How do you think she looked?"

"Pale and in pain. But she seemed very pleased that Sissy is back."

"That makes two of us," Kate said. "I meant to get over to the hospital myself, but there are all these last minute details I need to attend to for my next Powerful Woman seminar—it's this Saturday. I intended to tell you that last night, but with Mel's accident, I forgot to mention it. Anyway, I did talk to Mel and Sissy and her doctor on the phone. The doctor said Mel didn't have a concussion and her other injuries aren't serious."

I stared at her. It hadn't taken long for her concerned parent-substitute role to lose its luster. "She could have died last night," I said icily. "There was something wrong with the brakes. Mel slammed her foot down a couple of times, and nothing happened. If the car that hit us had been going much faster . . ."

Kate gripped my arm. "I know," she said quietly. "It came out badly. What I meant is I'm grateful that her injuries aren't life-threatening." Kate led me to the back of the house. "What I don't understand is what could have possibly gone wrong with the car. Roger always kept his car in impeccable condition, and Mel hadn't mentioned that she was having any trouble with the brakes."

We entered the kitchen where Kate had papers spread over the table. "I seem to do most of my work in here for some reason. Would you like something to drink?"

I shook my head. A thought had been nagging at me. "You mean you didn't know that there was something wrong with Mel's car?"

"Of course not," Kate said, her back to me as she cleared off some space for me at the table.

"Then why did you tell Mel to take your car last night?"

"I did?" Kate glanced over her shoulder at me, looking puzzled. "I don't remember saying it, but probably I didn't want the two of you to run out of gas at night. Mel is always trying to drive with an empty gas tank and then, when the car suddenly sputters to a stop, has to walk to the nearest gas station."

It was a plausible excuse—Mel seemed like the kind of driver who'd forget to check her gas gauge—but it seemed strange that Kate couldn't remember offering the girl her car.

Kate motioned for me to sit down across from her at the table. "By the way, the interviews you wrote are great," she said, patting the manila folder in front of her. "Bobby wants me to reconsider using the Robin Carter interview— which I may or may not do—but I plan to use the other interviews verbatim in my book."

"Terrific," I said. "I listed the hours I worked for you." Twenty hours at one hundred dollars an hour, to be more precise. I pulled the paper from my purse and handed it to her.

Kate glanced at it. "Fine. What I wanted to tell you about is the workshop Saturday. It's going to be different from the other ones, kind of a free preview of what the Powerful Woman workshop really is. This way I can clear up all the misunderstandings. Explain to the women what they can expect to get out of the workshop. Explain to the men, too—I mean, explain what they can expect if their wife or girlfriend or daughter becomes a Powerful Woman.

That part was Bobby's idea, inviting men to come to this preview lecture.''

"Interesting idea," I said.

"I should be getting great press coverage. I contacted the media this morning. You know that's one good thing about John Carter's and Larry Nelson's attacks on Powerful Woman. Reporters view it as a hot story."

"The any-publicity-is-better-than-no-publicity theory," I said morosely. It was a theory that made most public relations professionals—including me—cringe.

"I've invited some of the women who've already completed the workshop to talk about their experiences," Kate continued, sounding excited. "Most of them agreed to come. I also invited Sissy and Mel to attend. Sissy said she might come if they're still in town; she said she could use some extra power right now. And Larry Nelson agreed to come. I told him that it wasn't fair for him to criticize me without even knowing what a Powerful Woman workshop is like. He said he'd probably bring Tricia Whitmore. And, of course, Bobby will be there too."

I looked at her. Larry and Tricia. Sissy and Mel. Bobby. "How about John and Robin Carter? Did you invite them too?"

Kate ignored my tone. "No, but knowing them," she said, "they'll probably be out in front picketing."

"I need to get home," I said. "So if you'd like to just write me a check . . ."

Kate smiled ruefully. "Oh, I'm not sure what I've done with my checkbook. I'll send you the check."

That was what she'd told Lorna Bell, who still hadn't received payment for all her work at the earlier workshops. "I'll wait here until you find it. Why don't I check your purse while you look around the house?"

"You hard pressed for cash, Liz?" Not smiling anymore.

"Oh, I just figure I deserve better, Kate."

Kate stood up and marched from the room. She returned five minutes later with my check. "I must say," she said as she handed it to me, "that you've made big leaps forward in your assertiveness skills, Liz."

I smiled at her. "Yes, I have, haven't I?"

"So I'll see you on Saturday morning?" Kate asked as she walked me to the door.

Not if I had anything to say about it. "I'll let you know."

"You don't want to miss all the excitement," Kate said as she opened her front door.

There was something about the way she said it that made me shiver. Or maybe it was just the effect of the chilly night air as I hurried to my car.

# Chapter Twenty-five

I HAD FORGOTTEN WHAT IT WAS LIKE TO DRIVE ON THE freeway with my sister. But the memory, like a recurring toothache, came back with a sharp stab as Margaret zoomed onto the entrance ramp and started maneuvering in and out of traffic. "The woman in the gray Toyota you just cut off is shooting you the bird," I pointed out.

"Ignore her," Margaret said blithely. "I don't want to be late for this workshop."

"If you keep driving like this we might never arrive at all," I said sourly. I wasn't at all thrilled to be going to another Kate Quinlan lecture.

But Margaret had wanted me to go with her. "I'm sorry I said all those mean things about her before," she said. "I'd really like to go hear what she has to say."

I knew Margaret meant this as a conciliatory gesture. The relationship between us was still strained. Aside from discussing her kids, we barely talked to each other. I started to suggest that we do something else together instead. I didn't think she'd enjoy the lecture, and I figured I'd heard enough of Kate Quinlan's ideas to last a lifetime. But before I could speak Margaret added, in a small, totally un-characteristic voice that cut me to the quick, "I want for us to do this together. I miss you, Liz. I miss you being a part of my life." So here we were on our way to a lecture that I suspected neither of us really wanted to attend.

Accelerating, Margaret cut into the far right lane. Waving at the driver who was honking at her, she asked, "So what time does Nick get in tonight?"

"Five-thirty. I hope I'm still alive to meet him at the airport."

"You worry too much, Lizzy." Margaret exited the free-way at a speed not remotely near the posted limit. "Actu-ally I've had very few accidents." By the time we arrived at the workshop, the high-school auditorium was almost two-thirds full, with new arrivals pouring through the door. I spotted Mel and Sissy sitting in a back row. Mel's left arm was still in a cast. With her right arm she waved for us to join them.

I introduced Margaret to the two of them, then asked Mel how she was feeling.

"Better," she said dismissively, obviously tired of the question. "Did you see Drs. Whitmore and Nelson sitting over there?" She pointed a few rows ahead of us where, sure enough, Larry and Tricia were sitting, their heads close together in some animated conversation. Apparently they had moved beyond the "simple, get-acquainted dinner be-tween colleagues" stage.

Sissy turned to me. She looked more relaxed than when I'd seen her in the hospital. I could now see the humor in her deep-set eyes. "Mel wanted to march up to them to ask the woman why she'd returned to Roger's house on the afternoon he died. I managed to stop her."

Mel rolled her eyes at me. "She's worse than Kate. She pays more attention."

"Damn right," her mother said, but she was smiling.

From the corner of my eye I saw Tricia walk up the aisle to the auditorium door.

"I'm going to the rest room." Mel turned wide eyes on her mother. "That is if it's all right with you, Mommy."

"Sure." Sissy shook her head in mock distress as Mel left.

I patted Margaret's hand. "See what you have to look forward to when your kids are teenagers?"

Margaret groaned. "I don't want to even think about it. Liz, is that blonde woman with the curly hair over there Kate?"

It was. From the front of the auditorium, Kate waved at us. She looked as if she was coming to speak to us when Bobby Smythe stopped her and started talking animatedly.

Sissy leaned toward me, her voice low and confiding. "You know, considering how much I used to loathe Kate, I'm astonished that I've actually started to like her. We had a great conversation when I went to her house to pick up Mel's things."

"I was kind of surprised when Kate told me that you were coming to her lecture," I admitted.

"She talked me into it. I told her I could use a little empowerment about now." Sissy smiled ruefully. "But that's not why I started to like her. I changed my mind about her when she told me what a bastard Roger was. That I could relate to. She said that Roger was cheating on her too. With lots of women. He was even sleeping with their next door neighbor."

I turned to her, startled. "Which neighbor? Did she say the woman's name?"

Sissy thought about it. "Tricia? No, that was the other one, the one he worked with. I think it started with an A, a kind of long name. Annette? Amanda?"

"Allison?" I suggested, remembering the tall, dark-haired child psychiatrist I'd seen at the Quinlan house after Roger's funeral.

"That's right," Sissy said. "Allison. Apparently Allison's husband was very upset when he found out about their affair. He was the one who told Kate about it."

Which explained why Bobby and Allison were now getting a divorce. Sissy started to say more, but when she spotted Mel returning she changed topics. "Now how old are your children?" she was asking Margaret when I stood up to let Mel get to her seat.

Instead of passing me, Mel motioned for me to join her in the aisle. "I have something to tell you," she whispered when I was next to her. "I talked to Tricia Whitmore in the bathroom. She said that she did return to our house around three that Friday afternoon. She wanted to tell Roger that she'd been to the EEOC and if he fired her, she was going to file a complaint against him. But when she rang the doorbell no one answered."

Larry Nelson, I remembered, had said the same thing. No one had answered the door when he was at the Quinlan home an hour later. Had Roger already been dead by three? Or was one or both of the visitors not telling the truth?

"She could be lying, of course," Mel said. "But she didn't *look* as if she was."

I raised my eyebrows, surprised. I would have thought that Mel disliked Tricia so much that she'd distrust anything Tricia said in her own defense. Maybe Mel was a better detective than I'd thought. Perhaps Roger's killer had realized how good she was too.

At that moment Kate took center stage. The lecture was officially beginning. "I guess we need to sit down," I told Mel.

A movement behind us made me turn around. John and

Robin Carter were marching toward us, making their grand entrance. Although John was still limping he had the ramrod-straight posture and the arrogant expression of a conquering hero coming to claim his reward. By his side, Robin looked grim and uncertain, a woman steeling herself for an ordeal.

Still in the aisle, Mel and I had to step aside to let them pass. Carter nodded at me. Robin flashed me a tentative smile. I thought she was trying to tell me something, as I watched the two of them make their way to the front of the auditorium. But I didn't have a clue what it was.

Kate, beginning her remarks, pretended not to notice the Carters, who had moved to seats in the second row that someone had held for them. Mel and I moved back to our own seats.

"Who's that?" Mel whispered to me, nodding at the Carters.

"John and Robin Carter," I whispered.

"He looks better in person than on TV."

"Hush," her mother told her, holding one finger to her lips.

I settled back in my seat, wishing I were somewhere else. I watched Bobby Smythe, his expression grim, stride up the aisle of the auditorium and out the door.

A minute later Tricia Whitmore came in the door, returning to her seat next to Larry. In contrast to the Carters, Tricia looked like someone trying to be as inconspicuous as possible: a latecomer embarrassed by her tardiness. As she passed my seat, I saw her shoot an unfathomable look in our direction. Was Tricia wondering whether Mel had believed her explanation of her second visit to the Quinlan house on the day Roger died?

I only half listened to Kate's introduction, most of which I'd heard before. The auditorium was almost completely full now, a group of mainly women, with a sprinkling of men. Apparently fewer men than Bobby Smythe had anticipated were interested in understanding the Powerful Woman in their household—a fact that didn't surprise me at all.

I wondered if Nick were back in town today whether he'd have come to this lecture. Probably not. The concept of self-improvement turned him off. And while Nick, to his credit, always seemed to appreciate smart, independent women, I doubted that he wanted Kate Quinlan's blueprint for understanding them bettter.

I recognized a sizeable number of journalists sitting near the front: a woman who wrote a lot of freelance features; a *Chronicle* reporter with a photographer; a Channel 11 TV reporter with a cameraman. Obviously Kate had suceeded in contacting the local media. Or had John Carter, another avid publicity-seeker, contacted them?

Kate, I thought, had somehow made her speech sound more like advertising copy. She was telling basically the same information as in her earlier lectures, but this time the account of her personal story and the conclusions she'd gleaned from her experience seemed more succinct, her presentation more polished. Before Kate had seemed like a woman sharing her personal story with us. This time she sounded like a professional speaker. Every gesture, every clever quip seemed to scream that Kate Quinlan was marketing her little workshop for national exposure.

My sister, I noticed, seemed fascinated with what Kate was saying. Several rows ahead of us Larry Nelson was taking copious notes. Sissy, too, looked interested. Mel, on the other hand, was clearly bored and restless. I flashed her a sympathetic smile. I could relate.

Turning back to feign attention, a thought suddenly struck me. Neither John nor Robin Carter had appeared to recognize Mel. I leaned over my sister to whisper to the teenager, "Have you ever seen the Carters before?"

Mel shook her head. "Talked to her on the phone, but never saw either of them." She shrugged apologetically at me when her mother's glare abruptly ended our discussion.

But didn't that mean that John Carter couldn't have been the person who sent her the Mel-doll in the box? Whoever had sent that was well acquainted with the way Mel looked. The doll with its jeans and oversized black T-shirt, the straight, brown, shoulder-length hair was a very accurate rendition of Mel's usual appearance. Yet it was very clear to me from the way John Carter's eyes had swept over the two of us, then stopped only on me, that he had not recognized the girl standing next to me as Roger's daughter. Of course, maybe John had delegated the Mel job to someone else. Perhaps the same person who had spied on me. Or the one who'd killed Roger.

Kate was telling the group that we were going to do a little exercise she liked to use in the Powerful Woman workshops. Terrific. The ten-minutes-to-list-everything-in-your-life-that-you'd-like-to-change exercise. My favorite. This time Bobby Smythe, apparently Kate's new assistant, passed out the pencils and paper.

Irritably, I started listing anything I could think of. I still wanted to play the harpsichord, buy new furniture, move to Europe for a year. I still wanted to lose ten pounds—the same extra ten pounds I was carrying around from the last time I did this stupid exercise.

I stopped. On my left Margaret was scribbling away, a big grin on her face. I glanced over to see what she'd written. "Do your own work," she said and kept writing. My sister wanted to go to medical school! It was number one on her list. I wondered how serious she was about this ambition. I wondered why I never knew that she wanted to be a doctor. Then another thought: Margaret would be a very good physician.

Somehow that made me take the exercise more seriously. So, I thought, what did I really want to do with my life? The answer was so simple—and so obvious—I was startled. I was still writing, envisioning my new life, when Kate asked everyone to stop. I kept writing until Bobby Smythe was at our row to collect pencils.

I barely paid attention as Kate talked about what other graduates of Powerful Woman had gotten out of the class. Annette spoke for a few minutes about starting her own dressmaking business, saying she never would have done it without Kate's encouragement. The acerbic older woman from my first group (Beige Pantsuit) said that after attending Kate's workshop she'd decided to go back to college to become a CPA. "And it's been damn hard too, competing with all those twenty-year-old hotshots," she added. "But I guess it's better than being a bored-out-of-my-mind housewife."

"Hold on a minute." John Carter was on his feet. "While we're on the subject of women's experiences at your workshop I'd like to say something about what happened to my wife. Your workshop isn't always as beneficial as you claim it is, Mrs. Quinlan. In fact, my wife walked out of your workshop and tried to kill me."

I saw the flash of a camera, noticed that the bored-looking TV camera man was now on his feet filming.

Kate regarded Carter with a look of thinly veiled contempt. "Perhaps you should let your wife speak for herself, Mr. Carter. Let her describe her own experience at the workshop."

Robin Smythe stood up. She shot Kate a venomous look—also captured by the photographer. "Attending the Powerful Woman workshop was the worst mistake of my life," she said in a loud but nervous voice. "I would never have attempted to run over my husband if you hadn't goaded me to act now, do something, stop putting up with John's treatment of me. Everybody was chanting, 'You deserve better.' It was like a cult, like mind control, making me do something I never would have done on my own."

Kate regarded her calmly. "Did I ever suggest that you run over your husband?"

Robin shook her head. "Not in so many words, but you told me to stop making excuses, to stop putting up with his crap."

"Did I give you mind-altering drugs?" Kate continued. "Or torture you? Deprive you of sleep or food or water?" When Robin didn't respond, Kate answered her own questions. "No, I did not." The expression on Kate's face grew harder. "Even under hypnosis people don't commit violent acts that are against their basic values. So Ms. Carter, I suggest you take responsibility for your own actions—something I *was* trying to teach you to do in my workshop."

John was on his feet again. "It's *you* who don't want to take responsibility for what you did. You told these women that they should get rid of the men in their life—the way you told them that you did. It was men who didn't take them seriously, men who wouldn't give them the job promotions they deserve. You told them they had to correct this situation—to right all the wrongs that men had inflicted on them. And at least two of the women in that workshop took you at your word. My wife, who tried to run me over. And another woman who assaulted her male boss. Don't you think it surprising, Mrs. Quinlan, that two previously non-violent women suddenly turned on the men in their lives immediately after attending your workshop? They wanted to be a Powerful Woman—just like you."

Kate's face was flushed, but when she spoke her voice was still calm. "I guess I see what happened in another way, Mr. Carter. I told your wife and all the other women here to envision the kind of life they really wanted—a rich, rewarding life. Robin apparently decided that her life would be richer and more rewarding without you in it. If she had asked me for specific suggestions, I would have recommended divorce as a better way to accomplish that than homicide."

"She was brainwashed," Carter yelled, turning to face the camera. "And I have proof of it. Experts who saw her, who will testify to her mental condition." Kate moved to the edge of the stage. When she spoke her voice was softer, almost sympathetic. "It's hard to accept the fact that your wife hated you enough to want to kill you, isn't it, Mr. Carter?"

With a roar of fury Carter leaped out of his seat, pushing his way towards Kate. He was at the foot of the stage when Bobby Smythe tackled him. Someone screamed as their entangled bodies crashed to the floor.

That was the last that I saw. The people in front of us stood up to see better, blocking my view. A woman was still screaming when a police officer came rushing down the aisle to break up the fight.

"Everyone, please sit down," Kate shouted into the microphone. "Let the police handle this."

We sat. So at least I was able to watch the police officer in the front of the auditorium clasp handcuffs on John Carter while the cameras recorded it all. Heard Robin shriek, "John!" as her wild-eyed husband was taken into police custody. Glimpsed the stealthy look of satisfaction that passed between Kate Quinlan and Bobby Smythe.

Mel leaned over and touched my arm. "Hey, this was better than I expected," she said.

# Chapter Twenty-six

THE POWERFUL WOMAN FREE INTRODUCTORY LECTURE was over. "Well," my sister said, standing up and stretching, "I wouldn't have missed this one for the world."

Others apparently felt the same way—not necessarily for reasons that Kate Quinlan would want listed in Powerful Woman's promotional brochure. The reporters in the audience were clustered around Kate, looking for some last quote on her take of the morning's events. The audience members I saw filing out of the auditorium all seemed to be talking animatedly. "I bet Bill is going to be sorry that he didn't come with me," I overheard a tall auburn-haired woman tell a friend. "Particularly when he sees all the shouting tonight on the evening news."

Standing in the corridor, Bobby Smythe was beaming. When he spotted the four of us, he hurried over. "I think it really went well, don't you?"

I wondered about his criteria. Certainly the lecture had rated high in entertainment value and in media attention. On the other hand, I wasn't sure how many of the audience members had been persuaded to enlist in the real Powerful

Woman workshop—the one you had to pay for.

"Kate was cool," Mel said with genuine admiration. "I mean it didn't even faze her when that Carter guy started coming after her. And after the policeman took him away, she just went on with her lecture as if nothing had happened."

Bobby nodded happily. "Kate's a real professional." He looked at me. "And having Carter go ballistic like that in front of a roomful of people and a TV camera is the best thing that could have happened for our case."

"It certainly was a good thing that the police got here so quickly," I said. "Unusual too."

"Oh, I alerted the police the minute I saw Carter," Bobby said. "I had a feeling something like this might happen." He turned back to Mel. "How's your arm?"

"Okay."

He smiled a phony, paternalistic smile at her, a grown-up who wasn't sure what to say to a kid, but felt he should say something. "It's nice to see you in a dress for a change, though I see you kept the tennis shoes."

Mel sent Bobby a look so frigid that even he noticed. He turned his attention to Sissy. "I'm glad that Mel is going to be able to live with you. That seems like the best arrangement for everybody."

"Yes, it is," Sissy said. She waited until Bobby moved on to another group before adding, "The best arrangement for him too. This is a man who wants to be alone with Kate."

"I noticed that too," I said, remembering the way that Bobby had draped his arm around Kate's waist when he talked with her before the lecture, and their shared look of satisfaction afterward. Not to mention Bobby's tackling of John Carter when Carter was about to attack Kate.

"Didn't I tell you Mr. Smythe was hitting on Kate?" Mel asked me, looking smug.

I nodded, feeling preoccupied. Something was nagging at me. I had the sense that I'd learned something significant this morning, but I wasn't sure what it was. John and Robin Carter seeming not to recognize Mel. John Carter's uncontrollable fury, his irrational blame of Kate for his wife's actions. Trica Whitmore admitting that she'd gone back to the Quinlan house, but no one answered the door. Larry Nelson saying the same thing, but an hour later. Tricia and Larry, strolling out the door a minute ago, arm in arm. Kate and Bobby, another unlikely twosome, looking as if they too might be becoming a couple.

I waited until Mel was talking to Margaret then turned to Sissy. "When did you say that Bobby told Kate about Roger and Allison's affair?"

She shrugged. "I'm not sure. A while ago, I think. Kate said something about not being very sympathetic when he told her, because she was so busy working full-time and trying to make all the arrangements to set up her workshops."

Behind me I heard familiar voices. I turned in time to see Larry Nelson smiling down at Mel, saying something. Probably another inquiry about her health, considering the sudden scowl on her face. Next to them, Bobby Smythe was talking to Margaret. Whatever he was saying she was listening intently.

Sissy too had seen Mel's scowl. "I think we need to get going. I found a new place, a town house I'm renting in Bellaire, and we need to finish unpacking."

"So you decided to stay in town after all?"

Sissy nodded. "Mel has convinced me that she'll give up her detective stunts if we stay in Houston and she can finish out the school year." For a second, the worried look

I'd seen in the hospital returned to her small face. "I just hope it was the right decision."

I hoped so too. Before I could say anything, though, I felt a light tap on my shoulder. "I'm sorry to interrupt, ladies," Bobby said, "but Kate wanted to see you, Liz. She asked me to come get you."

When I looked hesitant—I was not up for another extended conversation on the career aspirations of Kate Quinlan—he added, "She said it would only take a few minutes."

"Okay," I said, not very graciously. I looked around for my sister, but she was nowhere in sight. "Would you tell Margaret where I am?" I asked Sissy. "She's probably gone to the rest room."

Sissy nodded and I followed Bobby down the hall. "Where are we going?" I asked as we passed the auditorium door.

"Oh, Kate's out in the back parking lot. She was taking something to her car."

And why couldn't she have just waited until some more convenient time to have this important conversation with me? I thought irritably. But no, everyone had to be at the beck and call of Kate Quinlan, Powerful Woman. Bobby opened a heavy door that led out to a small parking lot I hadn't seen before. I walked out. "Kate's not here," I said. Only Bobby's green Jaguar was parked there.

"She must have parked in the side lot," Bobby said quickly. "Come on, we'll drive over there to meet her." He took my arm, steering me toward his car.

"No, my sister is waiting for me." I pulled my arm free from his grasp. "Tell Kate I'll phone her this afternoon."

To my astonishment Bobby darted in front of me, blocking the entrance to the school door. "Your sister has already left. She had an emergency phone call from home. I told her I'd see that you got home. So you'd better come with me."

There was something about the narrow-eyed way in which Bobby was watching me that made a chill run down my spine. I'd seen that look before. In a documentary that followed a mountain lion stalking its prey. "What kind of an emergency was it?" I asked, trying very hard to sound calm.

"Something about her children. I think one of them had an accident."

Smythe caught my arm as I swiveled to make a run for it. "Don't even think about it," he snarled into my ear. He wrenched my right arm behind my back, jerking it upward until I screamed in pain. "Now we *are* going to my car."

The bastard was enjoying himself. I could hear it in his voice, the glint of satisfaction in his cold eyes. He'd probably be in ecstasy if he heard my bone crack.

Or if he got to commit another murder.

Smythe pushed me to the car. He unlocked the passenger door and ordered me inside. "Oh, and in case you have any stupid ideas about jumping out of the car," he said, pulling a gun from his briefcase, "I want you to know that I'm an excellent shot."

I believed him. He backed around the front of the car, keeping the gun aimed at me, while I glanced furtively around the parking lot. Where was everybody? I spotted a few cars parked at the far end of the lot, but no one seemed to be coming for them. I wondered if Bobby had really told Margaret that she had an emergency at home. Would she, or maybe Sissy, come looking for me when I didn't return?

Except by then it would probably be too late.

Bobby slid into the driver's seat, locking the doors after him, keeping the gun pointed at me. He turned on the ignition, put the car in gear and sped out of the parking lot like a man on a mission. A mission, I felt quite confident, that I'd rather not know about.

"Where are you taking me?" My voice came out an octave higher than usual.

"I'll let you know when I decide," he said, shooting me a sidelong glance. He made a sharp left out of the parking lot, heading away from the high school. At the next corner he turned right onto a multi-lane street, speeding through an orange light.

Now that we'd left the high school, Smythe seemed more relaxed. After a few blocks of silence, he turned to me, "If you do what I tell you, you'll be all right," he said, sounding more like the Bobby Smythe I knew: bright, bossy, compulsive and rather patronizing. "I am not an unreasonable man."

I myself questioned the validity of that last statement, but it didn't seem like the time to argue. I very much wanted to believe his assurance that he wouldn't harm me, but I wasn't sure that I did. "What . . . what do you want me to do?"

He turned to me. "I just want you to understand," he said in a small, sad voice.

I could feel my palms get sweaty. "Understand what?"

"I overheard you asking about Allison a few minutes ago. And I decided I needed to explain to you my version of events"—another sidelong glance—"since you're so interested."

Bobby seemed to be slowing down a bit as he started his story. Surreptitiously I glanced at the door, wondering if I could manage to unlock and open the door. Certainly there had to be another stoplight within the next half mile.

"I have always been faithful to Allison," Bobby was saying. "Always. My father was a man who had many casual affairs, and I saw what that did to my mother. She ended up killing herself after discovering my father in bed—their bed—with the new maid. The woman didn't mean anything to him. Daddy sobbed at her funeral; it was my mother who he'd loved—and who he killed with his selfish escapades. I determined then that I'd never cheat on my wife. I told Allison that before I married her, and I made clear how I felt about absolute loyalty and fidelity to one's spouse.''

I could feel Bobby's eyes on me again. "So you see, don't you, that I couldn't forgive her transgression with Roger? Even when she told me that the affair meant nothing and didn't affect how she felt about me—the same things my father said after my mother had died. I told Allison that I had made my feelings on the subject very clear at the beginning of our marriage, and she had chosen to ignore them—ignore them for a fling with Roger Quinlan of all people, that pathetic womanizer."

"So you decided to get rid of Roger?" I asked when he didn't go on with the story.

"Of course," he said irritably, as if I was being unforgivably slow. "I thought of sending the box to Allison, rather than Kate. But then I decided I had other plans for Allison—plans which would not announce to the world that my wife of twenty years had cuckolded me." He turned to me again. "Aren't you going to ask me what I'm going to do to Allison?"

Actually I wasn't, but I was getting a very strong suspicion that when his story ended Bobby intended for me to conclude as well. A criminal lawyer did not want a lot of witnesses for the prosecution walking around. "Okay, what are your plans for Allison?" I finally asked when I realized he was waiting impatiently for my question.

Bobby smiled. A smile so chilling that I would have risked leaping from the car right then—never mind the stoplight—if I hadn't at that moment happened to glance at the sideview mirror.

"I'm working on that right now," he said. "But first I need to take care of the unforeseen—and, I admit, unfortunate—consequences of Roger's death. I need to concentrate all my energy on getting Kate exonerated. It was very unfair that she's had to suffer for Allison's and Roger's sins. I hate unfairness, don't you? As I always told Allison, I am an extremely fair man."

And a very unbalanced one. I forced myself not to glance again at my side mirror. "I always thought you were fair," I agreed.

The car behind us started to honk.

Startled, Bobby glanced in the rearview mirror. "What the hell?"

I turned around, pretending this was the first time I'd seen the car. "It's Kate," I said. And Margaret. "She wants you to pull over."

He checked the rearview mirror again. "Who's that with her—the driver?"

"My sister." Who, besides laying on her horn, was now moving alarmingly close to us.

Margaret's car nudged our bumper. The impact slammed our car into the left lane.

"Is she crazy?" Bobby yelled as he pulled on the steering wheel.

"I always thought so," I muttered. "She's had a *lot* of accidents."

Margaret bumped him again.

This time we barely missed hitting the curb.

Cursing, Bobby managed to slam on the brakes. He'd planned on killing me, not both of us.

Unbuckling my seat belt, I reached for the door. Too late. Bobby jabbed the gun into my ribs. "Stay here until I come around to get you. You move and you're dead.''

By the time he was pulling open my door, Margaret and Kate were out of their car. Bobby yanked me from the passenger seat, the pistol at my head. "Do you want me to shoot her?" he yelled at the two women hurrying toward him.

"She is kind of a pain in the ass," my loving sister replied.

"Bobby, why are you doing this?" Kate asked.

I could feel the arm he had around my neck tighten. "I'm doing this for us, Kate," he said. "For you and me so we can make a new life together."

And he'd told *me* he was doing it because he wanted me to understand.

Kate's head tilted to one side, considering what he'd said. "How does shooting Liz help us?"

I could hear Bobby breathing heavily. I watched my sister's face, looking for some sign of what their plan was for getting me out of this. Margaret always had a plan. But the only thing I saw on her small, round face was terror.

"I want the two of us to be a team," Bobby was telling Kate. "To build something fine together. I can help you, Kate. We're alike, you and I. We're both winners. We both believe in ourselves. And we believe in being faithful and loyal to our marriage vows. Unlike Allison or Roger."

Kate's face was not giving away any clues on what she was feeling. "I agree. We are a lot alike. But what does this have to do with Liz?" The woman whose brains you're about to blow out.

"She'll keep us apart. We need to get rid of her. And Allison." He nodded at Margaret. "Her too."

"The way he already got rid of Roger," I pointed out. Maybe because I figured if I kept him talking he wouldn't shoot me. Maybe because there was something about the expression on Kate's face that reminded me of the cozy, conspiratorial look she and Bobby had exchanged after the police marched John Carter off to jail.

Bobby's arm tightened around my neck. "Shut up!"

"Let me get this straight," Kate said, not at all fazed by the fact that her attorney was choking me. "You killed Roger so we can be together?"

The pressure on my neck eased a bit. "Roger was unworthy of you, Kate. He didn't deserve a woman like you."

"I'll buy that. But why did you send me his body?"

A little less pressure around my neck. The man had his priorities: first woo Kate, then remove all obstacles. "I thought that if I sent you the body the police wouldn't suspect you. I wanted to get him out of your house because if you discovered the body there, you'd be the main suspect. Obviously I was wrong about this. I didn't think the police could trace the delivery back to your house. I'd used that delivery service before and they were very inefficient and disorganized. It was the last place I would have suspected of keeping decent records."

Kate, I could see, didn't look satisfied with his explanation. "Opening that box—seeing my husband's lifeless body spill out—that was *not* a loving act, Bobby."

"Well, I was angry with you too," Bobby admitted. Sounding like a little boy caught in a lie. "You were not very sensitive about my feelings when I told you about Roger and Allison. You just laughed it off. Made it sound like 'Grow up, Bobby; this is no big deal.'"

Kate sighed. "After all of Roger's affairs, one more wasn't a big deal to me. I'm sorry I was insensitive to you, Bobby."

"Okay, I forgive you," Bobby said, sounding happier. A pause. "Now are you going to help me or not?"

I saw Kate glance at Margaret and shrug. "Sure."

"Hey!" Margaret said indignantly. My sentiments exactly.

"A woman has to be pragmatic," Kate explained, moving next to Bobby. "We can't shoot them here," she said to Bobby. "Too many people driving by. The last thing we need are eyewitnesses."

Bobby considered it. "You're right, sweetheart. It would be better to drive someplace more deserted. I guess we're going to have to take her car. Mine isn't big enough for all of us."

He yanked me forward. "Move it. You get the other one," he told Kate.

"Give me the gun," she said impatiently. "You've got her in a chokehold. She's not going anywhere. I need the gun for the sister."

Bobby hesitated. "Give it to me," Kate barked. "You say you want to build a life with me. Now prove it."

His arm tightening around my neck, Bobby handed Kate the pistol.

She smiled at him. "Now get your fucking hands off her," she ordered, pointing the gun at him.

He stared at her, disbelieving. Keeping his arm around my neck. "You wouldn't shoot me," he said, moving slowly toward her, dragging me along. "I love you."

Kate kept her eyes on him. "Watch me," she said, and shot him in the foot.

Bobby was lying on the ground, moaning, when we heard the sirens.

"It sure as hell took them long enough to get here," Margaret said. She'd run up to hug me the minute Bobby hit the ground. "We called 911 from my car," she explained. "When I called home and there wasn't any emergency I knew something was wrong. Fortunately Mel went to check on you and saw Bobby push you into his car."

"You did good," I said. "All of you."

"And I am counting on the fact that you'll never, ever again comment on my poor driving," Margaret added. "Or my interfering in your life."

Fortunately at that moment the police car, lights flashing, arrived before my gratitude made me say something I might later regret. The officers hurried over to Kate, who was still holding a gun on Bobby.

"Now you've betrayed me," Bobby was screaming at her. "Just like Allison did."

"I betrayed *you*?" Kate shook her head in disbelief. "In the words of one of my therapist colleagues, you have a screw loose, Bobby."

# Chapter Twenty-seven

IN THE END, IT WAS ALLISON WHO PROVED TO BE Bobby's downfall. Ironically, considering that no one—the police or any of us amateur detectives—had ever thought to talk to her.

But it was Kate, fittingly enough, who set it all in motion. Kate who—after Bobby had been taken, in custody, to the hospital and the rest of us had all given our statements to the police—turned to Margaret and me and said, "We need to go talk to Allison."

"Why?" Margaret enquired.

"Because right now I'm not sure that there's enough evidence to convict Bobby of anything except abducting Liz at gunpoint. He'll get some hotshot attorney who'll make it sound as if we all misunderstood Bobby when he confessed to killing Roger or get his confession thrown out as inadmissible evidence. I don't want that bastard to get away with murdering Roger."

"And you think that Allison has evidence that will convict him?" I asked.

"Let's just say that I have a hunch that when Allison

hears that Bobby was planning to kill her, too, she might start remembering things that she didn't know she knew.''

Fifteen minutes later, Allison Smythe opened the door of her high-rise apartment, looking puzzled. Kate had called ahead to say we were coming, but she hadn't specified why. Allison ushered us into her sparsely furnished living room, apologizing that she hadn't had time to really get settled yet. We all declined her offer of iced tea and assured her we didn't mind at all sitting on straight-backed dining room chairs. The niceties covered, Allison finally sat too. ''It's so hard for me to believe that Bobby has been arrested,'' she said in a small, plaintive voice.

''Believe it,'' Kate said, not unkindly. ''He killed Roger and maybe Consuela too. And he was planning to kill you.''

''Me?'' Allison's already pale skin turned a shade paler.

''That's what he told all three of us,'' Margaret said, jumping into the conversation. ''And he said that whatever method he chose was going to be prolonged and painful because you'd betrayed him.''

I glared at my sister. Prolonged and painful? I myself did not remember hearing those words from Smythe.

Still, the message seemed to be having the desired effect on Allison. We could see its impact sinking in, as her thin lips tightened, her dark eyes grew hard. ''He's in jail now?'' she asked.

''Temporarily,'' Kate said. ''But he'll probably be out on bail soon.''

Allison, no fool, regarded the wife of the man she'd been sleeping with through narrowed eyes. ''And that's why you're here—to warn me that Bobby is planning to murder me?''

''Partly,'' Kate said. ''The other part, I hope, should prove mutually beneficial. I want you to help us find the evidence that will convict Bobby of killing Roger.''

Allison considered it. ''You've been assuming that I've been sitting on evidence?'' she enquired coldly. ''Because, unfortunately, I don't have what you want.''

Kate leaned forward in her chair. ''I'm not suggesting that you've been withholding damaging evidence, Allison. What I am suggesting is now that you know Bobby killed Roger, you might see certain events in a new light. Something you might have dismissed before could be significant.''

Allison nodded. ''Right offhand I can't think of anything. But let me get a pen and paper. Maybe we can brainstorm together.''

She came back with a yellow legal pad and a ballpoint. ''Now what kind of evidence are we looking for?''

''Did Bobby own a gun?'' I asked. I knew that Smythe was much too smart to shoot Roger with a gun registered to himself, but I also knew that older guns or guns purchased from someone else would not have been registered in Bobby's name.

Allison shook her head. ''I hate guns. I wouldn't allow Bobby to have one in the house.''

''How about packing boxes?'' Margaret suggested. ''Were there any of those at your house?''

''Sure,'' Allison said, ''lots of them. I was moving out, remember. Juanita packed a lot of the household items that I was taking with me.'' She scribbled notes on her legal pad then looked up to see the excitement on our faces. ''Yes, that could have been where Bobby got the box. Unfortunately, I couldn't say if any of them were missing, though maybe Juanita could. Was there any special markings on the box that might identify it?'' she asked Kate.

''Not that I remember. It was very large, at least three feet wide and around six feet tall, about the size of box a

refrigerator comes in. Aside from being addressed to me—
Kate Quinlan, Powerful Woman Workshop—I don't remember anything else about it. Except, of course, for its
contents.''

Allison stopped writing and studied Kate with a look of
real sadness. For a moment they gazed at each other, their
expressions unreadable. Then Allison said briskly, ''I'll
check today with Juanita about the box.''

We spent another half hour that way, throwing out clues
Allison might have noticed that indicated her husband was
planning a homicide. At the end of this interrogation, Allison admitted that she hadn't been around Bobby very
much in the last months she'd lived with him. She'd been
very busy with her own activities, she said, not looking at
Kate. She didn't know where Bobby had been the day
Roger had died or the day that Consuela had supposedly
shot herself. She didn't know if Bobby knew that Juanita
had a key to the Quinlan house. In fact, I thought, feeling
disappointed, Allison knew remarkably little about the man
she'd been married to.

Allison herself was apparently reaching the same conclusion. ''I'm sorry I wasn't more help,'' she said, as we stood
to leave. ''I'll talk to Juanita to see if she knows anything.''

On the way out, my sister pointed to several small vases
sitting on a walnut sideboard. ''Those are lovely. Do you
collect Chinese porcelain?''

Allison smiled slightly. ''Thanks. My mother collected
them. I inherited her collection.'' Walking with us to the
door, she stopped suddenly. ''That's it!''

''What is it?'' Kate asked.

''The gun. I said we didn't own one, but Bobby's father
has a big gun collection at his ranch. Bobby goes to the
ranch all the time to see his dad, who had a stroke a few
months ago. Bobby has access to dozens of guns, all kinds,

if I remember right. Rifles, revolvers, semiautomatics, antiques. I didn't think about it before because I hate the ranch and haven't been there for years.''

This time Kate smiled. ''That sounds very promising. Let me give you the detective's name to call to give directions to that ranch.''

As we walked out the door, Allison touched Kate's arm. ''I wanted to tell you this before, Kate. I'm sorry—for everything.''

Kate barely glanced at her. ''You should be,'' she said and continued out the door.

A WEEK later the police, armed with a search warrant, found the gun that had killed Roger Quinlan on Bobby's father's ranch. As Allison had guessed, the .22-caliber pistol was part of her father-in-law's large gun collection. The old man insisted that the gun had never been missing, but his housekeeper remembered the handgun had been gone for awhile, then was returned to its place in the gun cabinet several weeks later. When she'd asked the elderly Mr. Smythe about it, he said that Bobby had borrowed it because he was worried about prowlers.

Proving Bobby's connection to Consuela's death was more difficult. That gun, the cheap Saturday night special, was not part of the elderly Smythe's collection. Consuela's daughter could only give the police partial answers. No, her mother had not told her the name of the rich man who had given her money. When the daughter had enquired why he'd given it, Consuela had only said, her face stony, ''He did a bad thing, and had to pay for what he did.''

Had Consuela realized that Bobby had murdered Roger and tried to blackmail him? Juanita, the Smythes' former maid, told the police that she'd seen Bobby talking to Consuela outside the Quinlans' house, but Juanita hadn't thought much about it; Mr. Smythe was a very talkative man. She had noticed, though, that the key she'd had to the Quinlan house was missing from the box of keys in the Smythes' kitchen. When Consuela had misplaced her key and requested to use the Smythes' extra one, the key was nowhere to be found.

Perhaps Consuela had inadvertently provided Smythe with information on Roger's and Kate's schedules that he needed to plan the murder. Maybe she had pieced together the information she knew—Smythe's sudden interest in Roger's and Kate's comings and goings, the missing key to the Quinlan house, the packing boxes at the Smythe house, knowledge of Allison's and Roger's affair—and had decided that Smythe was the murderer. Maybe she had even offered to help him cover up evidence. It was certainly likely that Consuela would have been aware of the bloodstain on the study carpet. Her daughter provided the reason that Consuela had probably decided to go to Smythe with her suspicions rather than to the police. "She never trusted the police," her daughter said. "Mama thought they would always let off a rich, white man, and she would be the one who got in trouble."

News accounts of Bobby's arrest for Roger Quinlan's murder usually at least mentioned Kate's Powerful Woman workshops. Kate's free lecture also received a lot of publicity, mainly because of the excellent human interest photos available from the event: John Carter screaming at Kate, Bobby and Carter rolling on the floor, and Carter being led off in handcuffs. As a result, enrollment in Powerful Woman workshops tripled.

Kate was ecstatic. Without a trial looming in her future and no stepdaughter in residence requiring supervision, she was free to devote all of her energy to forging her Powerful Woman empire. "Soon you're going to be manufacturing

Powerful Woman T-shirts,'' I teased her the weekend following Bobby's arrest. Kate had invited Nick and me to brunch.

''I'm already working on that,'' she said seriously. ''I think the front should say I'm A Powerful Woman. What do you think we should put on the back?''

''Watch out?'' I enquired sweetly.

Nick snickered.

Kate smiled. ''I kind of like that. By the way did I tell you I dropped the charges against John Carter? I don't think he'll give me any more trouble. I heard he was very embarrassed about those newspaper pictures of himself being led off to jail. He thinks they'll hurt his business.''

I wondered how Carter was going to feel when he read Kate's interpretation of his relationship with Robin in *It's Your Life, Lady—So Start Acting Like a CEO*. Kate had decided, she said, to relate Robin and John's story in her ''Why Women Still Stay With the Frogs'' chapter.

Kate's eyes narrowed. ''I've been meaning to ask you something, Liz. I've been thinking that you might be ready to make a career change. I can see a lot of possibilities for marketing written materials through the workshop: manuals, promotional brochures, maybe even a second book. As I said all along, I think you're a wonderful writer, and the two of us make a great team.''

Nick kept a poker face while I thanked Kate for the offer, but said I had some other career changes in mind. Then I said Nick and I had to leave, it was great seeing her.

''How come you didn't tell her?'' Nick asked as we got into his car.

I shrugged. ''Maybe I was afraid if she knew I was quitting my job she'd really start pressuring me to come work for her. Or''—I smiled at him—''maybe I was afraid she'd claim in her book that I was another Powerful Woman success story.''

"It takes guts to do what you're doing," Nick said. "You should be proud of yourself."

I was. I also was scared about leaving a secure job and very sad to leave dear friends and an instituton I'd come to think of as my second home. As my friend Amanda O'Neil had pointed out on more than one occasion, I was a person who likes closure and tidy endings: all questions answered, all issues resolved, all loose ends tied up. Maybe that's why I wanted to write mystery novels: They always end so neatly.

But life, unfortunately, is seldom that neat. There was no guarantee that I was doing the right thing, that this new phase of my life was not a huge mistake. But I was doing what I'd always wanted to do since I was a child: write a novel.

I was giving myself a year to finish *A Therapeutic Form of Death* and see if I could find someone willing to publish it. A year was about as long as my savings would hold out—if I lived very, very frugally. And after that? I'd have to wait and see. Maybe I'd have to find another PR job or do some other form of freelance writing. Maybe I'd write another novel.

Nick, bless him, was incredibly supportive of my decision. He was excited for me and also a bit envious. "Maybe I could get a leave of absence and write that book I always wanted to write. You could work in one room and I'd write in another one, and we'd meet for lunch and a walk—or engage in other diversions." I said it sounded good to me. Why didn't he start working out the arrangements?

He didn't manage the leave of absence but he did phone his aunt to see if I could borrow her cabin in the Hill Country. She agreed, glad, she said, to know that someone was looking after the place. The cabin would be an ideal place to work: quiet and isolated, with a lovely view of a small, pristine lake—and rent free.

Nick promised to come visit on the weekends. We were tabling our marriage plans for awhile, but only my sister Margaret seemed upset by the news.

Margaret, though, was trying her best not to meddle, a real test of will for someone who believed that anyone who left a secure job and a willing fiancé to live alone in a rustic cabin plotting imaginary murders was not playing with a full deck. On the day I was to move, Margaret arrived with a huge ice chest stocked with frozen casseroles she'd made. "I don't want you to starve," she said, looking tearful.

"Thanks." I held up an institutional-sized box of Baby Ruths. "Mel Quinlan said the same thing when she brought these over this morning. She didn't want me going off without a lifetime supply of chocolate."

"Oh, how is she doing?" Margaret asked.

"She refused to discuss her injuries, but I think they're healing nicely. She likes living with Sissy. Her only complaint was now that Kate is selling the house and Mel will inherit a good sum of money, Sissy is making her save the money for college instead of spending it all on a new car."

"Poor kid," Margaret said, rolling her eyes.

"What about you?" I asked. "Are you still thinking about medical school?"

Margaret shrugged, trying—and failing—to look nonchalant. "I've sent off for catalogues and talked to Raoul. He said he thought it would be nice to have two doctors in the family."

"That's great," I said as the phone rang.

I picked it up. Kate's voice. "Liz, I just had this brainstorm. I'm going to write a new chapter in my book. All about Bobby, the whole story. I'm going to call it 'Who

Needs a White Knight.' What do you think?''

"Sounds great. Good luck with it.''

"I was hoping you'd be able to drop by so we could discuss it further," she said. "Maybe you could even take some notes and write the chapter in your spare time at the cabin.''

"I don't think so," I said. "Good-bye, Kate.''

I'd just hung up when Nick returned from the car. "I think everything is packed in. You ready to leave?" He was driving up with me, helping me to get settled.

"I'm ready," I said, not sure that I was. The three of us walked together to my car. I hugged Margaret good-bye, assuring her that I'd be back in a few weeks.

Nick was going to follow me in his own car. Waving at Margaret, I backed my car out of the familiar parking space. I drove to the edge of the parking lot and waited for a break in the traffic. Suddenly, unexpectedly, I had a sense of rushing out to meet my future. I was surprised—and pleased—to discover how exhilarating it felt.

# "Gerry Boyle is the genuine article."
## —Robert B. Parker

# GERRY BOYLE

## __LIFELINE        0-425-15688-5/$5.99

McMorrow senses a good story in Donna Marchant, an abused woman. But after the article is published and Donna is found murdered, he finds suspicion has fallen not only on her boyfriend, but on himself as well.

## __BLOODLINE        0-425-15182-4/$5.99

Jack McMorrow returns to track down the killer of a local girl who was just starting to put her life back together after having an out-of-wedlock baby.

## __DEADLINE        0-425-14637-5/$5.99

"A bone-cracking first novel."
### —New York Times Book Review

Reporter Jack McMorrow leaves *The New York Times* to edit the weekly paper in Androscoggin, Maine. When his staff photographer is murdered, Jack learns small towns can be as cruel as big cities.

Payable in U.S. funds. No cash accepted. Postage & handling: $1.75 for one book, 75¢ for each additional. Maximum postage $5.50. Prices, postage and handling charges may change without notice. Visa, Amex, MasterCard call 1-800-788-6262, ext. 1, or fax 1-201-933-2316; refer to ad # 531a

| | |
|---|---|
| Or, check above books    Bill my: ☐ Visa ☐ MasterCard ☐ Amex _____ (expires) | |
| and send this order form to:    Card#_____ | |
| The Berkley Publishing Group | |
| P.O. Box 12289, Dept. B        Daytime Phone #_____ | ($10 minimum) |
| Newark, NJ 07101-5289         Signature_____ | |

Please allow 4-6 weeks for delivery.   Or enclosed is my: ☐ check ☐ money order
Foreign and Canadian delivery 8-12 weeks.

**Ship to:**

| | | |
|---|---|---|
| Name_____ | Book Total | $_____ |
| Address_____ | Applicable Sales Tax (NY, NJ, PA, CA, GST Can.) | $_____ |
| City_____ | Postage & Handling | $_____ |
| State/ZIP_____ | Total Amount Due | $_____ |

**Bill to:**        Name_____

Address_____        City_____

State/ZIP_____

# EARLENE FOWLER

### Introduces Benni Harper, curator of San Celina's folk art museum and amateur sleuth

__FOOL'S PUZZLE        0-425-14545-X/$5.99

Ex-cowgirl Benni Harper moved to San Celina, California, to begin a new career as curator of the town's folk art museum. But when one of the museum's first quilt exhibit artists is found dead, Benni must piece together a pattern of family secrets and small-town lies to catch the killer.

__IRISH CHAIN        0-425-15137-9/$5.50

When Brady O'Hara and his former girlfriend are murdered at the San Celina Senior Citizen's Prom, Benni believes it's more than mere jealousy. She risks everything–her exhibit, her romance with police chief Gabriel Ortiz, and her life–to unveil the conspiracy O'Hara had been hiding for fifty years.

__KANSAS TROUBLES        0-425-15148-4/$19.95

After their wedding, Benni and Gabe visit his hometown near Wichita. There Benni meets Tyler Brown: aspiring country singer, gifted quilter, and former Amish wife. But when Tyler is murdered and the case comes between Gabe and her, Benni learns that her marriage is much like the Kansas weather: unexpected and bound to be stormy.

### *A Prime Crime Hardcover*

---

Payable in U.S. funds. No cash accepted. Postage & handling: $1.75 for one book, 75¢ for each additional. Maximum postage $5.50. Prices, postage and handling charges may change without notice. Visa, Amex, MasterCard call 1-800-788-6262, ext. 1, or fax 1-201-933-2316; refer to ad # 523b

| Or, check above books and send this order form to: | Bill my: ☐ Visa ☐ MasterCard ☐ Amex _____ (expires) |
|---|---|
| The Berkley Publishing Group | Card# |
| P.O. Box 12289, Dept. B | Daytime Phone # _____ ($10 minimum) |
| Newark, NJ 07101-5289 | Signature |

Please allow 4-6 weeks for delivery.        Or enclosed is my: ☐ check ☐ money order
Foreign and Canadian delivery 8-12 weeks.

**Ship to:**

| | | |
|---|---|---|
| Name | Book Total | $_____ |
| Address | Applicable Sales Tax (NY, NJ, PA, CA, GST Can.) | $_____ |
| City | Postage & Handling | $_____ |
| State/ZIP | Total Amount Due | $_____ |

**Bill to:**        Name _____

Address _____ City _____

State/ZIP _____